LEAGUE OF INDEPENDENT OPERATIVES
BOOK 2

ANTI-HERO

KATE SHEERAN SWED

To Susan
who always reads everything

FLICK HAD the kind of power that would have soothed most men away from fear, perhaps even as far as arrogance. Ten times faster than the average Olympic sprinter, he'd spent his career relishing the feel of knocking over the bad guys before they ever saw him coming. He'd once topped two hundred miles per hour while chasing down an armed Wave operative in a helicopter.

But Flick hadn't spent the last two years running. He'd spent them hiding.

His fortress was an adobe-bricked hut on the line where the Amazon jungle met the Andes in Peru, past the tourist hikes and selfie-spots, and a bit farther for good measure. Vines dripped from the trees, sheltering wildlife that ranged from beetles and butterflies to foxes and chinchillas.

Every three hours, dark or light, rain or shine, Flick's alarm went off. And every three hours, he stopped what he was doing —monitoring long-range radios, treating wool, caring for the alpaca that provided the wool—to patrol the perimeter. He never missed a round.

Even overnight. Flick rubbed sleep out of his eyes and slipped a coca leaf into his mouth, tucking it into his cheek and savoring the bitter tang of the stimulant as he stepped out of his cabin. When he'd moved to the Andes, he'd finally understood why the Milky Way served as a fitting name for the galaxy. Out here, the stars stretched across the sky like the river the Incas had dubbed them, a lacy streak of light that made the darkness at his fingertips that much more acute.

Sentimental nonsense. All the same, he couldn't help smiling at the stars. He wished his son would agree to come out here, see for himself what no cameras could properly capture.

January in Peru often meant bundling in rain gear and straining to hear through the pattering drops, but tonight was warm and dry. From the sky, at least. Mud squelched under Flick's boots as he slipped into his usual perimeter sweep, a path that zigged and zagged through the twenty-odd traps he'd set around the cabin.

Because Flick suspected that independent operatives didn't truly retire, and that eventually, someone would show up to call him back into service. Maybe it would be the league, come to ask his help after the fracture that'd scattered the original crew into retirement. Some of Flick's generation had balked at the idea of letting the younger IOs lead the way, and they might've been right. The kids had made a mess of it in the last few months, or so he understood. Coral unmasked, HQ revealed.

Of course, the old crew could've buried their sour stomachs to stick around and guide the kids away from trouble. Too late for regret. Still, the league might decide he was necessary, might come for him.

Or maybe Wave would show up to repay Flick for his crimes against them. He'd heard they were back, claiming they weren't the villains everyone had always said they were. Flick knew enough about goings-on in the league to suspect that was probably true.

They wouldn't find him, any of them. Only his son knew

where he was. Flick wished he could get the stubborn kid to hide with him, but he always refused.

In case someone *did* find him—and it paid to be overcautious about these things—he'd be ready.

Flick reached the first station, an old-fashioned trip line connected to a bunch of alarm bells—it'd been a while since he'd changed them, and he made a note to check the clappers in the morning to make sure they weren't rusting out—and stopped to listen. Nothing out of place, no human-sized footsteps or whispers. Just the usual dripping, rustling music of the jungle. And yet, a distinct feeling of unease began to trickle along his spine.

Rolling his steps, Flick walked quietly to the second station, a hole he'd painstakingly dug on his first days in the Andes and camouflaged with sticks and leaves. He ought to check this one, too; the rainy season tended to melt the walls into oozing mudslides. Too easy to climb. Perhaps he ought to line it in stone.

Tonight, even in the darkness, it was clear the trap lay undisturbed.

Flick never used his powers out here, never wanted to advertise his identity to hidden spies, however unlikely they might be. And so he inched around the circumference of the cabin at an un-enhanced walk, examining each trap with meticulous care while the uneasy feeling settled in the small of his back, sending thrills of nerves through his gut every time a bird squawked.

As Flick rounded the back of the cabin—halfway around the perimeter—something flashed white in the jungle ahead, a streak of reflection that vanished in a blink. Heart beating to a rhythm of I-told-you-so, Flick drew his dart gun out of his tool belt and breathed as slowly as he dared.

He didn't move toward the anomaly. He waited.

The white streak flashed again. Flick squeezed the trigger, but the streak was gone, the sedative-laced dart thunking softly into a tree trunk. As he scanned the darkness, Flick's mind burned with memories of the Pearl Knife. A worthy ally, that blade. When Dolly had wanted it to be. He'd seen her use it to slice information out of locked doors, hidden passages. Prisoners.

Flick had no wish to encounter the Pearl Knife again. This streak looked too thin to be the Knife, though; more like a child's glow stick. Who knew all that the blade could do? Dolly kept the truth of its powers close, and Flick doubted even she could describe its origins.

The streak flashed a third time, and Flick took off after it, his muscles only too glad to propel him forward at high speed. Tree trunks blurred around him, the stars melting into lines as Flick navigated his traps. It was like stretching his back after too long in one position, like letting go of something he'd been restraining.

It felt good.

The white streak doubled into a pair close ahead, beyond his perimeter. Flick surged forward, nearly there, as the two streaks ascended impossibly toward the trees.

Flick's heel hit the ground, and his next step caught in a familiar circle of twine. He tried to pull out before it could catch, but he'd designed this trap himself. And he'd designed it with enhanced humans in mind. Quick. Strong.

The rope pulled taught around his ankle, and the world stilled back to its normal pace as Flick's trap flung him into the air, the rope hissing over the tree branch as it lifted him upside down. He pawed frantically for the darts at his hip, leg burning with pain. But the white streaks returned, calm now, and attached to the cuffs of two very real arms.

Yes. Who else could have rearranged his traps and herded

him into one of them? The only independent operative with no enhanced abilities of her own.

"Coral," Flick choked as she disarmed him from above and flipped easily out of the tree.

He couldn't see Mary O'Sullivan's face in the darkness, couldn't make out much more than a silhouette below him. He remembered her as a girl, always shadowing the Inferno, always in training, always badgering anyone who showed an ounce of patience to give her lessons and information.

He remembered the other big argument in the league, the one that had happened right after Dolly had admitted to using the Pearl Knife to take down Mary's plane. The league had killed Alan and Celestine O'Sullivan.

And now, he supposed, Mary was here to claim her revenge. He wanted to tell her he hadn't known, not until it was over and done with, but he doubted that would save him.

Head swelling with blood, he flailed uselessly. "I hear they're looking for you," he said.

Something snapped—one of Coral's famous jewelry gadgets, no doubt—and she hovered close as a sharp sting bit into his neck.

"They won't find me," she said. "Unlike you, I know where to hide."

Flick opened his mouth but no words came. He tried to swallow, but his throat was dry as thatch, the bitter coca still burning in his mouth, the stars watching in silence as Coral's drug pulled him under.

THE PROJECTED light of Santa Monica's October sun beamed cold into the simulation room at HQ, where no number of space heaters could quite undo the fact that it was January, and the whole compound rested behind Niagara Falls. Eloise had on three sweaters, and still she shivered.

Eloise didn't particularly enjoy reliving the motorcycle chase she'd participated in last fall, and not just because the fake California light made her feel even colder. She didn't particularly enjoy motorcycles themselves, either. Or chases, or reminders of how frequently the Pearl Knife refused to obey her commands.

But Eloise never hesitated to do what needed doing, no matter whether she liked it or not. Still, no matter how many times she reviewed this chase, she couldn't see where she'd erred. With an urgent to-do list ticking away in her head, and an acute awareness that every moment she spent on non-league matters meant things could be going hopelessly wrong elsewhere, Eloise did her best to focus.

In the simulation, palm trees lined the streets, the sidewalks populated with bag-laden shoppers in tank tops and bikinis. Eloise watched the chase progress in slow motion, her eyes avoiding the spot where the woman in the polka-dotted sundress always leapt back to avoid Eloise's bike as it careened onto a pedestrian thoroughfare after the Wave van that held a kidnapped Agnes. Wave had captured LIO's star scientist to help them refine some dangerous serums, ultimately charming her into joining their cause.

Whenever Eloise's eyes drifted toward the polka dots diving away from her on the sidelines, she felt an overwhelming desire to find the woman and apologize for nearly killing her.

People should be glad to see her coming. Not afraid for their lives.

It hadn't been easy to assemble the simulation, especially without Mary's expertise. But with the help of Luke, the LIO support team's lead engineer, they'd managed to cobble something together from traffic cameras, security feeds, and agitated social media posts.

Eloise followed her mask-clad double along Santa Monica's Third Street Promenade, as she'd done a hundred times, watching herself go knee-to-knee with the other rider. She remembered the feeling of the Knife in her mind as it had urged her straight for a vendor stand; now, she could watch as it soared ahead of her with the grace of a shooting star. The source of her powers, the blade was as mysterious as it was powerful. Which this moment proved.

"Stop," Eloise said, and the simulation paused with hologram-Eloise practically bumping helmets with her visored opponent. Eloise stepped between them, staring so hard at the Knife that her head began to ache. "One frame forward."

The hologram twitched, and the Knife sliced, leaving a vertical band hanging in the air between Eloise and the vendor cart, a thin thread of silver. In the next frame, the thread unspooled. All in all, the cut stretched nearly ten feet. She'd measured.

For the following three frames, Eloise and the motorcycle disappeared.

She couldn't trust the stuttering simulation enough to reliably time her absence, but judging by the other bike's progress toward its crash into the stand, she couldn't have been gone more than a few fractions of a second.

Gone. Gone where? No matter how much she clicked from one frame to the next, no matter how closely she examined the picture from either side, she couldn't see the moment she'd passed through the silver line, or what might be on the other side. She certainly couldn't recall anything she may have seen there.

Here and now, the Knife hummed a tune into her mind, and Eloise gave it a twirl, the milky blade defying physics as it twisted around her hand. What was it made of? Where was it from? Not Earth, if she had to wager. She didn't even know whether to treat the blade like technology, or a sentient being. It felt like a bit of both.

Suppressing a shiver, Eloise clicked the recording to the other troubling spot, the moment when the Pearl Knife had refused to attack one of the motorcycles that had been escorting the van. She hardly expected to find any answers, but she didn't know what else to do.

When a notification chimed into her ear, Eloise practically felt her shoulders drop in relief. She'd never been happier to be interrupted by her former assistant, Gail, who was now in charge of the processing office aboveground. The world might know where to find the League of Independent Operatives, but that didn't mean they needed to be allowed in the front door. So Gail and her staff processed recruitment applications and fielded communications from the general public.

"We've got a code R up here," Gail said. "He's causing a bit of a stir."

The processing team also handled reporters. Until they got too pushy, at which point Gail called Eloise. She sheathed the Knife. She should send Ire or Nathan to deal with the interruption, but she was all too happy for an excuse to give up this useless chase.

"Hold tight," she said, shutting down the simulation. "Tell him I'll be there in a minute. Call Ire in, would you?"

Eloise didn't like to brandish the Knife without strong cause—she would be a hero, damnit, not a bully—and sometimes Ire's mere presence reminded troublemakers of what she could do. What they could all do.

Gail agreed, and by the time Eloise had collected her boots and parka, Ire was waiting for her at the elevator that led into the town of Niagara Falls. Gifted with enhanced strength after a chemical weapons accident—or saddled with it, depending on who you asked—Ire was the tallest man she'd ever laid eyes on, and wide to boot. He'd pulled a specially made sports jacket over his hulking muscles, a funny contrast to his spiky red hair.

"Will you be warm enough?" Eloise asked.

"Fine."

She nodded, and the elevator rumbled skyward, stopping when it reached its supply-closet door within the Niagara Falls visitor center. On the Canadian side, which was already causing headaches. The U.S. government had sanctioned LIO, eagerly handing over control of enhanced human incarceration, but the Canadian government had balked at the idea. The negotiations about who owned which slice of the headquarters LIO had built beneath the falls was enough to make Eloise want to scream with frustration.

But Eloise accepted the situation, because she had to. And because along with official acceptance came the power to recruit new members. The line between 'hero' and 'villain' may have blurred when it came to the past, but Eloise was determined to start fresh.

For now, the Canadians allowed Eloise and Ire to pass through the visitor center without incident, and they hurried along the sidewalk that wound toward the falls. January in Niagara Falls was not a pleasant month. The wind bit through jackets, the piles of plowed snow often rising above her waist. Ice coated every sidewalk so that she had to pick her way along to make sure she stayed on her feet.

And yet, the tourists still flocked. As Eloise and Ire walked toward the downtown area where the processing office kept its storefront, a man in a red baseball cap recognized them and called out to her. Eloise waved back, and suddenly more tourists materialized around them, cameras drifting away from the freezing falls to capture a couple of superheroes instead. Or so they seemed to see it.

Eloise had new insight as to what Mary had endured over the years, living her life in front of the camera. She wouldn't have minded some tutoring.

"Why do you always have to wave?" Ire grumbled. "Why can't you scowl and look like you don't want them around?"

"It's bad PR," Eloise said.

Ire grunted and shoved his hands into his pockets. "We're going to have to go back through the casino."

Eloise hated returning to LIO through the league's rented room in the casino hotel. They always had to stop for a drink, always had to mask their purpose there. Still, he was probably right.

They turned left to hurry up the hill to the processing office, casting a final wave back at the tourists—some of whom kept following, anyway. They called out questions and requests for selfies, which Eloise did her best to deny with grace.

By the time they reached the office, Eloise's fingers felt like they were ready to snap off, along with her temper. A feeling that only intensified when she arrived at the processing office to find the door wide open, the reporter in question holding it with his backside as he pointed a finger in Gail's bright red face. Eloise wasn't sure if the woman was going to bite him on the nose, or run away.

Eloise voted for biting.

"Heat costs money," Eloise said. "Shut the door."

The reporter stepped inside, his expression transforming into a mask of smiling respect. But if the reporter couldn't show respect to Gail, he shouldn't pretend to show it to Eloise. She knew better.

The reporter wore a well-fitted overcoat and boots scuffed with salt from the street, his phone in his hand and primed, she was sure, to begin recording.

When Ire shouldered in after Eloise, she began to wonder if they should have rented a space that was larger than a takeout counter.

"Eloise Reyna," the reporter said, extending his phone-free hand. "What a pleasure."

Eloise didn't shake his hand. "Explain to me," she said, allowing her irritation to leak into her tone like vinegar, "why you forced me to come in person to slap your hand for bad behavior instead of logging your press request like everyone else."

She'd done press conferences. She responded to every serious media request. She believed people had a right to LIO's story, and that the reporters were just doing their jobs.

She did not believe they had a right to bully her staff.

The man withdrew his hand, flexing his fingers as though to mask his attempt at friendliness. "Respectfully, I'm not here to talk to you. I'm here for Coral. Mary. And this girl—" He hooked a thumb at Gail, who flushed. "—says I can't log a request to speak with her."

Join the club, Eloise thought. She hadn't heard a word from Mary in over three months. They'd never gone so long without checking in.

Eloise kept her face neutral, crossing her arms over her chest. In her experience, when someone made a point of calling out their respectfulness, their behavior tended toward the opposite. Adding an adverb didn't make it true. "That's because I have no idea where Coral is. Which you must know, since I've repeatedly explained it to your colleagues. I'm sure a professional like you would have done your homework before showing up here."

The reporter flashed her the fakest smile she'd ever seen, nostrils flaring. "Respectfully, ma'am, the others might have bought that story. But I don't believe you."

"That's not very respectful," Ire said mildly.

The reporter dropped the fake smile as his eyes flickered to the strongman and back to Eloise. "Since October, we've all been aware of the enormous amount of resources that your... League of Independent Operatives... commands." He licked his lips. The idea of a superhero team was still fairly new to the world. "And since the U.S. government is now on your side, those resources would only have increased, which means taxpayers are now involved. I want to talk to Coral. And I believe you know where she is."

Eloise studied him placidly, considering whether it would be worth the bad press of stuffing him into a barrel and tossing him over the falls. Likely not. Though Mary probably would have supported the idea. In Eloise's mind, the Knife sputtered. If the blade had saliva, it might have spit at the man.

Easy, she thought, but the Knife still glowed, indignant on her behalf. Eloise curled her fingers around the handle, a movement she hoped could double as a threat and a hold on the Knife.

Because that was the Knife's other unfortunate behavior. It tended to get... upset with people when they argued with Eloise. Protective instinct, perhaps, but useless if she couldn't bring the wretched thing to heel.

Truthfully, Eloise had no idea where Mary had gone since splitting with LIO, much though she'd tried to locate her. She did, however, know that LIO's retirees—supposed heroes who'd worked alongside Dolly throughout Eloise's childhood—had been disappearing. Eloise kept tabs on them, as she had even before she'd known they might actually be criminals.

A month ago, Monster had vanished from his beach house in the Florida Keys. Two weeks ago, Carlisle had stopped showing up to his apartment in Sydney.

Eloise would have bet money on Mary's involvement. In Mary's mind, Eloise supposed, the retirees were connected with her parents' deaths, and with the murder and incarceration of Wave agents who may well turn out to be innocent of any crimes. Had Mary taken a moment to stop and think—had she trusted Eloise—she'd have known that Eloise had every intention of sorting through that part of the mess.

Mary didn't tend to stop. Or think. Eloise hadn't decided yet what she ought to do about her, particularly since she wasn't sure she disagreed with the basic premise of Mary's crusade. Assuming she wasn't murdering anyone.

The reporter was still staring at Eloise with such a look of entitled triumph on his washed-out face that she gripped the Knife both physically and mentally to keep herself—or the blade—from reminding this guy who held the power in this room.

Gail opened her mouth to say something, but Eloise held up a hand to stop her. "Who do you write for?" she asked.

The guy's creepy grin widened. "The U.S. Post."

Essentially a tabloid. Good.

"Right," Eloise said. "Gail, please make sure that the U.S. Post is banned from media requests in the future."

Gail nodded and scurried back behind the counter, while Eloise made a mental note to assign her some security support as the reporter's smile transformed to a mask of rage. "You can't—"

"I can," Eloise said calmly. "If you're spotted here again, Gail will call the police."

Eloise opened the door for the reporter, the Knife humming a satisfied tune in her mind as he shuffled back out into the cold. He knew he had no choice. That was the beauty of it. They could bluster all they wanted, but ultimately they obeyed. "Oh, and Mr... U.S. Post?" Eloise said as he started down the sidewalk.

The man stopped and looked back, eyes lit with hope. As if she'd change her mind after that display. The audience Eloise and Ire had collected on their way here had dissipated, and Eloise thanked the stars for small blessings.

"If you do see Coral," she said, "let her know I'm looking for her, too."

Nathan vaulted over the last hurdle at the center of the obstacle course, springing up from the mats as soon as he landed and sprinting for the rock wall that stretched halfway to the ceiling. He pulled himself up, attacking the wall with all the strength he had.

Which wasn't all that much, at the moment. The rest of LIO's new recruits were nearing the ceiling, with Len, the sticky-fingered cadet, already disappearing over the other side. Well, sure. If you could forgo the prescribed handholds, you could forge your own path.

Or if you could leap great distances like Tally, who had the audacity to grin back at him as she pushed off her foothold and rocketed to the top of the wall, passing several of the other recruits whose enhanced abilities—rain summoning, frost, and x-ray vision—couldn't help them here.

They'd been over the challenge course a dozen times today, and not one of the other recruits looked as tired as Nathan felt. The muscles in his arms protested fervently as he climbed, quivering with fatigue. He wasn't slow by any stretch, but he couldn't keep up with enhanced abilities.

And Ire had sweetened the prize this time by proclaiming

the winner of this race would get the first tour of LIO HQ when Eloise finally cleared them to visit. The man had actually encouraged them to use their enhanced abilities to get ahead.

As the thought crossed his mind, Rajni hit on a way to use her rain-summoning powers. And it wasn't to Nathan's benefit. Water sluiced down from the top of the wall, drenching the remaining climbers, and Rajni pushed past them through the deluge to slither over the wall. The others kept moving, except for Elle; without hesitation, she lay a finger against the wall, using the leftover water from Rajni's trick to send ice unfurling from her hand with audible cracks.

"It's hardly necessary," Nathan muttered, trying to regain his footing under the onslaught of ice. The other trailing cadet grunted in apparent agreement. Quin's x-raying abilities couldn't help them here, either.

Nathan tried to climb. Instead, his boot glanced off the next grip and he fell, landing on his back on the mat. Quin cast him a glance of commiseration—or perhaps to make sure he didn't require medical attention—before scrambling up the final ascent.

By the time Nathan reached the other side of the wall, the others were stepping through the final challenge, a brief tire run, and sauntering over the finish line past Ire. The strongman held a stopwatch and a whistle around his neck, giving Nathan sudden and painful flashbacks to grammar school PE class.

Nathan did his best to maintain his dignity as he finished the course, nodding to Ire before bending to stretch his legs. He wanted to collapse to the floor and stay there for the next year. But while the others chatted casually, congratulating high-jumping Tally on her win, Nathan couldn't help diving for his water bottle.

Well, he'd wanted to be an independent operative. This

was what training looked like. No movie montages to fast-forward the pain.

"Hey."

Nathan started as Tally approached him, grinning the way she had from the top of the wall. She had cropped blonde hair and a silver ring in her lip. He nodded, and her smile widened. "Coming to lunch?"

"If I can walk that far."

She laughed—more than the joke warranted, really—and knocked her shoulder into his. He had the distinct impression of being flirted with.

"I'll save you a seat," she said, winking, then headed off to join the others.

Definitely flirting. And maybe he'd flirted back? He hadn't quite meant to. He ran a hand through his hair and watched her go. No way he was ready for that. Not when he still spent half his time trying to sort through what had happened with Mary last fall, where he could have made things right between them. He fluttered regularly between guilt at choosing LIO and worry at Mary's current circumstances. No one had heard from her since they'd all parted ways in October.

As romances went, theirs hadn't lasted long. Still, it lingered.

When the other recruits had gone, Nathan collapsed on a bench by the wall to mop his face with a towel. "You know," he said, suppressing the urge to raise his voice over the hammering of his heart, "when I pictured working with the league, I thought I'd be... I don't know, on your side of the whistle."

Ire began folding the mats to prepare the space for afternoon exercises. Whatever that would be. Nathan hoped it wasn't sparring. "Thought this would be easy for you, Pearce. What with your police training and all."

"The worst thing about cadet training was my friend Steve

always beating my mile by a split second. These guys make it *rain* on me. I can't beat them."

"You've already seen LIO HQ," Ire said. "You don't need the prize. You're not supposed to beat them."

Nathan hadn't just seen LIO HQ. He lived there, in a room he barely saw. Somehow, that metal-walled world of tech and screens had become the norm, and yet it was still bizarre to him. In every way.

Ire stepped over to the rock wall and placed his hands on the sides, hefting the whole fifteen-foot monstrosity to the corner of the warehouse. Eloise wanted them to recruit new members, but obviously couldn't risk bringing uninitiated enhanced humans to HQ. Thus the training academy, a converted warehouse aboveground on the outskirts of town.

Ire brushed off his hands and started back toward the tires. "I never agreed with how they trained her, laying off the enhanced abilities when they sparred," he said finally. He picked up a tire under each arm, and Nathan didn't have to ask who Ire meant. Nathan had been hoping to train with Mary when he'd first thought of joining the league. Another independent operative without powers. An ally.

The thought of her made him ache. Where was she, now? Thriving without him, probably. She didn't need him. She never had.

And yet, he'd been the one to leave.

"You can't deal with enhanced abilities if you've never faced them," Ire said.

Nathan rolled his shoulders. It was only lunchtime. What kind of torture did Ire have planned for the rest of the day? His watch buzzed with an incoming call from his sister, and Nathan dismissed it with a glance. "Eloise has a power suppressant now. Can't we just use that?"

They'd been able to bring a sample of Mange's serum to the

lab after the fight in the Sea and Stars warehouse last fall. Wave had it, Eloise had reasoned, and therefore LIO ought to have it, too.

Nathan didn't disagree.

"You won't always have access to the serum," Ire said. "You have to learn to work around abilities. What better way?"

Nathan sucked down more water, blinking sweat out of his eyes and fighting the urge to stretch out on the bench for a nap. The recruits weren't even that much younger than he was. In fact, he thought a couple of them might be older. "I never imagined there'd be so many people out there with enhanced abilities."

Ire rolled a tire across the room with surprising dexterity. "Agnes did."

And now she was gone, too. Joined up with Wave. Among her closest friends, Ire didn't talk much about her. Maybe that put them in the same boat.

Nathan didn't realize he'd voiced the thought out loud until Ire stopped moving things and faced him. "We're not in the same boat," he said. "We're not in the same harbor. I chose against an unknown danger—one that took my powers and controlled my mind—over a danger I could help fix. Whatever LIO's past, I trust Eloise. Not that... Bradley person."

Ire kept his anger below the surface, rarely letting it boil over. Nathan could see it, though, simmering behind his carefully drawn breaths, his clenched fists. Definitely angry, but who with? Agnes? Dolly? Himself?

"While I abandoned Mary," Nathan said.

Ire shrugged, as if he didn't care. He did, though. It was part of why Nathan liked him. "You tried to choose between black and white in a world where the distinction doesn't exist."

Nathan refused to believe that. If a person couldn't say firmly and without hesitation what was right and what was wrong, then they didn't deserve to be a hero. Ultimately, it had been Mary's refusal to see that—her stubborn insistence on protecting her secret identity over the lives of others—that had made his choice all too easy. If bitter, too. He couldn't forget that.

Besides, Nathan had chosen what Chloe wanted. His formerly estranged sister, who'd now informed her children of his existence. They called him Uncle Nathan, when he picked up the phone. It seemed Chloe was always calling him these days, and sometimes—despite the fact that Nathan was glad for their reunion—he couldn't face talking to her.

For the sake of patching his relationship with Chloe, and with his father, he'd chosen the Pearl Knife over the woman he... well. It didn't matter now.

Nathan sighed and lay back on the bench after all, missing Mary. She'd have finished that obstacle course in front of the recruits. She'd have swung across the rafters, invented a gadget, or sassed them until they gave up.

On his wrist, his watch buzzed insistently, and Nathan silenced Chloe's call without bothering to check the screen.

THE FRESNO AIRPORT was hardly a swanky place to end up after completing a mission in Peru—certainly not compared to LIO HQ—but Mary's new life didn't allow for much choosiness. In the last day, she'd hauled a sedated Flick from truck to boat to drone-guided charter plane, and all she really wanted was a good meal and a hot shower.

She settled for a fried chicken sandwich in the parking garage, waiting until dusk before she swapped the license plates on the banged-up minivan she'd been driving for the last month. It was an eggplant-colored elder of a vehicle that smelled like peppermint mothballs, but it never hesitated to start when she turned the key. Mary might be accustomed to high-tech transportation, but the mechanic in her maintained high esteem for a car that kept chugging after such a long life.

She'd taken to calling it Grandma.

Mary paid the airport parking fee in cash and drove a mile under the speed limit until she left Fresno to cut away into the hills. As she left the city behind, Mary glanced back at her sleeping prisoner. She'd strapped Flick into the back seat and tossed an old army blanket over him so he wouldn't get cold. It felt like a strange thing to do for a person she'd kidnapped, but she wasn't like him, or Dolly, or any of them. She wasn't a monster. Not yet.

In the darkness, the LIO retiree was just a silhouetted lump. She wished he'd snore or something, so she'd know for sure he was OK.

He'd made it all the way from Peru. He could make it a little longer.

Mary passed into the Sierra Nevadas, trying to contain her eagerness as the forest closed around her like a cloak. With ice oiling the roads and no lights to guide her, she made herself take her time.

Patience had never been among Mary's top-ten virtues.

Finally, she left paved roads behind and forged along the narrow dirt switchbacks that led to the estate she'd purchased years ago. At Will's suggestion, strangely enough. He'd practically been on his death bed when he'd encouraged her to buy property, under an alias and entirely off the league's books. At the time, she'd thought he was giving her fatherly investment advice, and though she had business advisors, she'd been eager to grant any request he made. There'd been no reason not to do it; LIO could always use another surprise safe house. Or three.

Now, Mary looked back on the advice with more questions than answers. Had Will regretted the league's exploitation of her wealth? Foreseen her current situation?

Sprawled on the edge of a private lake, the estate looked like an oversized wooden cabin. Gables cascaded along the roof in tiers, as though whoever had built the place couldn't bear to create a single room without a view of the lake. With cobble-stoned walkways, charmingly overgrown gardens, and a stretch of dock reaching out over the water, the place screamed rustic luxury. *Yes, it's remote,* the wood paneling declared, *but there's also a swimming pool!*

When she'd bought it, Mary had christened the place

Aries, after her astrological sign. She saw no reason to stop calling it that now.

All this alone time was definitely making her soft.

Mary pulled into the driveway and opened the garage. Aries might look like your run-of-the-mill, multi-million-dollar celebrity escape from the outside. But on the inside, she'd seen no reason to hold back on the tech.

In Malibu, Mary had been forced to stuff all her tech into the basement. Here, she'd spent her first two LIO-free months outfitting the entire estate with her best toys, including her voice-operated home operation System. In Malibu, she'd had to limit her computer System's powers to the secret rooms, just like everything else.

At Aries, the System ran the house. And, not to personify things, but Mary felt that after so many years of emptiness and occasional visits from a caretaker, Aries rather enjoyed the attention.

Mary pulled Grandma to a stop, and the System closed the door behind her. "Welcome home, Mary," it said. She'd stuck with the Meryl Streep voice. It was comfortable, and made her feel like she still had a friend on her side. "I gather from the bundle of heat in your backseat that you'd prefer the prison entry?"

"Yes, please." As Mary got out of the car, stretching her arms above her head, the System pulled up the false wall at the back of the garage, revealing a second garage behind it.

Because some things still needed to stay hidden. If not underground.

One of Aries' previous owners had collected cars, or so she assumed from the sheer size of the garage they'd wrapped around the back of the house. The whole thing was shaped like an enormous L, the small garage leading into the bigger show-room. Even with the modifications she'd made, Mary could picture rows of Lamborghinis and BMWs on display here, their poor sad engines languishing from lack of use.

Or maybe the person had collected tractors. Who could tell?

Mary opened Grandma's sliding door and bundled a still-sleeping Flick out of the back, slinging him over her shoulder and waving away the System's offer of assistance via a hand truck. "Anything happen while I was gone?"

"A private garbage collector tried to talk me into enlisting their services."

"And?"

"Their prices are competitive."

Mary frowned. "You didn't—"

"Humor, Mary. I sent them away."

Mary let out a breath. She really should deactivate the sense of humor. But that made the System less fun to talk to.

The System shut the false door garage as Mary turned into the back stretch of the garage.

Not a garage anymore. No, she'd spent the majority of the last few months transforming the place into a line of high-tech cells. With three steel walls plus an invisible forcefield, each cell was more secure than anything even LIO would have been able to create without her.

The System dosed each captive with Mange's power-suppressing serum every day—which it could, blessedly, produce through the lab Mary had built for that purpose—and the forcefield acted as both a wall and a sensor, scanning the cells regularly and spitting statistics on body temperature, pulse, motion, and other indications that a prisoner might be regaining their powers or otherwise causing trouble.

Carlisle sat against the back wall of the first cell with his eyes closed, a thin blanket draped around his shoulders. Mary didn't know why he refused to sleep on his cot, but she'd never once seen the weather-working retiree using any of the furniture she provided. Maybe he just pretended to be asleep when Mary showed up. Couldn't blame him for that.

She could blame him for the part he may well have played in murdering her parents. Mary didn't know yet who'd been directly involved and who'd only known about it.

She intended to find out.

In the next cell over, Monster paced like a lion in a cage, blue scales glowing in the dim light. With his abilities, he wielded super strength like Ire's—but even with his powers suppressed, he was big, and his scales acted like armor. He'd rushed the forcefield when he'd first woken, trying to get to Mary. With his scales preventing him from feeling pain, the electricity had nearly fried his organs from the inside.

Now he stopped to stare at her, yellow eyes following her as she deposited Flick across the narrow corridor from him. His attention lifted goosebumps along her spine, but she forced down a shiver and kept her eyes ahead.

She'd grown up with these people. She tried not to think too much about that.

The System activated the forcefield around Flick as Mary stepped back with carefully deliberate movements. She needed to stay calm, not go running from a threat. Especially a confined one.

"Make sure Flick has something to eat when he wakes," she told the System. "Find out if he needs any medications or anything."

As she made her way upstairs, a tightness dissolved between her shoulder blades, loosening the knot of strain she always carried from the moment she abducted a retiree to the moment she deposited them safely in a cell. Even with their powers suppressed, they were dangerous. Someone like Flick might metabolize the serum too fast, try to run her off the road.

"I took the liberty of preparing the gin when you entered the perimeter," the System said.

"You're an angel."

"I'm ones and zeroes."

"Ah, but you're ones and zeroes that can cook. Salmon?"

"Already in the oven."

Mary made her way upstairs, carefully securing the prison behind her. If the Malibu house had been a stage, Aries was more of a playground. She'd kept all the fancy trappings—copper fixtures, wine glasses hanging from the ceiling, big stone fireplace—but she allowed her own touches to creep in. She let pieces of gadgets sit on side tables, bits of wire and stray tools taking up space on the shiny kitchen island. Gauzy curtains hid the view, which was pitch black at the moment, anyway.

And it was quiet.

"So, the garbage collectors," Mary said. She settled at the kitchen island with her plate and her drink, spearing a potato drenched in butter. "Were they cute?"

The System paused, typically a sign that she'd confused it. "I don't know how to answer that."

Mary shrugged. "Just making conversation."

"Oh, I see. I can assist."

Mary took a bite of salmon. "Be my guest."

"What do you intend to achieve by collecting all the retired league operatives?"

Mary paused. She'd been expecting something more along the lines of a knock-knock joke. Well, she *had* asked for conversation. "Justice," she said.

"Would you not do better to pursue it through legal channels?"

Mary gave her fork a wave, accidentally letting a potato loose. It spun across the room. She speared another one. "If we rush them into a courtroom, they'll all just defend each other. I need to figure out who knew what. I need a plan."

"So you kidnapped them before you had a plan?"

"I have the beginning of a plan."

Another pause. "Are you going to pick up that potato?"

Mary rolled her eyes and slid off the stool to retrieve the vegetable. "Eloise isn't going to do anything about her mother's crimes. She's not going to investigate."

"I have no data to corroborate that statement."

Mary did. Try half a lifetime of protocol-following nonsense. By that standard, a small voice whispered into her mind, Eloise would most certainly investigate.

But, the pragmatic side of Mary responded, Dolly was Eloise's mother. And sick. Even if Mary went public with the story, Eloise would probably get a pardon from her new government friends.

The more Mary protested, even to herself, the flimsier it felt. But she wasn't going to reach out to Eloise. Not now, not ever. "It's not about data," she said out loud. "It's about what I know."

"Without data."

"Yes. It's a human thing. You wouldn't get it."

"I suppose not."

Mary finished her dinner and dropped the plate in the sink, then sank down on one of the many couches in the room to fiddle with one of her new gadgets, something she'd been toying with as a way to neutralize the Trap's notorious poison. She'd bought the estate furnished, and she supposed the circle of couches and comfortable chairs meant Aries was supposed to be a place for gatherings. Families and friends around the fire drinking hot chocolate and telling stories or something.

She didn't even dare light a fire in here, since she hadn't

figured out how to program the System to sweep the chimney. It wasn't exactly a priority.

Who would even be here with her, if she did have an evening like that? Eloise? Agnes? Mary shut down that line of thought before it could get too painful. No use following that list to its logical conclusion. The best thing about this place was that she didn't have to keep pretend books around, which would only remind her of the one person who'd come into her life and actually read them.

Mary didn't realize she'd dozed off until the System woke her with an alert chime. She sat up, rubbing her eyes. Her mouth felt dry, her senses tired and foggy. She must be more exhausted than she thought she was, after all those hours of flying and driving and kidnapping.

"My sensors cannot locate Monster in his cell," the System said. "I detect no vital signs or heat signatures."

Heart in her mouth, Mary leapt to her feet and dashed for the stairs. "Is he hurt?"

"I do not have visual."

How was that possible? Those cells were as bare as she could make them without tipping into cruelty. There was nowhere to hide. Vision still half blurred from sleep, Mary tripped down the stairs and crushed her fingerprint to the security panel.

Nothing moved in the prison-garage, the whole place quiet except for the background hum of the forcefields. Flick still lay unconscious on his cot. She couldn't see Carlisle, but there was no movement from his side, either.

Mary faced Monster's cell. She hated what these people had done, but she wouldn't hurt them any more than she had to. She wouldn't let them perish under her care. If Monster was sick, she'd do what she could to help.

But Monster's cell was empty. "Turn the lights up," Mary

said, and the System did. Monster wasn't there. "Has there been a breach?"

"No breach. The nutrition hatch remains intact." If a computer could sound confused, the System definitely did. The nutrition hatch was nothing more than a password-protected door that bulged up at the top of each cell. Yes, it created a pocket. But a very small one. Two square feet, at the most.

Had the forcefield been glass, Mary would have pressed her hands to it, to peer in as far as she could. She felt it in the air, vibrating ever so slightly. "I can't see. Drop the forcefield."

"I can't recommend that," the System said.

"He could be hurt. Can you see under the cot?"

"I can. His mass exceeds the space in any case."

Mary stared at the empty space, helplessness flooding her chest. What would Eloise do here? She was running a prison now, too, after all. She must have a hundred protocols in place covering every conceivable situation.

Eloise wouldn't let someone struggle. She had backup, yes, but she'd check to make sure Monster was alive. If the System wasn't reading any vital signs, that just meant she needed to get to him. And fast.

Or maybe he'd learned how to leap through a forcefield. If he was running for the property's perimeter, Mary needed to know that, too.

"Drop the forcefield," Mary said.

"I must—"

"I hear your objection, and I won't hold you responsible. Let me in."

A bare few inches from her face, the air shimmered. The forcefield went quiet. For a beat, nothing moved. She could feel Flick's forcefield still working behind her, the shivers of electric energy it sent along her spine.

Mary stepped into the cell and looked up.

With a growl, Monster unfolded his body from inside the nutrition hatch and dropped, knocking Mary to the ground and dragging sharp claws across her back. She rolled, throwing him off, and leapt to her feet.

But Monster didn't engage her. Instead, he ran.

"I think the serum wore off," the System said mildly. The computer wasn't programmed to panic.

Mary was. She dashed after Monster, who had already reached the end of the corridor and turned toward the garage where she had Grandma parked. He looked back over his shoulder, baring sharp teeth as he ran.

"Did you know he could contort like that?" Mary asked. It was beyond comprehension that the hulking Monster should have been able to stuff his body into that tiny space. How had he even climbed up there?

"Negative. None of the league's files ever indicated such a power."

So either he'd just discovered it, or he'd kept it secret. She wasn't particularly psyched about either. "Well, he's about to reach a dead end."

But Monster didn't stop for the lowered garage door. Instead, with a catastrophic explosion of metal, he ran through it.

Mary cursed and leapt after him through the hole, the cuts on her back protesting as she moved. They were shallow enough, though she could feel warm trails of blood trickling down her skin, making her shirt cling to her back. She shoved the stinging pain away. "Raise the perimeter fields." She didn't hear the System's confirmation as she ripped into the woods, limbs tearing at her hair as she tried to catch up. At least the chill was carving away the last of her drowsiness.

"I wonder if he's developed a tolerance for the drug," the System said. "He may have been hiding it."

A twig whipped across Mary's cheek, drawing a strip of blood. She didn't stop. "And I wonder if you could activate the drone guard before he ambushes me."

"I am capable of multitasking."

Whatever his apparently many powers, Monster did not specialize in subterfuge. His size essentially forbade it. He practically crashed through the woods ahead of her, and she caught the occasional glint of his scales reflecting the moonlight.

And after a month with little exercise, he was slowing. Instead of running full tilt for the perimeter—where another forcefield would stop him, anyway—he wheeled around to face her.

Mary didn't stop. She leapt at him with a high kick, aiming for the head. He ducked, and she used her momentum to swing a fist against his side. It was like punching the side of a bathtub. Her hand smarted, the scratches on her back screaming as she whipped around to face him.

If Monster had anything to say to her, it was lost to his rage. "Those guards would be really great right about now," Mary said as he came at her again.

A dozen pinpricks of light materialized above her as the drones formed their humming circle, surrounding the fight from above. The lights made them look like a fleet of steady fireflies, the rest of their black bodies blending into the night, but they were far more useful than that. Mary couldn't help a spike of joy at actually getting to use her little army in a fight.

A girl had to appreciate the small things.

Monster ran for her, but the lead drone got him first, and he fell face-first to the ground, groaning and grasping at his neck where the serum-laced dart had hit him.

This time, Mary accepted the System's assistance in hauling him back up the hill to the prison.

"System check," she said, once she had him safely back in his cell. Carlisle was still asleep—definitely pretending, she decided—while Flick sat on his cot, watching her with dark eyes. He didn't say anything as she reactivated the forcefield around Monster's cell.

"The garage door has been breached."

"Yes, thank you," Mary said. "Let's skip the obvious bits. How did this happen?"

"You ignored my advice?"

The System couldn't have been more Eloise-like if Eloise had designed it herself. Since *Mary* had been the one to design it, that just brought up a lot of disturbing questions about her subconscious thought processes. "Rephrasing the question," she said. "How can we fix our setup so that doesn't happen again?"

"You can take my advice next time."

"Noted. And?"

"Additional sensors."

Mary touched her back and flinched. She had medical basics upstairs, with robotic arms for the System to assist her. Still, she'd have to take a few days off from hunting retirees to let her back heal. "Ceiling forcefield?"

"You do like forcefields. But yes, that could help."

Forcefields and sensors. She'd fled the beach house with plenty of gear, or so she'd thought at the time. Now, it felt like the bare minimum. She couldn't keep running down her limited stashes of money, and she certainly couldn't go buying expensive raw electronics. That would bring the league down on her for sure.

But she couldn't let the retirees escape, either. And if she wanted to shore up her defenses here for the long term, she was going to have to pay a visit to Malibu.

IT WAS NEARLY four-thirty in the morning by the time Mary reached Malibu and stashed Grandma in the parking lot of a public beach. She wanted to approach the house from the water, to try and avoid the notice of any reporters, LIO cameras, or even Wave spies that could be watching. So many enemies, so many eyes.

She already half regretted rocketing to Malibu without a second thought. The press might have given up searching for her, though she doubted it, but Eloise wouldn't have. There would be eyes on every entrance. She shouldn't go back.

But Mary couldn't risk ordering the parts she needed, either. And she definitely couldn't allow another escape scenario. So with parchment-dry eyelids and a running total of the hours she'd been awake clicking away in her brain—minus the brief nap at Aries, which hardly cancelled out the fight with Monster and the six-hour drive, never mind the new scrapes across her back—Mary left Grandma behind and started out along the beach.

The waves whispered greetings as she walked along the shore, hood raised, hands tucked into her pockets. Her feet ached, her back a wall of pain, and breathing the ocean air swelled emotions to the surface that she didn't like to face. Memories of her parents now mixed with the pain of the last few months, and it made her feel lost. It made her feel unraveled.

With her celebrity identity exposed and her independent operative life stripped away, Mary had no idea who she was supposed to be.

Since she didn't know, she'd decided to make it up as she went along. She was justice. She was retribution. She was doing what no one else would.

Mary rounded a curve in the beach, and the house emerged. It sat on a short cliff, its wide windows reflecting the pre-dawn sky. The house was dark and quiet, but otherwise exactly as it had always been. The glass windows looked out as though searching for her, the edge of her bedroom balcony sending a new surge of memories into her mind.

She was too tired to think clearly. She was coming undone. "This was a bad idea," she whispered.

As if to confirm that thought, a shadow peeled away from the cliffside and streaked toward her.

Mary flung herself toward the attacker, thanking her body for its muscle memory as it kicked her exhausted limbs into gear. Even so, she felt sluggish as she hit the shadow, her arms aching as she dragged them into motion, the wounds in her back stretching painfully. In the seconds it took to slam the dark-clad silhouette back against the rock wall, Mary knew she couldn't possibly be fighting a professional.

Tired as Mary was, a professional would have her on the ground by now. They might not win, but they'd have taken advantage of the upper hand.

Still, Mary pinned the person with an elbow to the collarbone, a knee to the hip.

"Wait," the shadow gasped, "stop."

"Who are you?"

"Dawn Kimble," the shadow said. "Reporter."

Mary dropped her arm, and Dawn sagged in relief, resting her palms on her thighs. "Damn," she said. "I better take another self defense class."

"It'll take more than one," Mary said dryly. "And *you* attacked *me*."

Dawn straightened, shaking her head. It was too dark to make out the details of her face, and Mary didn't recognize the name. She knew a few of the regular paparazzi, by sight at least, but Jenna's unveiling of Mary's secret identity last fall had drawn the rabid attention of much more respected publications. She'd seen the headlines, though she avoided reading. It didn't matter.

Dawn held up a mini recorder that she'd somehow slipped out of her pocket without Mary seeing. Dangerous. It could have been a weapon.

"I just want to talk," Dawn said.

"On record."

Dawn shrugged. "It's the job."

"How did you find me?"

The reporter tilted her head up toward the house. "You do live here. Don't you?"

"I haven't been back in months."

"No, but you can see how it's a logical starting point," Dawn said, like she was teaching third-grade math to a rocket scientist. "I'm just the only one who thought to watch the beach."

Mary pressed her palms into her eyes, her head swimming with the buzzy pain of fatigue. Of course there were others. Plus whatever Eloise had going, and she had to have something. Mary was almost impressed with the reporter's tenacity, waiting here all night. Some would have packed it in at midnight. Some would have packed it in a month ago.

Mary had known better than to come here, and she'd done it anyway. It wasn't as if she didn't have other methods for getting inside. Not only was she naming cars and houses, she was falling back on sentimentality. Risky. Dangerous. She could practically hear Eloise's voice in her head saying 'I told you so.' But if El had been here to warn her away from recklessness, would Mary even have listened? Probably not.

"All I want is an exclusive," Dawn said.

Mary dropped her hands to her sides. The waves murmured in the background, unhurried friends. She breathed. "Oh, is that all?"

"Don't you think people have a right to know what's going on? Whether they're still in at risk?"

"Not if sharing that information endangers me."

"Mary. Please." Dawn waved the recorder precariously close to Mary's face, the red light a streak in the darkness. Of course, the reporter would have been recording this conversation.

Mary snatched the device out of Dawn's hand and flung it toward the water, hoping she'd managed to drown the thing, but not at all confident in the current strength of her throwing arm. Maybe a seagull would peck it.

"That was unnecessary," Dawn said.

"Was it?"

"Talk to me," Dawn said, relentless, "and I'll let you escape back down the beach."

Mary laughed, throat stinging. "You'll let me? Are you that eager for another hand-to-hand demonstration?"

Mary wasn't sure she was up for a fight herself, even with a self-defense-class novice. But she had enough energy to bluff. Dawn hesitated, and Mary wished she could see the woman's face as she waited, contemplating escape. If Mary ran back down the beach, Dawn would follow; she might call someone who had a car, or who lurked closer to the lot where Grandma waited.

Call her sentimental, but Mary wasn't ready to showcase her ride. Especially since losing the van would require finding another one.

"Talk to me," Dawn said, "or I'll scream."

Oh, that was just what the headlines needed. *Rogue Independent Operative Terrorizes Reporter.* No doubt that one would show up in every publication that had someone posted outside her house.

It didn't matter how much Mary needed her materials. Coming here had been a huge mistake, half rooted in... what, nostalgia? Grief? She could have sent drones to get the things she needed. Should have.

Mary took a few steps back. Dawn tensed, probably ready to run after her, but Mary bolted past the reporter and leapt for the wall, scrambling easily up the familiar rocks and swinging herself over the side of the cliff. A motion-detecting light flashed on from the corner of her house, blinding her, and she swerved across the lawn, darting for the street by memory alone.

Mary didn't know who'd installed that motion light. It certainly hadn't been her.

Someone shouted, and footsteps pounded after her, too loud against the background noise of waves and whispering palms.

"Mary!" Dawn called, and Mary ran faster, scaling the gate that protected her house from the street—though not particularly well, she saw that now—and hitting the sidewalk in a graceless heap, barely biting back a cry of pain from the wounds in her back. They weren't even that deep. She was just... out of practice. That was all. She pushed herself to her feet as shadows pounded toward her from the direction of the front entrance, the vultures alerted to her presence.

"People have a right to know about you," Dawn yelled after her, and maybe she wasn't wrong, but Mary didn't stop. Feet numb, she made herself run, hopelessly aimless. Where was she even supposed to go?

Three figures appeared beneath the cool light of the street-lamp, men in t-shirts wearing identically hopeful expressions.

"It's like a goddamn zombie attack out here," Mary muttered. She tried to cut across the street, but another reporter materialized from that direction.

Of course, they had to know about LIO's secret entrance to the house, even if they hadn't pinpointed its location yet. They'd certainly be looking for a while. But they were working together, each with their own secret stakeout position, and she didn't need her paparazzi pin to know cameras were clicking, that the country would wake up to fresh pictures of Coral-slash-Mary-O'Sullivan tomorrow, whether she liked it or not.

Mary halted, head pounding, feet tingling. She turned to face Dawn, who'd huffed up behind her, a cluster of her colleagues hustling to catch up. Dawn held up her phone—smart of her to use the better device as a backup, and Mary wondered wryly if the reporter had been expecting the destruction of the first one—and Mary could see her face, pale and round beneath a ragged fringe of bleached bangs, eyes triumphant.

Mary hated losing.

She opened her mouth to speak, and a black sedan swung around the corner, headlights sweeping the sidewalk. It pulled to a stop as the reporters squinted, some shading their eyes, and Mary tried to decide whether to fight or run.

But she already knew the answer to that; if this person was

here to cause trouble, she'd protect the reporters as best she could. They were here because of her. She might not be ready to talk to them—she definitely didn't trust them—but she wouldn't allow them to get hurt, either.

The back door of the car swung open, and Jeff Hayes stuck his golden head out of the back seat. "Need a ride?"

"It was really smart of you to show your face," Mary said as Jeff's car skimmed along the highway, leaving Malibu and the swarm of confused reporters behind. "I mean really, that's like superhero 101. And I don't think open containers are allowed in cars like this. Do you trust your driver?"

The driver, who had to have heard her, didn't turn.

Jeff Hayes sipped his drink, an amber concoction with a pair of ruby cherries bobbing alongside the ice. Apparently unconcerned by her deluge of questions, he had a jacket on, his gray sweatpants distinguishable in the pulsing lights of the highway, and Mary wondered if her appearance had somehow roused him out of his bed. He certainly didn't seem like the kind of person who tended to usher in the sunrise.

Jeff leaned his head back on the seat and flashed her a lazy grin, one she supposed must help him to wheedle his way into various people's graces. Or rom-com scripts. "Mary, how lovely to see you. You're welcome for the save. Would you like a drink?"

She did want a drink. "I'd prefer a time machine."

"Darling, you should have said. Alas, I'm between time machine vendors at the moment."

Mary snorted. "Doing your impression of a charming person tonight, are you?"

"The Oscar on my mantel says I'm equal to the task."

"And yet you seem to be currently unemployed."

He waved the comment away, unconcerned. "Seriously, Mary, what are you doing in L.A.? I thought you'd be hiding somewhere dismally remote after you never showed up in Tahoe. Like Antarctica, or Cincinnati."

Jeff had actually ditched his entitled-asshole personality for a few seconds last fall, after Jenna's explosive broadcast had outed Coral's secret identity. Though Jeff had been recovering from a mind-control drugging, he'd helped them to deal with the press and offered to hide Mary while the story blew over.

She'd accepted. But then Nathan had chosen the league over her, and everything had been so confused. Jeff hated Nathan, which could have made him a good option, but in the end she hadn't been able to bring herself to trust anyone at all.

Mary leaned back and stretched out her feet. "You thought I was in Cincinnati, but you were watching my house? What were you even doing out there?"

"I hedge my bets, as you know. Besides, I live in Malibu. It's hardly a stretch."

"You should've hedged them more by staying hidden."

"Would you have gotten in the car if you hadn't seen my face?"

She wasn't sure she should have gotten in the car, anyway. But seeing as her other option had been an impromptu press conference in the middle of one of America's wealthiest neighborhoods, she supposed there hadn't been much of a choice. "No," she said. "I wouldn't have."

Jeff mocked a toast and took another sip, expression sobering. "You look exhausted."

Mary settled lower into her seat, fighting the urge to pull the hood of her sweatshirt back up. "Thanks. Haven't had much time with my stylist lately."

Jeff sipped his drink, the ice clinking against the glass. Did he actually have a cooler in here? Probably. If anyone had a cooler in a sedan, it was Jeff Hayes. "Have you seen yourself?" he said. "You're a disaster. When was the last time you washed your hair? Pearce might be gentle enough not to mention it, so I'll do the man a favor. You look like hell."

"And your car smells like feet."

Jeff looked at her. "Where *is* Pearce? Why isn't he helping you?"

Mary closed her eyes. The road hummed a lullaby, and the world tilted. "I appreciate your help," she said, her voice sounding distant. "Can you drop me at a hotel?"

"I can put you up, Mary. Pick a continent, I've got a house on it. Unless you're dead set on Antarctica, I suppose."

"They'll be watching you."

"You need help."

He actually sounded genuine, not that she could trust what she heard when it came to Oscar-winning Jeff Hayes. But when the walls squeezed in, he did prove himself an ally. If an annoying one.

"All right," Mary said. "But first, I need something from my house. And I want my car back."

It wasn't right, Grandma sitting all alone in that beach parking lot. She'd be out of place come sunrise, an eyesore among all the Bentleys and Teslas. Mary realized the thought was a silly one, but it made her sad all the same.

Jeff said something in response—possibly an expletive—but before Mary could form a comeback, sleep descended.

THE PARSE GALAXY, SECTOR 43.9123484A DRAGON'S LUCK
ORBITING CASINO

SLOANE HAD NEVER IMAGINED that a casino might be equipped with interrogation chambers, until she'd tried to rob one. Hindsight, and all that.

Archimedes Sol questioned troublemakers on one of the top floors of his orbiting gambling oasis, in a room with wide expanses of glass windows that overlooked the lush planet below, greens and blues and browns obscured by occasional golden cloud cover. A luxurious planet. A rich one, too.

But Sloane wasn't meant to admire the view; she was meant to fear the vacuum of space that extended *between* her and the view. Because the corner of the room featured the unmistakable arch of an airlock hookup, the perfect size for connecting a single-person skiff.

Or for shoving would-be thieves into the black, one by one.

Hands locked to the table, Sloane could only watch helplessly as one of Archimedes's thugs beat the shit out of her security officer. The thug packed a good punch, but he was wiry.

Sloane thought Oliver could probably have taken the guy, had his hands not been restrained behind his back. His lip bled freely, and if he survived today, he'd definitely end up with a black eye.

"I want damages," Archimedes Sol said, his thug punctuating the sentence with a blow to Oliver's jaw. Archimedes was a big man—he might have been better off doing the punching himself—with a full head of hair that was too inky black to be natural. His skin was bone-white, the backs of his hands tattooed in the style of the inter-planet dwellers, flecks of bright color arranged in a pattern that looked like meaningless confetti to Sloane. Oliver would be able to decipher it. He had his own set.

Archimedes Sol stood eerily still, arms hanging loose at his sides. "I want damages, and I want them with interest."

"What damages?" Sloane said. "We didn't actually steal anything."

Because their plan had been a shitty one. *Drop in from the ceiling*, Oliver had said. *It'll be easy*, he'd said. Sloane would have liked to think it was her criminal inexperience that'd swayed her, but in truth, she'd just wanted him to keep kissing her.

Big mistake.

"Of course you didn't," Archimedes Sol scoffed. "People don't steal from me. But you targeted my high rollers, and they saw you. That hurts my reputation, which in turn costs me money."

Please, Sloane thought. This patrons had loved the drama. She'd be willing to bet this little incident would help his business more than it hurt.

But she wasn't exactly in a position to negotiate. "Give us two weeks," she said. "We'll pay whatever you want."

"What I want is a million tokens in damages—galactic

tokens, not your useless Forgeian currency. And I want it in two days."

Oliver laughed, and the thug silenced him with a blow across the jaw that made Sloane cringe. The brutality was at odds with the luxurious surroundings, chandeliers glowing knowingly above, a duo of abstract marble sculptures guarding the entrance. She'd have thought the room had been hastily repurposed, if not for the handcuff-equipped tables and the two-way glass window.

"Two days," Sloane repeated. "That's not possible."

Archimedes Sol waved a huge hand. "Let them go. I'll enjoy the sport of hunting them across the galaxy." He shook his head. "I thought you were from the clean branch of the family, Ms. Tarnish."

Sloane cringed. He knew her name. Of course he did. And she *was* from the clean branch of the family, damnit, or she had been. Her father was going to kill her when he found out about this. No doubt Archimedes Sol would make the call himself, as soon as she'd gone.

The thug released Sloane from her cuffs, and then Oliver, who sagged in his chair as she rushed toward him.

"Two days," Archimedes Sol repeated, drifting out of the room with surprising grace for a man of his bulk.

Sloane offered Oliver her shoulder, and together they followed the thug down to the docks where their star schooner, the *Moneymaker*, waited. Along with the crew Sloane hadn't asked for and didn't want.

She'd half expected to find the thing blown to smithereens. But her uncle's old rust bucket was just as they'd left it.

Sloane wasn't sure whether to be relieved or disappointed.

"Bet I look roguish," Oliver slurred into her ear.

"Oh, totally," Sloane said. "They should put you on a fleet recruiting poster."

"That'd make it more honest advertising, anyway," he said.

Sloane forced a laugh, though she wasn't sure she completely understood the joke. She didn't know much about what it was like to be in the fleet, only how good the uniforms looked when a platoon came planetside. Though apparently, Oliver did. She'd have to ask him about that later.

For now, Sloane supported him up the gangplank and deposited him in the infirmary. "Don't move," she said. "I want to give you a full scan."

Oliver lay back in the patient chair and lifted a hand to his head. "Get us out of here, doc."

Sloane climbed the ladder to the navigation deck to where Hilda sat in her pilot's chair, scrolling through celebrity gossip feeds, her long gray braid flipped over her shoulder. Her green parakeet hopped across the dashboard, singing happily.

"Did we get the money?" Hilda asked, pausing for a longer look at a man with a particularly chiseled chest.

Sloane leaned over Hilda's shoulder and pointed outside. "There's a corps of armed guards standing right out there. See the scary guns?"

Hilda looked up, squinting. "Huh. So we should leave now?"

"If it's not too much of a bother."

Hilda waved her away as if to say it wasn't, and Sloane bit back another sarcastic remark as she slipped out of the navigation deck. She paused at Alex's door, curious as to whether the scientist had even noticed her absence.

"Did you do the thing?" Alex asked without looking up. She had goggles perched on top her of brown hair, and Sloane wondered if their presence ought to concern her.

"No," Sloane said.

Alex tsked and tipped something into a beaker. "Well, don't worry. You'll get it next time. Or my theory will prove correct and we'll make millions of tokens by engineering inter-system wormhole travel."

It was Alex's life's work, poring over wormholes and port-hole theories. Sloane had yet to see evidence that she'd made a single breakthrough. Or, for that matter, evidence for why her uncle kept Alex on his crew.

"Yeah, OK," Sloane said. "Keep working on that."

Alex frowned. "What else would I do?"

Sloane swung back down to the infirmary as Hilda navigated the ship out of the bay. No doubt Archimedes Sol had a tracking marker hidden on the *Moneymaker*—gods, she hated that name—one Sloane would never find, because she wasn't an engineer or a pilot or a criminal. She was a medical student whose loser uncle had saddled her with a broken ship, an inept crew, and a plea to get them back to him. Which required a journey across the stars-damned galaxy, for which Sloane had no funds.

Hence the attempted casino robbing. As if that could have ever been anything but a catastrophic failure. She'd let Oliver convince her, with his wide smile and his bedroom eyes. And now she needed twice the money she'd needed when this day started.

"I'm sorry to tell you this," she told the ship, "but we're basically fucked."

THE GLARE from the wall-sized screen in Eloise's office reflected in the surface of the Pearl Knife, which lay serenely on her desk as though in slumber. The rainbow lights from the live view of the Horseshoe Falls swam across the blade while Eloise stared, head in her hands. As if the Knife might yield its secrets as it dreamed.

Hours spent in simulations had taught her nothing more about what had happened in Santa Monica, or in the months since. The portal. The visions. The increasing difficulty in controlling the blade when it decided to go its own way. The Knife resisted all manner of scans and tests, its material as inscrutable as ever. Eloise honestly didn't know what else to do, so she'd taken to staring. Hardly a productive tactic, but it wasn't as though more scientific approaches had yielded anything more valuable.

A knock on the door made her jump, and she rubbed her cheeks as she called for the visitor to come in, wondering how long she'd been sitting here. Sometimes she couldn't tell if the Knife had pulled her into some kind of a trance, or if she'd simply been daydreaming on her own.

Nathan entered hesitantly, hands tucked into the pockets

of his jeans. "I saw the light on," he said. "Just thought I'd see if you wanted company."

Eloise rubbed her eyes. "It's not so late. Is it?"

The rainbow lights on the falls blinked off, as if in answer. Which meant it was midnight. Nathan shrugged, and Eloise got up to make him a drink. It always felt so old-school corporate, to have a wet bar in her office, but she had yet to regret the choice. At least she didn't have it transferred to crystal decanters. Though as far as power moves went, she could think of worse ones.

"How are things at the academy?" Eloise asked, pouring him a short glass of whiskey on the rocks to match her own. She had a feeling he preferred beer, but until she had taps installed, he'd have to settle.

Nathan gave a short laugh and dropped into one of the chairs beside her desk. "They are kicking my ass."

"Acting like a team?"

"Healthy competition, group lunches. I'd say so, yeah. Ire's doing a good job. If any more show up, though, you're going to need another teacher."

"Oh? That's good news." She settled back into her chair. "Who would you suggest?"

It was a genuine question, but Nathan's eyes widened a little in surprise. As if she hadn't invited him to LIO in the first place, made him a full member, and taken him into her confidence. Yes, he was training with the other newcomers, but he'd also knocked on her door tonight. He knew she valued him.

He still acted like his involvement here was all some kind of a mistake, like she might kick him out tomorrow morning.

"I don't know," he said slowly. "I think you could assign a non-enhanced team member to take up the next level of teaching. Ire's good at grounding them in their abilities. Beyond that, they're all so different. I'm guessing they'll need space to figure things out on their own."

"Are you volunteering?"

"Not yet," he said, without hesitating. "I've got to pass training, too." He stared into his glass without drinking. "It'd be good, though. For them to know from the start that non-enhanced operatives have a place here."

"It's sound advice. I'll talk to Ire about it, see what he thinks."

Eloise waited, curious to see if he'd mention Mary. She was a non-enhanced operative, after all. And if she could tame her restless impulses for a bit, she might actually enjoy the teaching. Eloise shook her head at that line of thought. She couldn't seem to stop thinking of Mary as a part of the league, no matter how long she'd been gone. As if she'd simply been off on a typical mission. As if she'd be back any minute.

"How's it going with Dolly?" Nathan asked, changing the subject. As he always did when it veered too close to Mary. They talked around her, always.

Eloise understood the impulse. Unfortunately, it was the same one she had whenever someone mentioned her mother. Eloise had stationed team guards outside of Dolly's room, confining her to her quarters, but she knew it wasn't truly enough. Not with dubiously guilty Wave operatives imprisoned beneath their feet, and Dolly's crimes out in the open, at least among members of the league.

Eloise hadn't even been to see her. It got harder every day.

Before she could form so much as the beginnings of a response, alarms shrieked into the room, lights above the door flashing neon panic. Eloise shot out of her chair, swiping the Knife off the desk as she bolted for the door. Nathan followed, his glass shattering as he dropped it to run after her.

"Attempted breach," Eloise shouted back to him as signals

pulsed yellow and green along the ceiling, though he probably already knew the codes. He seemed like someone who studied. "Casino entrance."

There'd never been a breach at LIO HQ, but they'd drilled for one. Eloise shut her panic away with practiced calm, taking care to keep breathing as she ran. Who the hell could have gotten close enough to HQ to set off a breach alarm? Her first thought was that U.S. Post reporter, but the idea was ridiculous. She'd be shocked if that man could investigate his way out of his own ego.

Team members poured into the corridors, hurrying toward their assigned stations in case the attempted breach became a successful one, many of them clad in pajamas. Engineers, computer scientists, weapons experts, and research assistants, readying themselves to fight, scour data, or retreat. Depending on Eloise's orders.

If Eloise fell, Ire would order them. If Ire fell... well, they were a bit short on veterans at the moment.

The Pearl Knife beat a discordant rhythm into her mind, objecting—she could feel it—to the idea of Eloise falling. *Don't worry*, Eloise thought wryly. *I'd object to that, too.*

But it paid to be prepared.

Eloise burst into the back corridor with Nathan on her heels. As per protocol, the area had emptied of team members, and they rushed for the elevator that led directly to the secret casino entrance. The elevator felt sluggish, and Eloise had to tamp down an anxious series of images that flooded into her brain as her adrenaline surged. Enhanced humans throwing slot machines around, injuring late-night patrons as enemies flooded the hotel suite the league owned under Mary's name.

When the doors opened, Eloise threw open the faux closet doors to find Ire fighting with a blur.

That was the only way to describe it. As they entered, Ire

was in the process of throwing his significant mass at a quivering burst of a person who hardly seemed to be there at all. Ire's fist met air, as if he'd been aiming at a hologram—except for the rush of wind that accompanied the other person's movements—and his momentum sent him crashing across the room and into an antique roll-top desk. The cover burst into splinters as he righted himself, staggering slightly with his own momentum. Ire wasn't clumsy, not at all, but Eloise could hardly see his opponent. It was no wonder he hadn't managed to hit them.

Nathan stood frozen at Eloise's side, watching in stunned horror as Ire attempted to catch the trespasser, who evaded his attempts by streaking over the bed and leaping onto the heater by the window, where they rocketed back and forth like a pinball caught in a trap. Eloise could barely follow their movements; it was like watching a race car zoom past.

But the person wasn't invisible, or holographic. Which meant they had to be moving at super-speed.

Ire ripped the phone out of the wall, ready to throw it at the intruder. Eloise held up a hand to stop him, opening her palm to shoot the Knife after the blur instead. The blade stopped just short of the heater, hovering. Holding back, at her command.

"I don't know which essential organ I might hit if you don't freeze immediately," Eloise said.

The blur stopped short, materializing into a handsome black man. Watching him stop was like watching pixels crystalize on a screen, from blurry to crisp in a blink.

And Eloise knew him. He had on a leather jacket and a pinstriped fedora, a combination that would have looked ridiculous on anyone else but which, of course, Steve Taylor pulled off with breath-stealing audacity. He raised his hands above his head.

For one hopeless summer, Eloise had let herself have a crush on this man. Oh, they'd been kids at the time—fifteen?

Sixteen?—and Flick had brought him for an uninterrupted six weeks of training. Steve had fallen in with Mary and Eloise on their adventures, sneaking around and out of HQ, causing minor trouble in Niagara.

She'd mourned his absence for a week after he left, then moved on. He'd visited again, of course, but by then she'd been too wrapped up in training to pay him much mind.

There was absolutely no reason his presence should make her heart skip now. Unless it was out of pure, unadulterated rage.

Somewhere beneath her surprise, Eloise wondered how the hat stayed on Steve's head when he ran a hundred miles an hour, or whatever it was.

"Sorry," he said. "I tried looking for the doorbell. I swear."

Eloise pressed her communication link. "Cut the alarms," she said. "Breach override. Everything's fine, you can all go back to bed." She called the Knife back to her hand, allowing herself a beat to breathe as she assessed Steve, doing her best to engage her sternest expression. "We also have a phone."

Steve shrugged, dipping his head as if in contrition. Except for the fact that truly contrite people didn't smile like that, a hint of mischief in their eyes.

Before Eloise could start asking questions, Nathan overcame his shock to step in front of her. "*Steve?*"

The man in question folded his fingers in a sheepish wave. "Hey, buddy. Miss you down at the station."

Nathan looked at Eloise, whose brain was quickly adding up two plus two. "You were Mom's contact. The one she had watching Nathan in Boston."

Nathan stared at her, unblinking. "What?"

Eloise stuffed the Knife into its sheath, suddenly embarrassed that she'd opted not to tell Nathan how closely he'd been on watch. She hadn't thought it important enough to share the details, that was all. "Dolly told me last year she had someone monitoring you, but that they'd stopped reporting in. That was you, Steve?"

Steve nodded, hands still lifted, and Eloise motioned for him to drop them. She should have realized that Steve would have stayed connected with the league, even after he'd gone off to college. Apparently when Flick left for good, Steve had, too.

But he hadn't given up his post, even after splitting from LIO. That was interesting.

"I did tell you we knew about your past, and your mother's involvement with Wave," Eloise told Nathan apologetically. "I just... didn't realize we were still watching."

"Via my best friend in the force. Who's an independent operative." Nathan scrubbed a hand through his hair, and she could almost see him thinking that while he'd searched for IOs all those years, there'd been one standing right beside him.

Steve hopped down from the heater and clapped Ire on the shoulder, a move Eloise would not have attempted just then. He had a pair of gold studs sparkling in each ear, and the same dimples as always. "You all right, big guy?"

Ire grunted and gave Steve a sour look. "Next time call first."

Steve nodded and caught Eloise's eyes, his expression sobering. "I didn't mean to crash in like this, El, honest, but I need your help. It's my father. He's missing."

▭

Back in her office, with the Knife still secured at her waist and the muted falls hiding in the dark, Eloise breathed her heart back to its normal pace by contemplating the changing of the guard that LIO was still undergoing. Six months ago, she'd have been consulting with Agnes, Mary, and Ire. Now, Nathan was cleaning up the glass from the drink he'd spilled, while Steve took his hat off and collapsed into a chair, legs crossed, eyes pinched with worry.

At least Ire was still here, leaning against the wall with his arms crossed. From the looks of it, he had one foot out the door. If not for the academy, Eloise suspected he'd have gone Mary's way. Off the grid.

"So Flick is missing," Eloise said, sitting on the edge of her desk and resting her palms beside her. It felt too... boss-like, to go for the chair behind it. "Are you sure he's not just stuck in his panic room?"

It came out sounding like a joke, though she hadn't meant it as one. Eloise was well aware of the paranoid, survivalist tendencies Flick had developed since her father's death and Dolly's abdication had fractured the original league. After everything Eloise had learned since then, she hardly blamed him.

Flick's reaction might even be a mark in his favor.

"Believe it or not, I checked," Steve said. "El, you've got to know that the old guard have been disappearing. Monster, Carlisle, now Flick. All vanished. Unless you're hiding them here?"

Eloise caught Nathan's eye, and he raised an eyebrow. Apparently Steve didn't trust her, or the league, any more than his father did. One part of her couldn't blame him, but the other... the other wanted him to see her and believe she could make everything right. That she *would*.

"I do know," Eloise said. "But my plate is overflowing. I don't know how I can help."

Steve leaned forward, his eyes like dark pools of pain. He had to be beside himself with panic. "Please, El. I'll lead the effort, I just... I need your resources. I need your expertise. I wouldn't be here if I had any other choice."

That comment stung, but it didn't surprise her. What did surprise her was that no matter what his thoughts on the league as a whole, Steve thought she had any expertise to offer. The retirees—the operatives Steve called the old guard—had spent days screaming at each other when her mother had named Eloise head of LIO. And once they'd been all screamed out, they'd slammed the doors and abandoned the league in a huff. Leaving Eloise alone to manage the team, not to mention Mary, Agnes, and Ire. And her ailing mother. Who also happened to be a criminal.

And Steve thought Eloise had *expertise*? She should correct him, explain how little control she actually had. But he was looking at her with such hope...

Eloise sighed. "I can't," she said. "I'm not... we can't really spare any people for this. Not in the field, anyway. You're welcome to stay, use our resources to find out what you can. I'll grant whatever clearances you need."

Mary would have balked at that, said something snarky about protocol. But Eloise actually wished Steve would stay. With him back on the team? Well, one more ally would be to their benefit.

Maybe she *should* reallocate some people to help him with his search, assign a few team members to the task. Gail was busy, but Pete might have time to help with surveillance.

"I'll help," Nathan said, and Eloise shot him a look. But that didn't keep him from continuing. "It's her, isn't it? You think Mary's been kidnapping the old guard."

Eloise hesitated, but she supposed Steve would have to know that if he meant to find Flick. She needed time to think. She thought of her mother, under guard but still in her room rather than the cell she'd admitted to having earned. "And I'm not sure she's wrong to do it," Eloise said.

Eloise would have gone about it a different way. But that

was why she'd always needed Mary. And Mary needed her. Where could she be stashing them?

Steve frowned—he'd grown up with Mary, too, though more in an 'I'm here for vacation' kind of way. Was he surprised at her potential involvement?

Nathan said, "Partner me with Steve. I can help."

Nathan was too close to this, too eager. She didn't want to tell him that if anyone could drive Mary further away, it was him. "I'm not sure that's a good idea."

"I can handle it."

She wasn't convinced that he could, but she said, "You're not the one I'm worried about."

She liked Nathan, she really did. But sending him after Mary felt like a betrayal. Sending *anyone* after her felt like a betrayal.

Surely sending help couldn't be a betrayal. Eloise had seen the blurred images of Mary standing outside her house in Malibu, the accounts of how she'd escaped into an unmarked sedan. By the time Eloise sent team staff out to search for her, Mary had been long gone. What was she up to? And what had made her slip up like that?

However Mary was managing it, Eloise thought it was probably past time to send help her way. Whether she wanted it or not.

Unless she'd exposed herself to the press on purpose. Eloise rubbed her temple, trying to delay an oncoming headache. It seemed inevitable at this point.

Nathan swas still staring at Eloise, gray eyes boring into her as if he could will her to make a decision in his favor. "She'll try to crush you," Eloise said.

"Maybe."

Steve was looking back and forth between Nathan and

Eloise, eyebrows drawn together in confusion. "I missed something."

"Nathan and Mary dated," Ire said. He pushed away from the wall. "If we're caught up on last week's soap operas, can I go back to the academy now?"

One foot out the door. "Of course," Eloise said, and he stalked out of the room. He didn't quite slam the door behind him, but she made a note to check on him later anyway—he had to be missing Agnes—before turning back to Steve. "I'll message Pete in the surveillance lab and let him know you'll need access."

Steve stood. "Thank you."

Eloise tapped her fingers on the desk. "I'd like a word with you," she said to him. "Alone."

Nathan cast one more glance at Steve and gave his head a little shake as if to dispel his lingering confusion before following Ire out of the room.

Steve faced her, thumbs hooked through his belt loops. "It's good to see you, El," he said.

She looked him in the eye, and for a breath she was sixteen again, his smile catching her just under the ribcage. "Yes," she said, summoning the most businesslike tone she could. "You, too."

Steve cleared his throat. "I think we should bring the old guard here. Offer them shelter. They could be in danger."

Eloise picked up a stack of papers and shuffled through them as though they held an answer, stalling. She didn't know why she should be nervous to talk to him, to ask him anything. It was ridiculous. "And I think you should join the league. Officially."

Steve lifted an eyebrow. "Extortion? I wouldn't have expected it of you."

"No," Eloise said, flustered. She set the papers down, trying to hide it. "Not extortion. We'll help you. But we desperately need senior operatives."

Steve crossed the room and came to lean beside her on the desk. No one would have dared that with Dolly. Well, maybe Mary would have. His sleeve brushed against hers. "El, I want to stay as far away from LIO as I can manage. I'm only here because I'm desperate."

Eloise swallowed a wad of regret. It seemed she'd always be paying for her parents' crimes. Still, there was hope here. He *had* said she had expertise, hadn't he? "And I don't trust the old guard," Eloise said. "I won't bring them here unless I have to."

Steve let his chin drop to his chest, but Eloise couldn't let his disappointment sway her. There was too much at stake. The original LIO members might not all have been involved with the murder of Mary's parents, but some of them surely had been.

"But otherwise your help isn't contingent on me joining?" Steve asked.

"Of course not."

He pushed off the desk and retrieved his hat from the chair, flipping it back onto his head. "Then good night, El. I'll let you know what we find."

Eloise watched him go, wishing she could call him back—someone who remembered the old days here, even a piece of them—and refraining. She needed to maintain control over LIO, and she wouldn't accomplish that by unloading her emotions on someone who'd once been a friend.

Sighing, she unsheathed the Pearl Knife and laid it back on her desk.

MARY WAS ALWAYS glad to absorb herself in a tech project. Back at Aries after her ill-advised stint in Malibu, she crouched above Carlisle's cell, the nutrition hatch open at her side as she screwed sensors into the gap that had allowed Monster to hide. It was still hard to believe that the huge man had tucked himself into a space the size of a couple of shoeboxes, enhancements or not. What had he done, dissolve his bones?

She needed to know more, but enhancements weren't her area of expertise, and she could only handle so much at one time.

After spending a single night in Jeff Hayes's guest room, Mary had done what she should have done in the first place and sent drones to collect the materials she needed from her beach house. She'd taken a perverse pleasure in flying them over the heads of the reporters who ambled around outside of Jeff's house, waiting for her.

The press might know who they were dealing with now, but they still had no idea what she was capable of. Maybe it was wrong of her to hold the past against them. Maybe she didn't care.

Getting out of Jeff's house without being seen had taken a bit more maneuvering. Not to mention swallowing a fair amount of her pride. Taking a room for the night was one thing. Hiding in the trunk of a sedan? A different matter entirely.

Accepting help from Jeff Hayes, of all people. She had to be out of her mind.

She'd spent her first night back at Aries installing a force-field across the prison ceiling while the System nattered at her about dangerous technology and lack of sleep. But there was no one else to do this work. It was just her. So she took her time, avoided getting zapped into next week, and breathed more easily knowing there were extra precautions in place.

Lack of sleep or not, she always enjoyed her tech work. Even when its purpose was distasteful. She'd be enjoying it even now, if not for the prisoners themselves. She'd taken care of Monster's cell first, just to get it out of the way. Now, Carlisle stared up at her with doleful eyes, unable to sleep—or feign it—with her tromping around over his head. At least the power suppressant seemed to be holding.

Mary screwed in the last bolt on Carlisle's security upgrade and activated the new sensor, ran a quick test, then secured the hatch. Picking up her tools, she hopped over the narrow gap to Flick's cell, careful of her footing. She really didn't need to fall into a forcefield today, and not only because she dreaded the lecture the System would give her.

When she opened Flick's hatch, he too looked up at her, and all at once she couldn't take it anymore. The silence. The mournful stares. It was really getting on her nerves. "OK," she said, "one of you guys has to say something. Want to make a special request? Hot chocolate? Spaghetti? I can get you those things."

Flick just watched her. He was a compact man, with wiry

muscles and light brown skin. She'd provided them with changes of clothing, of course, and the System retrieved laundry through the ill-named nutrition hatch, but Flick still wore his hunter green vest. He watched her, his dark eyes unreadable.

"Maybe you want to yell at me," Mary said, when he didn't respond. "Or threaten me. As in, someone knows you're here. They're closing in. Your allies will cut me to ribbons."

Flick didn't respond. Mary drilled a hole in the side of the hatch and secured the sensor ribbon with a heavy bolt. This one was acting stubborn, refusing to bend the way she told it to. If she didn't line it up correctly, it wouldn't communicate with its partner on the other side.

"Come on," she said. "I could really use the conversation. Maybe you want to try to talk me into believing I'm misguided. Off the rails. That could be fun."

"Sounds like you're the one who thinks so," Flick said quietly.

Mary snorted. Well, she *had* baited him into talking. What did she expect him to do, thank her for his incarceration? She smoothed the willful sensor into place and bolted down the other side. "I'm only doing what no one else will."

"How long have you known?" he asked. "About the plane?"

Mary realized she was scowling at the second sensor, and she smoothed out her expression. Amateur move, giving away her emotions. She was out of practice. "A few months."

Flick still hadn't moved from the bed. He just sat there, hands in his lap, looking up at her calmly. The creases by his eyes and the wrinkles on his cheeks suggested smile lines. He certainly wasn't smiling now. "It's why I was hiding," he said.

Mary twisted the last bolt in place and sat back on her heels, peering down into Flick's upturned face. "You're telling me you were more afraid of the league than of Wave? Or the criminals you socked over the years?"

He just looked at her, as if he knew he couldn't convince her and didn't see a point, and all at once she realized how alone she really was. So desperate for conversation that she'd coerced her prisoner into talking with her, then disbelieved what he'd said. She was the one picking fights here.

Satisfied that the new sensor now worked properly, Mary started to pull the hatch back over Flick's cell. Before she could shut it, though, he said, "I don't blame you for this, you know. But I do hope you'll find a way to sort it out."

"So do I," she said, unnerved by his politeness.

"Don't wait too long to go after her," he added, settling back against the wall. "She'll be ready for you."

Mary closed the hatch, securing it tightly. There was no question in her mind of who Flick meant; he was talking about the Trap.

Mary made herself double check the other hatches before descending, even though Flick's words made her want to flee upstairs as fast as she could. That was the point; she knew that. He wanted to throw her off, to play the victim. To scare her, even. Why else bring up the Trap? But if the league had frightened Flick into hiding, it was only because he'd known what they were capable of—and he hadn't split with them until years after her parents' murder. Until he'd found *himself* in potential danger.

Heroes should care about more than their own hides. She repeated it like a mantra as the System ran checks on the new sensors, then activated the ceiling forcefield. As soon as she could, Mary retreated upstairs, forcing herself not to run.

If she was really this desperate for conversation, she needed to teach the System how to play twenty questions. Not goad her prisoners into getting under her skin.

The truth was, Flick wasn't wrong about the Trap—and that was the problem.

It didn't matter. She'd get all of the retirees here—every single one—and then she'd figure out what to do with them. Eloise might be comfortable letting them get away with what they'd done, but Mary wasn't.

Feeling off balance, she flipped on the television in the living room. A little background noise, to take the edge off her isolation-induced foolishness. The Trap probably didn't even know Mary was picking off her old colleagues. There was no reason to fear her.

The first thing that came on the TV was a red carpet event. Awards season. Right. Mary sat on the arm of the couch, gripping the remote as if it could somehow save her as she watched the parade of glitter-clad celebrities making their way through the gauntlet of interviewers with carefully prepared quips and beaming smiles.

Without meaning to, Mary searched the crowd for Jeff Hayes. She caught sight of her ex, Parker Chapman—she hadn't seen him since Jeff's disastrous foundation party—and other familiar faces, but no Jeff. No Alexa, either, though that was hardly surprising. Mary's producer friend was a known Wave affiliate now, and likely keeping a low profile. She'd probably gone underground entirely, though Mary had no idea where.

Mary had always hated attending these events. The secret identity, the patches over her scars, the simpering smiles. And yet... and yet, something ached in her throat at the sight of people living her old life, continuing on without her. What did they think about all the revelations? What did Parker think?

Mary turned off the television before an interviewer could ask one of them that very question. She got out her tablet instead and settled in at the kitchen island to work.

There was no time for missing her old life, any part of it. There was only time for her mission. Now that the cells were fixed up and she'd had a chance to rest, it was time to get back to work.

"Maybe I'll work on my Diana trap," Mary said. Not because of Flick, but because it needed doing. "Can you unlock the prototype?"

"I see what you did there," the System said. "Because Diana is the Trap."

"Can't get anything past you." Mary opened her design software to run a simulation on her latest attempt. Despite her denials to Flick, she'd actually thought about looking for Diana first; the Trap was one of the few retirees she hadn't located yet. But Diana's powers made her a tricky mark, and Mary didn't want to enter an encounter unprepared.

The software on the screen showed a revolving model of her prototype, which essentially looked like a metal glove. Lurking inside each carefully designed fingertip? Needles to inject the power suppressing serum straight under Diana's poison-laced fingernails.

Mary didn't know if it would work. But it seemed the fastest way to try and neutralize Diana. And if Mary ran into her, she'd have to be fast. As she watched the screen, the System delivered a tray of parts from the gadget-delivering dumbwaiter she'd installed beneath the counter.

Drawers would have been fine. Hidden dumbwaiters were cooler.

"Seems a bit cruel for you," the System commented as the software demonstrated the needle part of the equation.

Mary rolled her eyes. "And you think Diana won't do the same thing to me if we run into each other?"

"I hardly think it would behoove her to inject serum into your fingers."

Mary opened one of the armored gloves and started to unscrew the tip of the thumb. She'd only installed about a third of the syringes. "You know what I mean. If you think she'll be taking any high roads, or avoiding cruelty, you'd be wrong."

The System was quiet for a moment, though the computer really shouldn't need to think things over. It should be able to plan out forty different tracks for this conversation in a blink.

"My records indicate that you are correct," the System said finally. "The Trap is prone to outbursts that indicate she does not shrink from violence, or even cruelty. But I have footage of roughly sixty-three fights in which you have been engaged in the last five years—"

"*Roughly* sixty-three? That's a pretty precise number."

"—and in those fights, you had twelve opportunities to attack someone from the back, fourteen opportunities to turn deadly weapons on your opponents that would have killed or incapacitated them, and three opportunities to let someone die instead of falling from a great height. Most of those opponents, based on their records, would have killed you given the chance."

The System's voice was apparently neutral, as a computer should be. So why did Mary feel... accused? She clamped a mini screwdriver between her teeth, squinting to focus. "More light. And your point is?"

"The anomalous behavior isn't Diana's. It's yours. You've always avoided hurting other humans. Now you're incarcerating them and designing torture devices."

It wasn't a torture device. It was a beat-Diana device. Mary inserted the syringe into the finger of the glove and checked the springs. She'd need some kind of a remote timer so she could activate the serum once the gloves were clamped on.

She wasn't actively hurting anyone. She was doing what she needed to do. But she didn't want to argue morality with a computer. "Times change," she said. "Now make yourself useful. While I'm doing this, see if you can find out where Ranger's staying."

▭

Mary's leg had still been in a cast when Dolly had told her about the plans for her parents' memorial. Scheduled a full month after the plane crash, the service would take place in Malibu. And Mary would need to attend.

Eleven years old, grieving and trying her best to settle into a new life at LIO HQ, Mary had balked at the idea of going out in public. Dolly couldn't accompany her and risk continuing Mary's association to the league, and nor could Will. Instead, they'd formed a plan to send her with the Trap.

Diana's secret identity was just that—a secret. She was a nobody, essentially.

And she'd resented the assignment. In hindsight, Mary thought she understood Diana's hatred; Mary's parents had been Wave operatives, and Diana had been stuck babysitting the enemy. Or so she'd apparently seen it.

Mary wanted to think she'd have approached the situation differently. She wasn't the best with bedside manner, but she'd have tried. She'd certainly have responded to a terrified child's attempts to make conversation on the flight out to L.A. But Diana had just slumped silently in her seat across the aisle, playing with her gloves and finally exploding with a threat to sedate Mary for the remainder of the trip.

Nice lady.

When the flight landed, Diana had replaced her signature crimson gloves with plain black ones, glaring at Mary the whole time.

Mary had spent the days leading up to the service thinking about her parents. About what the church would be like, if anyone would expect her to speak, and if she would be able to hold the tears back if they did.

She hadn't considered the reporters.

When Mary's LIO-driven car had pulled up at the church, it was as if they'd arrived at a red-carpet event, except for the fact that everyone was dressed in black. Reporters lined the sidewalk and clustered along the stairs, lanyards around their necks and cameras held high as they strained to reach over the chains someone had set up to keep them back—someone who'd thought of reporters, even if Mary hadn't.

Right, she could remember thinking. *I can do reporters.*

But before she'd even managed to maneuver her crutches out of the car, the reporters had begun shouting at her. And they hadn't shouted the usual questions.

Tell us about the crash how are you feeling what were your mother's last words did they have any enemies could it have been a malfunction could it have been Wave what did the Pearl Knife say where does the Inferno live where have you been staying what did you see were you afraid were you awake do you remember what was it like to what was it like to what were you thinking when—

And Mary had just... frozen. Right there in front of the church, with all those voices competing for her attention, none of them asking about Mom's latest film or Dad's favorite suit or when she might start her own acting career. The flashes had glared at her, the clicking and narrating nearly as loud as the shouted questions.

And then Diana had appeared at Mary's side to usher her past the reporters and into the church, a hair too fast for comfort. Mary's arms had been sore from working the crutches, her dress sticking to her tights. They'd settled into the reserved front row of the church, where Diana flexed her fingers, scowling. She'd had her black hair tied into a messy bun, and wore a black pant suit, black heels.

"Thanks," Mary said.

Diana began ripping the memorial program from the corner, working it into strips. "Dolly asked me to do a job. I'm doing a job."

The service, the eulogy, the flowers. To this day, Mary remembered none of it.

What she remembered was going to the bathroom after the service, Diana tapping her gloved fingertips on the edge of the sink while she waited for Mary to finish.

What Mary remembered, vividly, was snapping. It might have been that precise moment, in fact, when she'd forever stopped caring about protocol or pleasing other people. As Diana had shoved the bathroom door open before Mary had even washed her hands—or checked her reflection, a pre-press necessity—eleven-year-old Mary had just... snapped.

"Why don't you like me?" she'd asked. "Why are you treating me like a misbehaving kid?"

"News flash, highness," Diana had said, propping the door open with her back. "Not everyone likes you."

"I already know that," Mary had said. "I've seen articles that go over everything about me. My hair. My clothes. My tutoring. My weight. Why would I think everyone *likes* me?"

Her parents had tried to shield her from all that, but there'd only been so much they could do. Just thinking about it had made her eyes burn with tears, her bottom lip tremble.

Diana had rolled her eyes. "Boohoo."

Mary had barely restrained herself from stomping a foot. "Why won't you be polite, even if you don't like me?"

Diana had just smiled. "Because I don't have to," she'd said.

And then she'd walked out of the bathroom, leaving Mary alone. Against orders.

Mary had watched the door close before turning to the sink to furiously wash her hands. She'd splashed water on her face, not caring whether she smeared her makeup. Just as she was patting herself dry with a paper towel, a blonde woman wearing a black suit almost identical to Diana's had stepped out of a bathroom stall, a press badge fixed to her waist.

"OK?" the woman asked, checking her own reflection in the mirror.

Mary had nodded.

The woman had turned, leaning back on the sink, and smiled down at her. "That lady is your guardian?"

Mary had shrugged. "I guess."

The reporter had propped her palms on her knees, bending so her eyes were at Mary's level. "What *was* it like, Mary? On the plane?"

Looking back—because she had all the time in the world for that, at present—Mary was sure Diana had propped a back door open, or somehow informed the press of Mary's location. Because as Mary rushed out of the bathroom, she'd found herself surrounded. Voices had crashed into her ears in a cacophony, indistinguishable from one another, and Mary's breath had caught high in her throat. She'd stumbled back against the door, where the blonde woman was leaning against the door frame with a recorder in her hand.

Diana had been nowhere in sight. There'd been no way out.

Mary had tried to catch her breath as waves of heat rolled through her body, spots covering the reporters' faces and crushing them into a single mass. She'd tried to back up, but she'd left her crutches in the bathroom and her balance was unsteady. A screeching whine poured into her ears as she'd gasped desperately for breath.

And then, to her undying shame, Mary had fainted dead away.

Agnes Jenson removed a clean syringe from its tray and dipped it into a vial of her latest formula, drawing 2ccs of the clear liquid. It might not resemble the neon-colored serums that Mange had created, but this little concoction had already allowed a strength-enhanced rodent to jump three times higher than his previous best. Repeatedly. If she got it right, her little enhancement booster could change the world.

Now, Agnes rolled up her own sleeve and dosed herself with the liquid. The Wave tech working beside Agnes looked at her askance, biting her lip, but she didn't say anything. The others rarely said anything to her. Three months in Wave's headquarters, and most of them acted as if they fully expected her to run back to LIO any moment to spill all the intel she'd learned from Wave.

They were wrong. Agnes dropped the syringe into a tray and watched ten seconds tick by on her watch.

Aware of the tech's eyes on her, Agnes opened her senses to the energy of the light around her, imagining she could perceive the individual photons swirling in the air. She tugged at them—that was how it felt, like enticing bits of light just slightly out of alignment—and the tech gasped as Agnes warped the light around her and blinked out of sight.

Usually, wrapping herself in invisibility was like putting on a cloak. The science worked the same way, but in waves across her body. This time, she'd been able to feel the light every-where at once. And with only 2ccs. That was progress.

Her treacherous mind went straight to thoughts of how excited Ire would be when he saw what she'd done, and how much this could augment his already momentous strength, before she remembered he wouldn't see it. He wouldn't know.

A bittersweet victory, without her friend here to celebrate with her. Agnes reinstated her visibility and began typing notes into her tablet, trying to reclaim the surge of accomplishment. She felt the tech's eyes on her, and she looked up to find the woman still gaping. Agnes gave the other woman her friendliest smile, but the tech just looked away.

Suppressing a sigh, Agnes finished her notes and carried the tray of used syringes to the sink as Alexa Mannes drifted into the room. Typically the highest ranking Wave official onsite, the poor woman looked as out of place among the white coats and chemical smells as she did everywhere in Wave HQ.

High rank or not, she was trapped here just as fully as Agnes was. And she seemed to think of Agnes as a friend, though they'd never met before their arrival here. Maybe it was the Mary connection. Or maybe she recognized that Agnes felt equally out of place.

Alexa joined Agnes at the sink, looking around as though for a way to help. Alexa's heels brought her exactly to Agnes's height, and she had her brown hair pulled into a low ponytail. Well into her fifties, Alexa maintained her impeccable eye makeup despite the odd situation.

"How are you holding up?" Alexa asked. "Can I dry that?"

"They need to air dry," Agnes said. "Today was good. I think I can scale up the enhancement boosters."

"I hope you're not testing too much on yourself, my dear. There are risks, in such an endeavor. And we're not exactly close to a hospital."

That they were not. Transportation to Wave's headquarters involved accessing one of their hidden entrances on the coast—Agnes didn't know how many there were, or how many coasts featured them, though she suspected the answer was *many*—and catapulting through an underwater tunnel for hours on end.

Agnes didn't know where they were, exactly, except that the dome was located under the ocean. The Pacific, she suspected, since her entrance point had been Long Beach, California. But who could say?

"I'll be careful," Agnes said, finishing her last syringe and placing it onto the drying rack. "Would you like to come for dinner? Tam would love someone to talk to that isn't either eight years old or a boring scientist."

Alexa patted her hand. "You're hardly boring, my dear. And I'd love to. You lead the way."

With a parting wave to the other scientists and technicians —which went ignored—Agnes led the way into Wave's corridors. While similar to LIO HQ in essence, Wave's home base distinguished itself through a layer of luxury that the league had never prioritized. Where LIO's halls were defined by metal and glass, Wave had taken care to add touches of warmth. Lush blue carpets, decorative sconces, artwork on the walls—actual paintings that depicted country landscapes and sunlit cities and rooms full of laughing families. There didn't seem to be a theme to it, just a patchwork of pictures that someone happened to like.

At first, Agnes had expected the place to smell like a moldy underground lair. Instead, it smelled like fresh flowers. They had fully functioning kitchens, apartments, recreation rooms, laboratories. Just like LIO HQ, and yet so very different.

"The transition is treating you well?" Alexa asked as they walked together toward one of the residential pockets of the dome. It was hard to imagine that their surroundings sat somewhere on the seabed; Agnes frequently wondered how they'd engineered this place.

Mary would have had a field day examining every inch. And the transportation tunnels, too.

"The transition is fine," Agnes said. "Not without its hitches."

"Well, sure," Alexa said. "I missed the Golden Globes."

The corridor gently sloped around to the left, and Agnes nodded to a passing scientist she'd seen in the lab here and there. He ignored her. Alexa noticed, clucking her tongue. "They'll come around, doll," she said. "They have to respect your expertise."

"I wouldn't trust me, either," Agnes said honestly. If a former Wave associate joined up with LIO? She doubted anyone would.

Agnes's daughter, Lucy, greeted them at the door with exuberant hugs and rapid chatter about winning an invented card game against Tam. The prize, apparently, being a huge cone of chocolate chip ice cream—which Agnes only hoped they could procure for her. Lucy shared Agnes's brown complexion, her dark eyes bright with the excitement of her mother's return, and a dinner guest to boot.

Lucy dragged a laughing Alexa away to try her hand at the game, and Agnes joined Tam in the kitchen. Her wife hummed to herself as she stirred soup on the stove, her chin-length auburn hair tucked behind her ears. She'd touched her lips with gloss, a detail Agnes couldn't help but notice. When was the last time Tam had put on lip gloss? Agnes hugged her from behind, and Tam leaned into her embrace briefly before swatting her away to assemble salads.

"I hear you owe Lucy ice cream," Agnes said. "Can we get ice cream?"

Tam tsked, but she was smiling. "You still haven't been to the cafeteria, have you? They have make-your-own-sundaes."

"Are they fish flavored?"

Tam's answering laugh was like bells. "Only for you, weirdo. I hope Alexa knows Lucy is going to crucify her in that card game. The rules only make sense to her."

Lucy and Alexa had their heads bent together in serious concentration as they looked over a set of construction paper cards.

"It's nice to have a guest," Agnes said.

"It's nice to have *you*." It was true that Agnes had split her time between family and LIO before now, keeping her wife and daughter separate and secret. For good reason, too. Only Eloise had known they existed, though Agnes had been thinking mainly of protecting her family from the criminals she'd been fighting, rather than the supposed heroes she'd been fighting with.

No, that wasn't fair. Mary, Ire, Eloise... They were still heroes, no matter that they'd been tricked into taking down some innocent Wave operatives that Dolly had framed to try and prevent the organization from re-forming. The league had still stopped Wave-neutral crimes. Hundreds. And what about Ire holding up that bridge?

Agnes tossed the salad, absently contemplating the route these lettuce leaves must have taken to make it all the way here. Never mind the tomatoes. Or maybe they had some kind of a greenhouse, with sun lamps. She really ought to take a day to explore.

At the table, Lucy threw her head back and laughed victoriously while Alexa buried her head in her hands, feigning misery at an apparent loss.

It *was* good to have so much time with her family. Still, Agnes could hear the unspoken 'but' hanging at the end of her wife's sentence. *It's nice to have you,* but…

Tam let it hang, though. She didn't say it.

"It's nice to have me despite the circumstances?" Agnes said.

Tam ladled soup into a pair of bowls, pausing to wipe the drips away with a towel. "I'm an artist, love. Weird experiences come in handy. But I am starting to wonder when we can stop living 20,000 leagues under the sea."

"When it's safe," Agnes said. That was what Bradley Archer kept telling her, anyway. Not that she'd seen him in weeks.

"And when will that be?" Tam stepped away from the food to face Agnes, smoothing her hair away from her face.

Agnes just shook her head and kissed her wife, lingering on the strawberry taste of that lip gloss. She didn't know what Wave's plan was at the moment. She didn't know when it would be safe.

"At least I'm just working in the lab," she said, kissing Tam again before picking up the salad bowl for dinner. "At least I'm not doing anything dangerous."

ONE OF THE mind-boggling qualities Ire possessed, Nathan thought, was how completely the man could transform a space —without assistance—in a very short amount of time. For two weeks, the recruit training center had been a gym; in the space of a lunch break, Ire had transformed it into a laboratory. He'd arranged three black lab tables in the center of the space, each with a microscope, a Bunsen burner, and two stools.

Nathan picked one, propping his foot on the bar and watching as the others entered. Ire had worked with Agnes in the labs, once upon a time. Maybe he planned to teach them some chemistry.

Whatever it was, Nathan was grateful for a day to sit down. Or even just an hour.

"I feel like I'm back in high school," Quin said, settling onto the stool beside Nathan's. Quin had their black hair swept out of their eyes in waves that settled over their ears, and they carried a particularly large backpack today.

As the other recruits paired up at the rest of the lab tables, Nathan couldn't help but agree with the high school assessment. He caught Tally's eye—she'd added a strip of pink to her blonde hair—and she winked at him. He narrowly avoided cringing in response.

"Glad we get to be lab partners, then." Nathan nodded to the pack at Quin's feet. "What'd you bring today?"

"Ice packs, extra bandages."

Nathan blinked. "Why? You've been doing fine in training." Sure, Quin didn't have a physical enhancement like the others did, but they'd still ranked highly in several challenges.

Quin raised an eyebrow. "They're for you."

Nathan swallowed a choke of surprise. "Ah. Thanks?"

Ire kept saying it wasn't about who won the challenges, but about how much they improved. Nathan, who'd finished last in every race, didn't find this particularly comforting. But he had no intention of giving up.

Every day, he came here to train. And for the past few nights, he'd then gone back to HQ to help Steve try to track down his father, to no avail. If Mary really did have Flick holed up somewhere, it might be a long time until they found him. Mary knew how to hide.

Which was why the pictures from Malibu—plastered all over the internet these days—were so confounding. Why would she have shown up at the house, unless she'd wanted to be found?

These were the questions that made it impossible to sleep. Which made it impossible to win, or even place, in physical challenges against enhanced humans.

"That was a joke," Quin said, "because it was a nosy question. Officer. I just have books to return to the library."

Nathan laughed. "You're right, it was nosy. Sorry."

Quin shrugged, grinning, and leaned their elbows on the table. "What's the lesson today, do you think?"

The science of enhanced abilities, as it turned out, complete with blood draws, cell studies, and experiments that involved freezing and heating the cells. Ire stalked into the room at exactly eight AM and started lecturing them on the various ways their abilities could be affected by temperature and other conditions. They shouldn't be caught off guard, and if they were, they should know how to study.

"Don't you have a staff to handle this kind of stuff?" Tally asked, before they started the experiments. "I saw it on the news."

Nathan expected Ire to snap at her, but the strongman was nothing if not a patient teacher. "LIO has a staff team that includes scientists," he said. "But at the very least, you need to be able to understand what they tell you. And some of you might not want to go out fighting crime. Some of you might be more comfortable in a lab."

"Not me," Tally said. Rajni and Elle nodded. Apparently they objected to the idea of going back to school. Nathan didn't; he hadn't attended university, and he wasn't about to turn down an opportunity to learn. He'd wanted this for too long.

Quin, he noticed, didn't join in the nodding. Next to Elle, sticky-fingered Len looked at his hands, as though he, too, thought the idea of a lab career sounded pretty good.

Ire laced his hands casually in front of his body. "Let me put it this way, then. LIO's got a staff team, but you're not in LIO yet. Until you are, you'd better learn to understand your own abilities."

A draft of cold air coiled through the room, and Nathan looked up to see who had entered. For a moment, he felt like he was staring at a ghost.

It was Chloe. His sister was here, in Niagara Falls, wearing heels and a long beige coat, a black purse tucked under her arm. Tall and ginger-haired, she had a fringe of blunted bangs and freckles scattered across her face. Something about her demeanor made her look as if she'd just walked into a board meeting. One she intended to run.

Nathan clutched the edge of the table as though to keep himself upright, a web of hot emotions tightening across his chest. The last time Nathan had seen her in person, Chloe had told him there was nothing he could do to make things right, that their father would be better off if Nathan just left. That they'd spent five years—between Nathan's thirteenth and eighteenth birthdays—pretending they could forgive him for carrying a bomb into an office building.

Pretending, Nathan had interpreted, that they could still love him.

It hadn't mattered that he'd been tricked, or that he hadn't known. Regardless, Chloe had never even tried to believe in the innocence of his mistake. So Nathan had moved to the States, become a police officer. He'd tried to prove he could make things right.

And now that he was an independent operative, Chloe apparently thought so, too.

"New recruit?" Quin said, shaking Nathan out of his daze.

Nathan slid off his stool. "Nope. That's my sister." He caught Ire's eye, half wishing the strongman would insist he stay to perform the exercise. But Ire waved him toward the door and continued his lecture.

Nathan understood that he'd been a child when he'd carried that bomb into the office, a child heartbroken over his mother's long absence. He understood, too, that Wave believed they'd used the bomb to thwart another terrorist plan, though that part of it made no difference to Nathan. Right was right, and bombs were wrong. Especially when you handed them to a thirteen-year-old kid.

Nathan also understood that no matter the circumstances,

his family should have been there to help him. He understood all of it. Intellectually.

Emotionally, though, he couldn't tamp down the guilt that spiked through his gut at the sight of his sister. The longing, and above all, the treacherous joy.

"What?" Chloe said, as he paused beside her at the door. "No hug?"

Nathan hugged her, the brief embrace cursory and awkward. "Are you here to tell me to pick up the phone more often?"

Chloe giggled. It sounded girlish and strange alongside her professional attire. "No, no. I mean *yes*, of course you ought to answer my calls—" She batted at his arm. "—but I'm actually here with my enforcers."

Her accent sounded like home. "Enforcers? Isn't that a hockey term?"

She tsked. "You do like American sports, don't you?"

"I really do." Aware of the darting glances of the other LIO students, none of whom were listening to Ire's explanation, Nathan offered Chloe his arm. He wanted to ask her to come back later, or wrench her out the door to talk on the sidewalk— anywhere but here—but he didn't want to give the recruits any more gossip fodder than they already had. And something about Chloe's spotless clothing, the too-flowery musk of her perfume, made him want to show her he had nothing to hide.

"Come on," he said. "If we're lucky, there'll be coffee in the break room."

"America is ruining you. Tea?"

"Probably."

He could feel her drinking in the whole operation, eyes scanning the space as he led her across to the makeshift kitchen Ire had installed in the corner, with a fridge, a kettle, and a small sink. More of a break area than a room, really. Open to the rest of the training area, it didn't even have cubicle walls; but at least it was *behind* the working recruits, which meant they'd have to turn around to stare at him and thus risk incurring Ire's wrath.

Nathan found an unopened package of Earl Grey—an American brand, one he didn't recognize, but Chloe didn't complain at the sight of the box—and started coffee for himself.

He had a feeling this conversation would call for coffee.

Drinks acquired, small talk completed, Nathan sat across from his sister at one of the card tables Ire had arranged here. While her tea steamed, Chloe slipped a card out of the pocket of her purse and slid it across the table to Nathan. Her name appeared in blocky letters beneath the red-tinted title: *Enhanced Ability Enforcement Association.*

"EAEA?" Nathan said.

She smiled. "Why do you think I prefer to call us enforcers?"

He'd have wagered a different guess. "What is this?"

"Don't look so serious. We're on your side."

Nathan stirred a packet of sugar into his coffee and took his time mixing it in. "What side is that?"

"The League of Independent Operatives, of course." Chloe waved a hand toward the room where the recruits were busily helping each other draw vials of blood. "This. Recruitment?"

"You're not associated with us." At least, he thought Eloise would have mentioned it.

Chloe glanced out across the warehouse floor, watching the recruits. "Of course not. But we've got a solid lobby going in the U.K. We're making traction with elected officials there, and in Europe as well. The American team called me over to prep them for a round of legislative meetings this month."

And, if he had to wager a guess, to investigate the league's recruitment center through her brother, who'd let her straight in the door without blinking. Too late to regret another foolish choice. But not too late to find out what the hell she was talking about. Nathan abandoned the coffee and folded his hands on the table, meeting Chloe's gaze as levelly as he could. "But what are you lobbying *for*?"

Chloe didn't shift, but her smile was too frozen. "People with enhanced abilities are dangerous, Nathan."

"LIO's not."

She tapped her hand on the table, a quick, emphatic movement. Like a visual exclamation point. "Exactly. That's exactly it. We think everyone with enhanced abilities should be under LIO's umbrella. Registered and sanctioned."

Nathan didn't like the sound of that. He wondered whether Eloise knew about this EAEA, and their hopes for the league. "And if they're not?"

Chloe looked at him with wide eyes. She took a sip of her tea and grimaced. "I read the league is in charge of incarcerating enhanced humans now."

Nathan couldn't quite hear his own thoughts through the thudding of blood in his ears. She couldn't possibly be implying that enhanced humans who refused to join LIO should be jailed.

Though, it wouldn't be at all inconsistent for her to judge an entire group of people without knowing who they were. "Not every enhanced human will want to join LIO," he said, working to keep his voice level.

"And why not?" Chloe asked, suddenly prim. "I'd question their motives."

Nathan dragged a hand through his hair, glad he hadn't had more of the coffee. Jitters enough in this conversation without it. "Because LIO is like... it's practically a special operations unit. It's not for everyone."

And enhanced humans didn't deserve to be incarcerated simply for living.

But the league acted as jailers already, didn't they? Not that he dared say it out loud. Chloe's knowledge of it was hardly a surprise; it wasn't as if Eloise's new government friends had made a secret of their plan. They'd practically trumpeted it, in fact. With the unveiling of the League of Independent Operatives, facilities incapable of containing enhanced humans had rushed to shuffle the problem over to other enhanced humans. Problem solved, or at least out of sight.

Those enhanced humans were convicted criminals, however. Chloe was suggesting something entirely different. Still, a vague sense of unease trickled across his spine, lifting goosebumps along his arms. If Dolly's testimony had slammed the door on those Wave prisoners—that was who most of them were—then who was to say that some of them, perhaps all of them, were not innocent?

For that matter, why hadn't Nathan taken the time to stop into the prison level? To see how the prisoners fared? He'd known full well that they were living beneath his feet at HQ, Jenna among them. Perhaps he just hadn't wanted to face it.

And yet... and yet, he was supposed to be here trying to make things better.

Chloe still sat there, hands wrapped around her mug, waiting patiently for him to continue. As if he should have to explain why interning innocent enhanced humans was wrong. That was what she was suggesting, wasn't it?

She blinked her eyelashes at him. It grated. "Not everyone wants to be in law enforcement," he said, trying to sound more patient than he felt. "Some people want to be lawyers and hairdressers and pizza deliverers."

"All at once?" Somehow, she made it sound condescending. Like she was laughing at him.

Nathan shrugged. "If that's the dream. The point is that LIO's not set up for the world you're describing."

Chloe leaned across the table and squeezed his hand. "And *my* point is that it should be." Her tone was sugary sweet. "This little recruitment center is very nice, Nathan. But there are too many bookshelves and too few targets."

Ironic words, coming from the woman who'd shunned him for accidental violence. Nathan barely restrained a grimace. "Ire wants to teach people to handle their powers. Filter them into the league in a way that makes sense to them."

Scientists, engineers. That was the dream. It was a nice one, too.

Chloe twisted her lips in distaste. "And cut dangerous people loose?"

Dangerous people. Like him, in other words. She didn't say it, but the suggestion lingered in her eyes, in the twist of her mouth, like a threat.

He longed to pull his hand away from her. If he did, she might never offer it again. Memories clattered across his mind—Chloe delivering a bouquet of carefully selected wildflowers to their father on a rare day trip to the Lake District; Chloe insisting they rescue an injured kitten from behind a restaurant dumpster; Chloe begging Nathan to take her on the Ferris wheel at a local fair and rocking the car until he nearly threw up all his cotton candy.

And Chloe, little more than a child herself, lecturing him on his responsibility to leave their home the instant he turned eighteen.

Even with that memory lodged through his heart like a stake, part of Nathan insisted he had to be misunderstanding his sister's intentions. Surely, she couldn't mean... but stronger men than he had turned their back on dangerous truths, to disastrous effect. He wouldn't be one of them. The injustice of what she was suggesting? It was too blatant to ignore.

Still, Nathan couldn't pull away. She'd take his family; she'd take his father, again. Cursing himself for caring, he chose his next words carefully. "Enhanced doesn't automatically mean dangerous."

Chloe shook her head. He half expected her to roll her eyes at him. "You've always been sweet, Nathan. But you're also naive. Think of all the trouble these people could cause."

She paired that last part with a meaningful eyebrow raise, as if to emphasize the kindness she showed him by not mentioning the bombing. Even though Nathan had bombed that building without a single enhanced ability to his name. Where was the connection? His naivety, he supposed.

Nathan refused to accept that believing the best of people equated with some kind of clueless innocence. He leaned across the table, searching for the little sister somewhere beneath this plasticky politician. "Surely you can see why forcing enhanced humans to join LIO—to *fight* with LIO—or go to jail would be wrong."

Chloe gave his hand another squeeze and released him, digging into her purse for her phone. "We'll have to talk about it later. I just stopped in to let you know I'm stateside." And, Nathan thought, to check out LIO's recruitment center. "The Canadian branch wants my advice before I head across the border. The U.S. looks promising, but Canada's hesitating to grant us a meeting." Her smile was disconcertingly sunny. "They'll come around. They've an obligation to listen to their constituents."

Chloe stood, and Nathan followed her toward the door. The conversation, and its abrupt end, had his head spinning uncomfortably. Chloe blew him a kiss, and then she was gone.

WHEN THE *MONEYMAKER* docked at the X-Tra Lux Factory Outlet Station, Sloane assumed mistakes had been made. Oliver had promised to guide them to some top-secret black market, not a shopping-spree haven for bored socialites. His plan was to pick up... well, she wasn't sure, exactly, but he claimed to have an idea. Something about controlled tech.

Sloane watched as Oliver detached weapons from the wall in his cabin, shoving them into holsters at his hips, thighs, calves, and shoulder blades. Despite having spent several nights in his cabin, she hadn't thought twice about the array of guns and knives that lined his walls. Not to mention mysterious tech she didn't recognize, rectangular black boxes and ebony coins that sparkled with multicolored lights as Oliver pocketed them.

"I realize we need gear," Sloane said, "but this is a designer outlet station. The last time I was here, I bought a Gemini Ferange handbag on sale."

Fifty percent off. Last season's design, but still.

Oliver shoved a palm-sized laser pistol into his upper breast pocket. She didn't understand how he could move with so much gear strapped to his body, let alone punch people. Though she supposed punching would be secondary, given all the weapons. "With the right tech, we can pull off any job," he said. "You have no idea how far we'll be able to reach."

How he intended to pay for this tech, he didn't say. Clearly, the man had a plan.

"In that case, we should've visited here *before* the casino gig." She sat on his bed, ankles crossed in front of her, hands clenched in her lap.

Apparently satisfied with the arsenal he'd arranged about his person, Oliver tossed her a heavy vest. "This place is a last resort, babe. Put on the armor, and let me do the talking."

If another med student had talked to her that way, Sloane would have slapped him in the face. Here and now, she supposed she had to admit to being out of her depth. She held up the vest. "It doesn't look like armor."

Oliver kissed her forehead. "I like you when you're clueless," he said. "Come on."

Sloane considered thumping him on the head with the vest. Instead, she strapped it on, fumbling with the buckles. He was probably messing with her, dressing her in some sort of virtual reality game wear just to freak her out.

They'd landed at a *mall*. Sloane refused to be freaked.

To Sloane's surprise, Oliver stopped at Alex's lab as he led the way through the res deck, dipping his head through the doorway while Sloane paused behind him. "Need anything while we're station-side?" he asked. "Wires? Gears? Black market... crystal ball things?"

Poring over a notebook at the standing desk beside the sink, Alex didn't even look up. "Nope. Bye."

"Beep us if you think of something," Oliver said.

At that, even Alex raised an eyebrow, though she kept her eyes trained on her work. "Um," she said. "OK. Thanks?"

Sloane followed Oliver through the tight crew quarters corridor and down a grated staircase to the *Moneymaker*'s cargo hold, where the exit hatch was located. She had to work hard to match his strides. "What was that about?"

Oliver didn't pause. "What?"

Sloane hooked a thumb back over her shoulder toward the lab, though Oliver continued down the stairs, practically skipping across the cargo hold. "Checking to see if Alex needed anything? I don't even know why the hell Uncle Vin keeps her on this crew."

"She's doing important shit." Oliver made for the hatch control panel and banged on the cover to open it. Rust marred the edges, just like it marred half of everything on this stupid ship. The currently empty cargo hold smelled like medicine, beer, and honey, all mingled together, and Sloane wasn't sure she wanted to know the details.

She popped her hands on her hips, suspicious. "Since when do you think Alex is doing important work?"

"Since always." He hit the panel again. "You just never asked. Besides, we're a crew. We help each other out. Why isn't this working?"

A crew. Sure. Sloane hadn't seen Oliver ask Hilda if her pet parrot thingy needed seeds. She shoved him aside and wiggled the panel to side it open. "It just needs a little finessing."

With a groan, the *Moneymaker*'s hatch dropped into a gangplank. Clearly Sloane wasn't so clueless, after all. She'd have liked Oliver to acknowledge that, but he just started down the ramp while it was still moving. Sloane waited, following only when the shuddering had stopped.

No rush, she figured. As soon as Oliver left the dock and stepped into the main corridor, he'd take one look at the shop windows and realize his mistake. This wasn't the black market he'd been aiming for.

Oliver stopped at the glass doors that separated the dock from the rest of the station. They should have shuffled open without delay—at least, they'd done so when she'd visited before—but they stayed shut fast. A scrolling sign on the door indicated that they'd landed after hours. *Come back at 10am Galactic Standard Time and enjoy a complimentary cocktail on us!*

At 10am, Sloane hoped they meant mimosas. Come to think of it, she wouldn't have minded one right about now. Or four. "Looks like we're stuck," she said.

Oliver didn't seem worried. He paused to enter something on his holo-tab, grinning over his shoulder at her when the doors parted. Like a proud little kid.

When she'd been here last, every shop window had glittered with retail goodness, the carefully arranged window displays overflowing with purses and shoes, dresses and tunics, in styles that spanned the best of the galaxy. Jewelry. Makeup. Perfume.

The hall even smelled like leather and hot pretzels, as if the ghost of the luxury outlets were just out of sight.

Given the changes she could see in the place, Sloane doubted she'd run across a designer scarf outlet anytime soon. The lights in the hall shone a dim green, and it seemed to Sloane that most of the businesses were shuttered—until a man in a long black coat ducked into one of them, glancing behind him as he slipped through the door.

The shop directly across from the *Moneymaker*'s dock was the only one she could see with a window display, and it was a far cry from anything she'd seen before, in any mall. Jars full of yellow-brown liquid filled the shelves, and when she squinted, she could see *things* floating in the them. Tadpole shapes and finger shapes and, in one, what looked like a human face. Just the face.

Sloane stared at the hollow-eyed face in horror until Oliver laced his fingers between hers. She jumped. "Don't feel too bad," he said, tugging her away and swinging their hands between them as if they were simply out for a walk in a nice, safe, Central Galaxy park. "Welcome to X-Lux After Hours."

Sloane shook her head, disbelieving. The galaxy's most famous shopping mall was a cover for criminal activity. Because apparently, nothing was sacred. What else didn't she know?

A lot, if she had to guess.

Oliver led Sloane through the corridor, where she tried very hard not to look at the shop windows that did hold displays. Every glimpse was more grotesque than the last; apparently only the gruesome places showed their goods off to the world.

The shop windows, however, felt safer than the other After Hours clientele. Everyone she passed packed as many weapons as Oliver. Some glanced around, furtive, while other strode confidently through hall, which sloped gently around to the right. A circular runway, she remembered, with several layers of shops. But how? How was it so different by day?

It wasn't nearly as crowded as it had been when her father had brought her here last year, and thank goodness. Still, Sloane decided to keep her eyes on the floor.

They reached the center of the circle and took an escalator up. Oliver moved comfortably through this place, even nodding to a few other criminals—that's what these people had to be, all of them—as they passed by.

"How is this possible?" Sloane said finally. "I swear, the last time I was here—"

"The floors in the station move," Oliver said. "Every twelve hours, the businesses... switch. When your socialite friends are here shopping, the black market's trapped in the center. When we're here, the lux goods are locked up tight in the same spot.

"I'm not a socialite," Sloane said. "I'm a medical student. Or at least, I was."

Oliver shrugged. She couldn't tell if he was teasing.

Finally, Oliver stopped outside one of the shops with tinted windows. He entered a few numbers into his holo-tab, and the door opened with a click.

One step inside, and Sloane understood why the After Hours shops elected not to display their wares for every criminal to see. Wall-to-wall cases filled the store, every one of them filled with holo-tab strips and comm links, security bracelets and payment chips.

And that was basically the only stuff Sloane recognized. The rest of the items were definitely tech, all of them sleekly black or silver, many of them blinking or scrolling like the weapons in Oliver's stash. She had no idea what any of them did.

She wasn't sure she wanted to know.

As she looked around the store, a tall man stepped out from behind a velvet curtain in the back of the store. His ears peaked into little points from the sides of his bald head, his lips verging on orange, and Sloane wondered if he could be part Wringer. Far from his side of the galaxy, if so. Very far.

"Good to see you again, Mr. Smith," the maybe-Wringer said, steepling long fingers in front of his chest.

"How many Smiths come into this place?" Sloane asked.

Oliver shot her a 'shut up' look, but the maybe-Wringer merely stretched his orangeade lips into an approximation of a smile. "All of my clients are named Smith," he said. "What can I do for you today?"

Oliver pulled out his holo-tab, hesitated. "We have business in the back shop."

The black market had a black market? Because of course it

did. Sloane tried to look nonchalant, but she had a feeling she was breathing too hard to pull off that particular illusion.

The Wringer scoffed a laugh. "I sincerely doubt that, Mr. Smith. Based on your purchase history, you're squarely a front-shop man."

Oliver punched a code into his holo-tab and swiped it over to the proprietor, who pulled out his own device and stared at the screen, lips parted. "I see," he said, setting his tab aside with a hand that trembled ever so slightly. "Coming up in the world, are we?"

What, by getting a job on the *Moneymaker*? That seemed unlikely. But what else could Oliver have shown the man? Sloane looked at Oliver, who tossed her a wink.

Fine. She wouldn't mess up whatever scam Oliver had going by running her mouth. She might not be a good criminal, but she could handle that much.

"All right," the Wringer said, "but first time visitors stay in the front. I'm sorry, Ms. Smith, but I cannot bend that rule."

Sloane shrugged—she'd just as soon leave this to Oliver—and the two men disappeared behind the velvet curtain. She didn't quite understand what kind of a criminal crew her uncle had put together here, but Oliver clearly knew the ins and outs of the underworld.

What kind of tech did the Wringer have that could help them steal money? And from where? If Sloane was meant to stand in for her uncle as the leader of this crew, she was doing a pretty poor job of it. But if Oliver could get them out of this mess—if she could just deliver them back to Uncle Vin and go back to her life—then she couldn't object to letting him take charge. Surely he'd fill her in later.

SOMETIMES, Eloise thought, talking with people via video screen—rather than an old fashioned audio-only conference call—was more of a curse than a blessing. Curse number one: checking and double checking every surface of her office for sensitive items before her call with Travis Bertram, the junior security counselor assigned to act as a liaison between LIO and the U.S. government.

At least, she assumed he must be junior, given that he looked like a frat boy who'd been scrubbed clean and propped at a desk, all blond and freckled. As soon as they'd exchanged a set of wooden niceties, Travis had started talking. And for the last twenty minutes, he hadn't *stopped* talking, even to hear answers to the questions he'd asked.

He had a green stain on his tie. Eloise couldn't tell if it was avocado, asparagus, or a smear of lime toothpaste. She took vindictive pleasure in imagining him squeezing it out of a Ninja-Turtle themed tube.

It shouldn't matter, but the longer he talked, the more the stain distracted her. Eloise had, admittedly, lost track of the conversation. Lecture.

Travis Bertram—she'd have bet the Pearl Knife that the

name was followed by a Roman numeral, if not a trust fund account number—turned a page in his notebook and looked up at the screen for the first time since he'd started prattling.

Maybe the green smear was actually a bit of lettuce. If she squinted, she thought she could make out edges.

"Everything seems in order," Travis said, and Eloise wanted to ask how he could know that, since he'd talked over every answer she'd given him. Checking off boxes.

Someone knocked on the door, and Eloise called for them to enter. Maybe it would be Gail with an emergency to rescue her from this conversation.

It was Steve. She motioned him in, and he dropped into one of the chairs on the other side of her desk. He'd left his hat behind today, and he laced his fingers comfortably across his stomach.

"Thanks, Travis," Eloise said, turning back to the screen. Travis didn't seem to have noticed Steve's arrival. "I have a couple of—"

Travis held up a hand, and Eloise pressed her lips together in annoyance. Behind her, Steve hissed in a breath. Clearly she wasn't imagining the kid's rudeness. She decided to think of him as a kid, partly out of spite and partly to keep herself from lashing out at him.

"There've been a couple of robberies the task team is concerned about," Travis said. "We think they're being perpetrated by enhanced humans."

In her mind, the Pearl Knife stirred. As if it, too, had been asleep. Eloise imagined it stretching. She tapped her fingers on the desk behind her. Maybe if she got a bigger one, she could add a huge chair and set it up so she loomed behind it when she spoke to Travis. That might make her satisfyingly intimidating. Though it would also require her to rearrange the entire setup of her office so that her chair faced the screen—which was currently situated behind her desk, along with the camera—and Eloise wasn't sure Travis Bertram was worth the effort.

"What makes you think the robbers are enhanced?" she asked.

Travis turned a page. "We can't figure out how they got into either place. Super-secure vaults, in both cases."

Belonging to important people, if Eloise had to guess. "I take it no one was hurt?"

"No one saw them. They didn't even leave fingerprints."

The Knife swirled a sudden band of colors into her mind, interspersed with a vision it hadn't shown her in months: a patch of redwood trees, with sunlight flickering through the boughs. The Knife had sent her that image repeatedly last fall, during LIO's disastrous attempts to corner Wave. She figured it had given up, but now the trees were back. And the Knife felt almost... excited. As if it meant to respond to Travis's words.

Eloise blinked, trying to clear the vision. "Gloves?"

"No way to know."

And no way to know if they were enhanced, either. "Inside job?"

Travis adjusted his tie, dislodging the flicker of green. Lettuce, then. She hoped. "We'd appreciate it if you could investigate."

Redwood trunks pierced Travis's face, the whole room flickering uncomfortably. Eloise tamped down a surge of nausea, bracing her hands on the desk behind her and willing the Knife to calm down. "The league isn't a branch of the FBI, Mr. Bertram," Eloise said. "We haven't really got the resources for this sort of thing."

Except, wasn't that what they were here for? Eloise was used to defining missions herself. And she didn't prioritize enhanced humans, necessarily; she prioritized citizens in danger. She couldn't send her people after every thief in the country.

Travis closed his notebook. The trees thickened. Vomiting in front of Travis would significantly compromise her professional demeanor. "Please, Ms. Reyna," he said, deigning to raise his gaze for the second time. "Oh. And... colleague." He blinked, and Eloise realized that she, too, had forgotten Steve's presence. "We'd appreciate the help on this."

In her mind, the Knife... bounced. There was no other way to describe it. *Is this related to the trees?* She asked it, annoyed. *Or is it something else?* But the Knife just bounced again. Eloise sighed. "Fine. I'll look into it."

The Knife pulsed, insistent, and Eloise sent back a wave of dizzy frustration. If the blade thought she understood what it wanted, what she was supposed to do, it was wrong. If anything, the damn thing was just going to make her fall over.

"Thank you." Travis Bertram said, reburied in his notebook and oblivious to her discomfort. "I'll check in next week. The director would like to schedule a tour."

"Schedule it with Gail. Goodbye, Mr. Bertram."

The screen went black, and Eloise allowed herself a breath. Her stomach was roiling as the Knife's emotions mixed with hers. She had no other way to describe the feelings; just nausea-inducing emotion. Impulses that felt like commands, pushing her to abandon everything until she'd located that damn patch of trees.

If it's so important, she thought, *why did you drop it for three months?*

"El?" Steve said. "Are you all right?"

She wasn't all right. For one thing, she'd forgotten about him. Again. Eloise stood up from where she'd been sitting on the edge of her desk, and the room tilted around her. She stumbled, catching herself on her desk chair as the Knife flashed the redwoods again, double images flickering across her vision.

Steve leapt to her side—one second sitting, the next holding her elbow—and helped her into the chair. He didn't move away. "Have you eaten today?"

"It's not my blood sugar," she said, swallowing a wad of saliva. If the Knife made her throw up right now, she'd never forgive the damn thing. "It's the Knife."

His gaze dropped to her hip, where the blade gleamed.

"I don't..." Eloise touched a hand to her temple. Once she said the words, there'd be no taking them back. She felt exposed. "How do I know I can trust you?"

Steve crouched down beside the chair, tipping his head back slightly to look her in the eye. "You don't," he said. "But if there's something going on with your abilities... we've known each other a long time, El. Maybe I can help."

They had. And despite his declaration against the league, he'd kept their secrets for years. He'd watched Nathan, and he'd kept tabs on other possible Wave connections.

Eloise's father was dead. Her mother had admitted to horrifying crimes. The closest person she had to a sister was off doing god knew what, and might never forgive Eloise for the sins of her parents. Tears throbbed in her throat, and she shoved them savagely away. "I can't control the Knife," she said.

Again, Steve's eyes dipped to the blade. "You controlled it the night I arrived."

Eloise met his eyes. He didn't look scared, though he ought to. The Knife could decide to kill him right now, and she might not be able to stop it. The blade sent indignation through her, protesting the thought, but she knew it was true.

Steve only looked concerned. About her. He didn't understand.

"It partners with me sometimes, when it wants to." When it

agreed with her, apparently. "In L.A., it opened a portal. It won't do it again."

His eyebrows twitched. "A portal? To where?"

She shook her head. "It carried me through a vendor stand when I was chasing some Wave operatives. A blip. I just... skipped it." She stared at him, hard, trying to gauge his reaction. But he just sat there quietly, listening. It was nice to have someone listening. "During the same fight, it refused to take down one of the operatives."

Steve tapped his index finger on the arm of the chair. He had long fingers, and she suddenly remembered him sitting in the corner of a LIO holiday party as a teenager, playing Beatles songs on the guitar. No wonder she'd been head over heels. As a kid, of course. She wondered if he still played.

"Have you asked Dolly about it?"

Eloise ran her fingers along the arm of the chair, tracing the grain of wood with a thumbnail. "I'm not sure I can trust anything she'd tell me about the Knife."

Or anything else. Eloise half expected Steve to haul her to her feet and drag her to see her mother now, to demand answers. If he did that, the Knife might actually attack him. For all its mysterious faults, it did have a tendency to protect her.

But Steve didn't move. "Could Dolly still be controlling it?"

"I don't think so. It seems to be sending me messages."

"What does it say?"

"Trees."

Steve blinked. "Trees," he repeated.

"The room is full of redwoods. Right now."

But why? What was the Knife trying to tell her? And why had Travis Bertram's mission ignited visions the blade had given up on showing her several months ago?

Steve glanced around in obvious confusion, and Eloise actually smiled. But that almost made her laugh, which almost unchained the tears, so she forced herself to stop. "It's trying to send me to a place with redwoods. There's something it wants me to see. It showed me the same trees last fall, for a few days, and then it just... stopped. Something Travis said got it all riled up."

"Travis?"

Eloise nodded toward the screen. "The G-Man." Kid.

"Gotcha." Steve glanced around again, as if he might be able to see them this time, then settled his warm gaze back on hers. "Maybe if you go out west, it'll pick up a stronger signal."

She shook her head. "I can't leave HQ. I've got too much to deal with here."

Steve gave her a long look, as if he could read her thoughts, as if he could understand everything she didn't want to say. Eloise didn't have control of the Knife, and she didn't have control of LIO, either. If she left, who could say what might happen?

"You trust Ire?" Steve asked.

"Of course."

"Nathan?"

She nodded.

"Then let them handle things for a few days. Go pick a spot in California, or Oregon. See if the Knife can tell you more from there. From where I'm sitting, it seems like it needs a trigger. Maybe a reminder."

Eloise looked at her hands. Leaving the league, even for a few days, could invite any number of disasters. What if a breach happened while she was away? Everyone had responded adequately to Steve's arrival, but what if something more serious happened?

They needed her for guidance. They needed her—and the Knife—for protection, too.

Still kneeling, Steve gripped the arm of the chair. "El, you know I'm not the league's number one advocate."

"I do know that," Eloise said. "But I don't know why."

She wished she did.

"Suffice it to say I'm cautious. But if anyone can change that, it's you." He didn't move closer, didn't touch her, yet she felt the intensity behind his words. "I'm not sure there's anything more important to LIO's survival than you getting a handle on that Knife. We don't know what it is or where it's from. We do know what it's been used for. We need answers, and maybe... maybe following it will give us some."

He did understand the danger, then. And she appreciated the 'we.' As if, all of a sudden, she no longer faced this alone.

"And if it's making you sick," he added, "I'd just as soon work out a fix for that, too."

Eloise bit back a retort about not needing anyone else's protection. She didn't need it, but it wasn't bad to have someone on her side, was it? Not that she could quite see why he'd want to protect her, given their opposite stances with regards to LIO.

"If I go out west," she said, "where will you be?"

Steve shrugged. "I'll keep you company. If you want me."

"What about your father?"

Steve leaned in, and Eloise found herself wondering what she'd do if he touched her hand. She found herself wanting him to. "Like I said, I don't think there's anything more important to LIO right now than figuring out that Knife. Dad would agree with me on that."

Eloise nodded. He was right; she'd put this off for too long. Any longer, and she could put everyone in jeopardy. "In that case, we'd better start packing."

Suburbs gave Mary the creeps.

Seriously, who in their right mind wanted to live surrounded by grocery stores and dollar depots and houses with weirdly planted trees to strategically separate them from friendly neighbors? Give her solitude or give her people, but don't try to pretend both could exist simultaneously.

Not that Malibu was so much different, in its own way. She supposed money presented the illusion of solitude, rather than the real thing.

Mary hadn't been surprised to learn that Ranger had been working for a zoo for the last two years. The LIO operative could communicate with animals; it only made sense. She had, however, been surprised to learn that he was a maintenance worker for a petting zoo in a nothing town she'd already forgotten the name of, outside of San Antonio.

If she'd had the power to command animals, she'd have wanted to ride elephants or play fetch with tigers. Instead, the guy fed goats and mucked out pig stalls. Or maybe he convinced the animals to do that part themselves; she wasn't entirely clear on the limits of his power.

Mary watched the petting zoo entrance from a scraggly

copse of trees in the park across the way, nose itching from the mulch and manure smells as families came and went. It was chilly, and she pulled her jacket tight around her, missing the warmth of her Coral uniform and promising herself she'd come up with a solution. Some anonymous, in-between outfit to wear that didn't belong to Mary O'Sullivan or Coral. A warm one.

Families came and went, most of the kids so small Mary doubted any of them stood as tall as her knees. Finally, an elderly docent ushered out the last few and switched off the lighted sign in the little ticket booth.

The docent gathered her things, donned a scarf that made Mary shiver with jealousy, and left.

Ranger didn't appear.

Mary waited, listing the ways this escapade could have been streamlined, were she still with LIO. They could have pulled Ranger's work schedule, studied his habits. Which would have required team members to tail him for a while, but as long as it wasn't Mary, that was all right.

And with LIO, there was always the bonus that Eloise would have reminded Mary to check the weather before showing up. Mary would say something about Texas being hot, and Eloise would say something about it being a huge state with multiple climate zones, and ultimately Mary would have ended up here wearing something more substantial than a thin jacket and leggings.

Finally, as dusk tipped into evening, Ranger appeared at the ticket booth, looking much the same as he ever had. Short, stocky. She couldn't make out the details. He had on a baseball cap and thick work boots, and he wasn't alone. A thin guy walked beside him, his features muddled by the oncoming darkness.

Mary cursed as Ranger and his friend ducked into the

ticket booth—to clock out, maybe—then locked it tight behind them as they started down the sidewalk together.

She'd been planning to confront Ranger right here, to dose him with the serum and toss him into Grandma's back seat without alerting anyone to her presence. If she'd expected the guy to have a friend with him, she'd have waited in the car, followed him home.

LIO would already know the location of that home.

Mary stayed on her side of the street, working the shadows as the park melted into the best imitation of a downtown area the suburb could manage. Which was to say, she passed a tire shop and a closed hair salon before Ranger and his friend disappeared into a bar with a neon 'open' sign in the window and a sign that dubbed the place 'Crabby's.'

Great. More staking out, and with no tall buildings to lurk under, no fire escapes to hide on, no alleys to squeeze into.

Suburbs.

Stifling a sigh, because she was still that much of a professional at least, Mary backed into the shadows of the hair salon's doorway and waited.

The last time she'd been in Texas... it had to have been at least five years ago, during the golden years when Will had been alive and Dolly was in charge. El had had fewer burdens dragging her down. She and Mary had been the side-mission experts back then. Cleanup crew, saddled with the job of rounding up any un-enhanced henchmen who tried to get away.

In this particular case, Mary and Eloise had ended up in San Antonio proper, chasing a couple of con artists along the River Walk and all the way to the Alamo. Mary would wonder why criminals always felt the need to hide in national monuments, except that the league had themselves set up behind

Niagara Falls. Though Dolly was a criminal, too, so maybe the thought processes were similar.

For whatever reason, those two con artists had tried to hide out in the Alamo. Mary still remembered trying to keep from cracking all the exhibit frames, the cool stone rising around her with the feeling of a temple as she beat the hell out of the criminals. Until Eloise had calmly ascended and cut the chains on the ringed chandeliers to trap them.

No stakeouts on that job. But even those had always been easier with Eloise. The woman had all the patience Mary could never count on herself. She didn't even know how many hours of twenty questions they must have wracked up over the years. Hundreds. El definitely wouldn't be fidgeting in this doorway. She'd have made them stay in the car.

What had made them such a good team? Was it the balance between recklessness and care, impulsiveness and thought? El might deny it, but she certainly had a bit of both.

Mary, well. Mary tended to act now, clean up later.

For some reason, that thought made her think of Nathan. She didn't want to picture him hanging out at LIO HQ, couldn't quite slot his clean-cut cop persona into the place where she'd grown up. But it wasn't a persona, was it? Not in the way that Jeff Hayes wore mask after mask. Not in the way Mary did. Nathan was just... Nathan.

He'd probably made friends with half the team by now.

The door to the dingy bar banged open, and Ranger stumbled into view. He missed a step on his way out of Crabby's—damn, that was a stupid name—catching himself on the side of the building and narrowly avoiding a face plant onto the perfectly maintained sidewalk. Too bad. That might have made her job easier.

As it was, his tipsy state could only help her. Though if his friend followed, she'd have to call it a night. Sleep in the car. Try again tomorrow.

But the friend didn't show. Ranger headed down the sidewalk alone, swerving ever so slightly and whistling an aimless tune.

Mary followed, keeping pace with him this time, until Ranger turned down a residential street with fewer lights than the supposed main drag. No cars. Just sleepy homes with families no doubt preparing spaghetti dinners, or whatever it was normal people did.

Forcing herself to focus, Mary followed the retiree up a small rise, where he moved to cut through a patch of a park that appeared to separate this sleepy neighborhood from the next one over. Nice and dark.

Every once in a while, things decided to go Mary's way. Ranger started up a set of stone steps, placing his feet with tipsy care, and she cut through the grass and moved past him up the hill.

She paused when she reached the top of the steps. He still hadn't seen her. He still didn't know. She bent to unsnap the syringe carrying the power-suppressing concoction out of her boot.

Half a moment. Yet when she straightened, Ranger had paused. Because someone else had stepped onto the handful of steps that stretched between Mary and Ranger. Someone with a fringe of blonde bangs.

"Dawn Kimble," Mary said. "How the hell—"

"I followed you," Dawn interrupted. All the way from California? It shouldn't be possible. "I'm a good reporter."

With awful timing. Because Ranger was a good operative. Without warning, he leapt for Dawn, catching her neck in the crook of his arm as though to use her as a shield.

This was why reporters were bad news. They got in the

way, they got themselves into trouble, and they complicated everything.

"Come on, Ranger," Mary said. "You don't need a shield. You know better than to think I'd try to shoot you."

She wasn't that far gone, whatever the System said. Not yet.

Ranger squeezed out of a laugh, an ugly rasping sound. "I was the backup plan, you know. For the plane. I was supposed to send birds into the engines if Dolly's Knife failed. Glad I didn't have to kill the poor creatures."

Mary sucked in a breath, Ranger's comment landing like a punch to her chest. Just as he'd meant it to. She blinked away the memories that cascaded into her mind, worse these days than they'd ever been before she'd known the truth. A broken wing. A tail of smoke. Lately, the memories were harder to banish.

"You're a regular Disney princess," Mary said. Her voice almost sounded steady.

The corner of Ranger's lip lifted in a sneer. He'd brought kittens to HQ once to entertain Mary and Eloise, a wriggling pile of gray and white cuteness. Dolly had put them up for adoption. "My point is," Ranger said, "that we have no idea what you'll do in the name of revenge."

We? The implication hit her mind—*we*—a second before the blow hit her back, knocking her off the top step. Mary rolled, controlling the fall as best she could with her limbs battering the stairs. She landed on the wide slab of a step where Ranger held Dawn and leapt to her feet to aim her syringe-holding hand at Ranger's neck. He loosened his hold on Dawn, who immediately sagged. Thrown off by the sudden rag-doll shift in her weight, Ranger let go, and Dawn rolled her body away from the fight. The girl knew a thing or two about self defense, after all.

She should work on the part where they told you to avoid a fight, if you could. Instead of jumping straight into one.

Ranger aimed a clumsy punch at Mary's head, but she avoided it easily, scampering up a few steps. A coyote howled, too near for comfort, and Mary risked a glance toward the top of the steps. And her second attacker. Tall and dark-haired, she wore a crimson-lined uniform with matching red gloves. Mary should have noted her arrival, the vinegar smell of her poison-tipped fingers.

"Your parents knew what they were doing," the Trap said.

Great. Caught off guard, with a reporter to protect, and Mary didn't even have her Diana trap prototype. Assuming she survived tonight—and Mary always made a point of assuming she'd survive—she'd never leave Aries without the robo-gloves again. And she'd think of a better name for them, too.

Where was Dawn, anyway? Mary risked a glance at the grass, but couldn't see the reporter anywhere. Better to act as if she were still in the vicinity, though Mary hoped she'd run.

"Hey Diana," she said. "Good to see you. Nice heroing, pushing a girl from behind."

The Trap just smiled. She wore her long, dark hair loose around her shoulders, as if to say she was too powerful to heed the basic common sense when it came to her fighting apparel. "You should know by now," she said. "There's no such thing as heroes."

Diana leapt, and Mary stepped back, aware of Ranger still cowering below her on the staircase. As Diana came at her, Dawn cried out, and Mary had to force herself to stay focused on her opponent instead of looking the reporter's way. Diana had removed her gloves, which meant she was here to kill. Or at least to maim.

Diana always aimed to touch skin.

Mary met Diana's offensive, aiming an elbow at the other

woman's temple that Diana batted away with a laugh. She might be older by a couple of decades, but she'd clearly kept up her training over the past couple of years. She moved fast, testing for cracks in Mary's defenses, trying to drag her fingers across Mary's uncovered neck.

But Mary was fast, too. She met Diana wrist-to-wrist, and the other woman only had time to press a stinging fingertip to the back of her hand before Mary was pushing her away. She kicked Diana in the stomach, and the Trap stumbled back.

Mary took the opportunity to leap up onto the grass, where Dawn stood motionless on the hill, eyes wide. To Mary's eyes, it looked as if a tree had captured her within its limbs.

Because it wasn't enough that Ranger and Diana had teamed up. They had to bring camouflaging Rocker, too. And he'd turned his arms into tree branches. Totally normal.

Mary knew when she was outnumbered, and she knew better than to stay in a fight she couldn't win. While Diana shouted at Ranger to move, Mary dove for Rocker's ankles, taking him out with a full-body slide. He could camouflage all he liked, but the man couldn't grow roots. They all went down together, and Mary untangled Dawn, pulling her to her feet as she grabbed a shockdisk out of her boot.

Her last shockdisk, actually, and no materials to make more. Pity she'd forgotten the gloves. Pity she wouldn't be able to bring the Trap in tonight. Or all three of them, together.

Too late for regret. Mary only needed to escape. She threw the disk as hard as she could, watching the glint for a moment as it sliced through the air toward the retirees. She didn't wait to see it fall, instead pulling Dawn away, down the hill and through the park.

Behind her, a percussive pulse told her the disk had landed.

It wouldn't stop them for long. She hoped it would be long enough.

Dawn scrambled after Mary as she stepped out of the park and surveyed the trees for the darkest route back to Grandma. This was why people did stakeouts from inside cars, she knew that, but ultimately she'd been too restless and too sick of sitting around.

Eloise would have known better. The LIO retirees certainly had.

"You want to tell me how you found me this time?" Mary said as Dawn scrambled along behind her. "And don't say you followed a hunch to watch that petting zoo."

"All right," Dawn said, breathing hard as she ran, "but first you tell me what *you're* doing here."

"I'm dispensing justice. Or I should be."

The retirees must have been guarding Ranger, waiting for her to appear to take him as she'd done with Flick and the others.

Dawn's feet scuffled in the grass. She made far too much noise. "I mean what are you doing playing the shadows like this? Shouldn't you be out saving people?"

"Funny, I thought I just saved you."

"Only because I followed you here."

"My point exactly."

Dawn huffed. "I mean, shouldn't you be out, I don't know, stopping criminals? Like those enhanced guys who keep drilling into banks?"

"Hadn't heard of that one."

"But shouldn't you have? Shouldn't you be listening to scanners and watching the news, and trying to help people?" She sounded almost scandalized, as if she couldn't believe that the reckless vigilante who'd abandoned the league and disappeared could do anything but the right thing.

Well, Dawn Kimble had a few lessons to learn about IOs.

There was no right thing. There was just what needed to be done.

They'd almost reached the main street, and Mary paused. She'd stashed Grandma behind a Victorian style house someone had turned into an office building, right along this stretch. Through a couple of back yards, maybe over a fence, and she'd be there.

Mary doubted these people had motion lights, but even she could exercise caution occasionally. If she moved along the fence that separated those yards from the businesses facing the main street, she might be able to avoid activating any hidden alarms.

"Excuse me," Dawn said, "remember me?"

"Sherlock Holmes? Yes, I remember you. Be quiet. I'm scheming."

"I'm a reporter, not a detective."

"Lois Lane, then."

Dawn pointed to the street. "There's a line of parking lots between the fence and the businesses. Go that way."

That was it. "Hey, you were useful. Thanks, Lois."

"It's Dawn."

"I know."

Mary started toward the street, ducking through two empty back parking lots. Ten points to the reporter.

Who was still trailing her. And, dim as the lighting was, she definitely still looked pissed. It was like being trailed by an angry dwarf or something.

"Thanks for your help," Mary said, "but I'm not in the market for a sidekick. I'll file your application in case of an opening."

"If you want to thank me, just tell me what you're doing here."

Mary headed for Grandma, not bothering to hide the car's

presence from the reporter. She'd have bet money Dawn already knew exactly what kind of car Mary drove. She fumbled for the remote and slid the door open. She'd been hoping to deposit another retiree into her vault. Instead, she had a feeling she might have to lie low for a while. Frustration made her clench her teeth until her jaw ached uncomfortably. She really, really could have used something to throw right about now. Not *at* anyone, just... to throw. Angrily.

Dawn still waited, arms still crossed, her face pinched in annoyance. Mary brushed off her hands. "If *you* want to thank *me*—the person who saved your butt back there—then you can explain how you tracked me from California to Texas."

Dawn looked at her feet, avoiding Mary's eyes, and suddenly Mary got it. "You're enhanced," she said. "How?"

The reporter opened her mouth, like she might actually respond. Instead, she just licked her lips and shook her head. "Never mind. I'll see you later, Coral."

"Great," Mary called after her. "You do know you led them straight to me, right? What did you do, catch my scent back in Malibu or something?"

Dawn ignored the question, spinning on her heel to traipse back across the parking lot. It didn't matter how her powers worked, anyway. The more important question was, had Dawn found her way to Aries? Mary cursed to herself. She'd never considered the possibility that someone might be able to track her through an enhancement. She'd never heard of one like this. Not for the first time, she wished she could call Agnes. Lean on her friend's expertise.

Dawn kept going. Mary knew she should leave, take off right now, but she couldn't help it. Maybe it was the reckless thing, or the lonely thing. Maybe it was just her unending need to get in the last word. Whatever it was, she kept talking. "You know what Lois Lane's problem is, right? Because you've got the same one. Swooning after stories, chasing after heroes."

This time, Dawn slowed.

"The problem is that for all her evil intentions, Diana's right," Mary said. "There's no such thing as a hero."

Nathan was surprised to find he already had access to LIO's prison level, where a fingerprint opened the initial set of doors as easily as it did his own room. Not that he'd been denied entrance to any part of LIO HQ, but some part of him thought that freedom might not extend to the compound's highest security area. Even after the fingerprint worked, he thought the pair of team guards would turn him away, citing security protocols; instead, they simply nodded and stepped aside so he could complete a retina scan.

Nathan had filled Ire in on Chloe's intentions, but Eloise was apparently off on a mission with Steve—she'd left instructions with Ire, who was in charge with Nathan second in command—so together they'd decided to wait until she returned to fill her in. He wasn't sure what might have drawn her away from HQ, but it must be important if Steve was willing to put his own search on hold. Besides, politics was slow, and a shiny business card didn't mean anyone planned to take Chloe seriously.

And yet. After his conversation with Ire, after reaching a decision—which felt strange enough without Eloise to consult —Nathan had spent the night staring at the ceiling of his room, running the conversation with Chloe back through his mind. Chloe's crusade could become a problem, certainly, but only if people actually started listening to this madness. Regardless, the idea of punishing enhanced humans simply for existing made him nearly breathless with rage.

What kept him awake, though, was the prison right here beneath his feet. The league was already incarcerating enhanced individuals. Nathan hadn't bothered to ask about them, or check on how they were being treated, even knowing that Dolly's word was a large part of the reason they'd been jailed in the first place. If they'd had trials, her testimony would have been key.

They could all be innocent.

Nathan didn't know what his presence could do to change that. He only knew he couldn't ignore it anymore.

The prison doors slammed to a close behind him, and Nathan paused for a moment to assess. Two long rows of cells extended to the back of the level, dusty silver boxes about twice his height with flat tops that capped each one several feet from the ceiling. Green lights blinked along the floor. He moved farther into the room, where odors of plastic and hot metal sent uneasy thrills through his gut.

At first, Nathan thought the cell walls were completely opaque, that it would be impossible to see through them. No bars, no windows, just cold metal. As he stepped between the rows, though, the two walls facing him melted into clear glass. Or at least, something that resembled glass. Strange tech might explain the strange smells, he supposed.

He didn't risk touching it.

In the cell to his left, an older man sat hunched over a desk, scribbling on one of a dozen papers scattered around him. He pushed dirty bifocals up on his nose and raised his head, giving Nathan the impression of a startled owl. "Is there a schedule change today?" he asked. "Or did I lose track of time again?"

The cell looked comfortable enough, with blankets on the bed and a curtained corner that must contain a toilet, and possibly a sink.

Nathan cleared his throat. "No schedule change. I just—"

"He came to ease his conscience."

The voice came from the cell at Nathan's back, and he turned to see a woman with white hair flowing around her face, illustrated cards spread before her on a green carpet. She had no desk, but the same pile of blankets sat on her bed, the same bathing area curtained in the corner. She spoke softly, but with confidence. As if she knew what she was talking about.

And she did. What enhancements did she have, that she could speak to his jumbled thoughts like that? "Not if it shouldn't be eased," Nathan said carefully.

Her attention on the cards, the woman tipped her head to the side. "Officer?"

"Jo," the man with the desk said, a warning tone in his voice. "Don't forget yourself."

She sat back on her heels, gazing at the doctor with unworried calm. "What will they do? Lock me up? This one's different, doctor. Look at him. He's not a guard."

He wasn't. Which was probably why he had no idea what they were talking about.

The doctor huffed. "They'll dose you to the heavens, is what they'll do."

"Trust me," she said. The doctor sat back in his chair, looking older than he had a moment ago, expression sagging in worry.

And Nathan had thought he'd been out of his depth when he'd first learned about LIO. He'd caught up quickly then, and he'd catch up now. He glanced at Jo, still examining her cards, and he thought he understood. Whatever Jo's abilities were, the serum didn't stop them from working. Some form of mind reading, perhaps?

"Very good," she said. "It's mostly emotions, actually, but you're thinking right at me. Sometimes it mixes together."

Nathan watched her as she touched her cards, a Tarot deck with whimsical moons dancing across each face. He couldn't see the details, though he thought one of the figures might be thumbing its nose at the viewer.

"I won't say anything," Nathan said. "I don't see how reading emotions would help you escape, unless you can control them, too."

"Nope. Just read them. You can check my file, I'm sure."

Nathan wasn't sure he trusted anything LIO files said— especially since they didn't seem to know about her immunity to the serum—but it could be a start. "And the cards?"

"I use the cards for clarity. This one's yours." She held up a card featuring a figure whose a profile was shaped as a crescent moon. Its face contorted with glee, it was at once grotesque and somehow... alluring, in a way. Standing on the edge of a cliff, the figure appeared ready to leap into nothing. Though Jo held the card upside down, Nathan could read the title well enough: the fool.

It wasn't a label Nathan felt he could deny.

"I pulled it before the doors opened," Jo said. "I don't know why the cards speak to me, as such, but they do. Emotions are complex. The cards tether them for me."

"It's upside down," Nathan said, his throat dry.

Jo placed the card on the floor. "I drew it that way, and so it stays. The meaning shifts, you know."

Nathan felt himself moving closer, until he stood just a foot from the glass. Or whatever the material was. "What makes it my card?"

She smiled. "It's balanced on the edge. Just like you. You have decisions to make, officer. The trouble is, you don't know what you don't know." She looked up at the doctor. "He'll keep our little secret."

To Nathan's surprise, the doctor sat back in his chair and let out a breath. He, at least, trusted Jo's interpretation implicitly. Appearances could certainly be deceiving, but at first glance? These people didn't seem dangerous at all. If anything, the doctor seemed terrified, Jo resigned.

"Oh, I could've told you that," a third voice chimed in, and though the walls were dark, Nathan could hear Jenna's voice with surprising clarity. "That's Boy Scout Nathan Pearce. Or whatever version of the Boy Scouts they have in England."

Jenna Carpenter's guilt, at least, he could confirm. But she still deserved a fair trial. Was that paperwork underway? Or would they just sweep her under another pile of enhanced abilities fear?

Nathan stepped between the next pair of cells, and the wall dissolved to reveal Jenna standing in the center of her shoebox of a room, staring straight out at him. Petite and pale, her brunette hair had inched past her shoulders.

Her cell held no desk, no carpets, no books or papers. In the cell behind hers, a thin figure was curled into a ball on the bed. Sleeping, or pretending to. It felt like interrupting a private moment, to peer in without the prisoner's knowledge. With shame heating his face, Nathan turned back to Jenna.

"How many times have you tried to escape?" he asked Jenna, wondering again at that burned metal smell. They were checking her response to the serum, weren't they? He'd have to think of a way to suggest it without implicating the others.

Jenna grinned at him. "Four."

"Five," the doctor corrected. Nathan could still see inside the doctor's cell; the walls stayed clear for a good long stretch.

With a pang, Nathan wondered whether the doctor and Jo wished they could spend more time looking at each other. Clearly, they were friends.

"Where is she?" Jenna asked, her voice a low hiss that made him cringe.

She meant Mary, he assumed. Nathan folded his arms, willing Jo not to answer for him. Whether she heard his wishes, or whether she simply knew better, she said nothing.

"Hasn't forgiven you, I suppose," Jenna said. "Too bad. You look like you could use a good—"

"Surely you don't expect me to tell you anything," Nathan interrupted. "Although I'm sure if you behaved yourself, Eloise would let you have pancakes."

Jenna gave him a wry smile that made his stomach crawl. "So self-righteous. Well? Is your conscience eased yet?"

Nathan wasn't sure it ever would be, but he schooled his expression to neutrality. Lots of practice with that at least, as a cop.

Jo's power might let her read emotions, but Jenna read weakness without any enhancements at all. Nathan turned his back on her and rejoined the other two prisoners, who watched him openly. The rows of cells extended another fifty yards at least. How many were full? How many were innocent?

Surely Eloise would deal with the prisoners eventually, do what she could to sort right from wrong. But her plate was overflowing. And maybe Nathan could help. He stepped back in front of the doctor's cell, waiting for Jenna's walls to shift back to metal—or at least, metal-esque—before speaking again.

"I'd like to help you, if you'll let me," he said. "I'd like to hear your stories."

IT WAS weird coming to Jeff's house now, Mary thought as she woke in his guest room in Malibu for the second time in under two weeks. After the near-fiasco with Ranger in San Antonio, she'd thought it best to avoid Aries until she could figure out how to ensure Dawn Kimble wasn't going to lead Mary's enemies straight to her door.

Still, it was weird to stay in the house where the whole mind-control drugging thing had gone down last fall. The exposure of Nathan's Wave connection. The death of a friend. She twitched the curtains aside to look out at the pool, an elaborate setup with crisscrossing bridges and two thatch-covered bars. The sun sent sparkling rays dancing across the blue water, and even with the bad memories of this place, Mary couldn't help a spike of gladness at being back in Southern California.

She put on a sweatshirt and went downstairs, following the sound of the television to where Jeff Hayes stood at his kitchen island wearing gym shorts and a green t-shirt. The man was gloriously tanned. What did he do, sand away his blemishes? He was watching the television—which spanned the wall in the connected sitting area—with such entranced concentration.

Strange, to be granted a moment to see him without armor.

"Morning," she said.

Jeff jumped, spilling coffee all over the counter. "My god, woman. Have you not heard of a doorbell?"

Mary snatched an orange out of the fruit bowl on the counter and sat across from him on a stool with a polished brass seat. It was cold. "The idea was for me to come in and out without anyone knowing. So I did."

Jeff grimaced and pulled a towel out of a drawer—Mary couldn't help a twinge of surprise at the fact that he not only had towels, but knew where to find them—and tossed it onto the spill. "Yes. True. I did assume, however, that *I* would know."

Mary dug a fingernail under the orange peel, trying to remember the last time she'd bothered to eat fresh fruit. A while. "Your first mistake."

"Oh, no. I imagine this mistake ranks somewhere in the middle of a list that seems to be growing uncomfortably long. How did you get in?"

"Scaled the trellis."

Jeff shook his head. "So did Pearce, when he came to accuse me of Wave membership last fall. Delightful person, by the way. I suppose you trained him."

Mary didn't want to talk about Nathan. She didn't respond.

Jeff's house wasn't at all what she'd expected when she'd first met the man. Understated, as much as a Malibu home could be. Minimalist. It reminded her a little of her own house, except that he didn't bother much with the props. A few candles stashed in the corners, a copy of *Popular Science* on the coffee table—that was a surprise—and overly waxed hardwood floors. Even the pictures on the walls looked as if they'd been selected by a hotel decorator, bland collections of abstract shapes shaded in beige, black, and metallics. Nothing to object to. Nothing to offend.

Not at all like the man who owned them.

The talking head on the TV, a man Mary vaguely recognized—from a party, or maybe a red carpet thing, she didn't know—was finishing a report about a series of mysterious robberies that had been cropping up across the country. A Chicago CEO's art collection had been raided last week, and a New York Senator's jewelry vault the week before. Despite the varying objectives, the crimes appeared to be connected by virtue of their similar mysteriousness—though the details weren't being released.

"That's vague," Mary said, as the talking head finished his report and slid the story back to the anchor. Nobody had said the words 'enhanced abilities.' They didn't have to.

"Sounds like your territory," Jeff said.

"I'm all booked up. What are you even doing at home? Aren't you expected on set, or in an important meeting?"

Jeff slid a mini bottle of Macallan single malt out from under the counter and dropped a dash into his coffee. When she raised an eyebrow, he said, "It's your fault. For the scare. And I know you're out of practice, but I'll remind you that no one in Hollywood wakes up before noon."

Myths. People out here worked their asses off. "Not true."

"Fine. No one in Hollywood expects *me* to wake up before noon, and I hate to exceed their expectations. Do it once, and they'll be scheduling 5:30 meetings every Monday."

Mary sensed an evasion—undoubtedly an actor of Jeff's stature would have been called to various sets at all hours of the day—but she decided to let it go. Jeff's schedule was his business.

Before she could think of another question to annoy him with, the news split into a double screen, with the TV anchor in one box. And Dawn Kimble in another, her face dusted in makeup, her expression serious under that fringe of bangs. Mary grabbed the remote and turned the sound up.

"You know her?" Jeff said, and Mary shushed him as the anchor started talking again.

"We all know the White House has sanctioned the League of Independent Operatives as an official national security affiliate," the anchor was saying, "with the Pearl Knife at its head. Most people think of it as a good thing. Eloise Reyna's been forthcoming with the press, even welcoming, offering an open channel. We've talked with her ourselves."

"And I appreciate that stance," Dawn said. "But I also think there's more going on than Ms. Reyna is admitting, and that the public has the right to know what that is."

Mary leaned back against the counter, unable to wrench her eyes from the screen. Damn, that little reporter worked *fast*.

"Can you give me an example?" the anchor asked.

"Sure," Dawn said. "The whereabouts of the original league members."

The anchor blinked, though surely he'd have been prepared for her to say that. Maybe Dawn had surprised him with the direction of her story. "They're in retirement," the anchor said, "or so I understand. Dolly Reyna passed the mantle to her daughter, and the Inferno is dead."

Mary shook her head. "They didn't even know there was a league until last October. Now they're experts."

Jeff was looking at her oddly, his brow furrowed in question, but she ignored him.

"I've been tracking them," Dawn said. "Monster, Carlisle, Flick. They're missing. Someone's abducting them."

Mary jumped off the stool. "That *bitch*."

"Language," Jeff said. "If I used that word, you'd throw me in the pool."

"I'd throw you all the way to Antarctica. Shut up."

"Missing," the anchor repeated. "Is this OperativeWatch gossip, or actual reporting?"

Dawn flushed as the corners of the anchor's mouth twitched up ever so slightly. Mary didn't know who was surprising whom with this, but she didn't care about reporter politics.

Dawn wouldn't dare name Mary. Would she? Yes, the reporter had been pissed the other night after the whole Ranger fiasco, but lives could be at stake here. Surely she knew she should be discreet.

And she was. Sort of. Mary clutched the counter as Dawn finished her spiel without naming Coral, or Mary. But by the time she'd finished talking, she had the anchor half convinced that there was something strange going on.

When Dawn ended the interview with a call to action for reporters to investigate the disappearances, Mary threw her orange at the TV, and Jeff shut it off with the remote.

"OK," he said. "So clearly you've got something to do with this, and though I have the benefit of your citrus-chucking reaction to judge by, I imagine there are others in your life who could work it out. Dawn did."

"Yeah, well, Dawn was there."

He blinked. "She was there."

"Apparently she's got enhanced abilities that let her follow me. Fun, right? I saved her from some pissed off retired IOs. And coyotes."

"Coyotes."

"Possibly. I'm not feeding you lines here, Hayes, stop repeating everything I say. Yes. Ranger sicced some on us a couple nights ago, and I saved her."

"Right before you trussed him up and tossed him into your soccer mom van, if I understand what she's implying?"

Mary glared at him. "I might have missed the boat on that one."

Jeff leaned his elbows on the counter, rubbing his face with both hands. "She's going to out you."

"She hasn't yet."

"Because she's waiting on evidence. And let me take a guess why you chose today to grace me with your illusive presence. These ex-superheroes are after you now, and you didn't want to lead them to whatever jail you've got going."

Jeff was, unfortunately, somewhat smarter than he looked. Mary picked up the orange peel and set it back down. She needed something to do with her hands. She missed her seashells, but she'd thrown most of them away, and the ones she still had only made her think of Nathan.

Jeff poured another generous dose of whisky into his coffee and took a long drink. "I'm afraid to ask this," he said, "truly, it pains me. But why are you collecting ex-super-spandexers and trussing them up in the back of your hideous car?"

"I'm not sure Ranger ever wore spandex."

"Mary."

"He was more of a forest-green uniform type thing. Smoky the Bear. Only he smoked."

Jeff just drank his coffee and stared at her until she threw her arms up in frustration. "Someone has to bring them to justice," she said. "They deserve to be punished for what they did."

Jeff eyed his coffee as though he wanted to replace the whole cup with liquor, then set the mug down carefully. He shifted personalities so regularly, she never quite knew who she was talking to. Still, he had to be remembering the fact that he'd been the one to connect the league with Mary's plane crash. He'd been the one to reveal it to her. "Maybe you should rethink your methods."

"Trust me, I've thought this through."

Jeff pressed his lips together, as if he wanted to contradict her on that. "What about those enhanced guys out there causing trouble? Shouldn't we go after them?"

"We? Are you an IO now, or are you researching a role?" Mary slid off her stool. She was done with this conversation. "This was a mistake. I should go."

"No, wait." He came around to her side of the counter and leaned back against it. "I'm sorry. I just... I'm new to this whole vigilante thing."

"Add it to your list of mistakes."

"I'll keep my end of the bargain," he said. "I'll trust you."

Mary took a step back. "I don't need your trust."

"Well, you have it. And the guest room, whenever you want it."

Mary nearly cringed at that. He was right that she hadn't wanted to lead the retirees back to Aries. In her frenzy to find a safe place to stay after driving from San Antonio, she'd told herself that Diana and the others wouldn't dare come after her at Jeff's. But that had probably been a mistake. She hadn't meant to put him in danger. Jeff's house was one of the more obvious places to look for her, with or without Dawn's eerie tracking abilities.

A reporter who could track her. That was so, so unfortunate. After the whole reporters-making-her-faint thing at her parents' funeral, Mary had returned to HQ to find that Eloise had not only hidden every recent magazine and newspaper, but also blocked Mary's WiFi access. Simply to keep her from seeing all the awful things they'd written about her.

She had a thicker skin, now. But that didn't mean she trusted a single one of them.

Now, standing in Jeff's kitchen, Mary sighed. "I really should get going."

Jeff smiled, but it seemed like a stretch. Like he was trying too hard to make amends. "Where to this time?"

"I'm not sure I should say."

"Someone ought to know where you are." He held up a hand. "Someone unconnected to any and all vigilante organizations. Just in case."

She studied him, but he really did seem sincere. Despite his clenched fists. Or maybe that was part of it. Was Jeff Hayes trying to be a good person? Or was he just watching out for himself, as per usual?

In any case, he was probably right. And if someone had to know where she was, it might as well be someone she disliked. No use making herself vulnerable again just to get her heart trampled on by cops gone rogue.

"I'm going to New York City," she said. The home of a former LIO member who hadn't shown up last night, and whose location she actually knew. "I'm going see a magician about some rabbits."

Before Agnes's arrival at Wave HQ, family game nights had been a rare treat, squeezed into Agnes's too-infrequent visits along with bowling alleys and amusement parks and Lucy's busy school schedule. These days, game nights were practically a nightly phenomenon, yet no one seemed to have gotten sick of them yet.

Stirring mugs of hot chocolate at the counter, Agnes couldn't help enjoying the scene at the table. Her wife and her daughter, eyeing each other's Monopoly real estate and plotting their routes to first place. They were both so competitive.

Agnes dropped extra marshmallows into the mugs and delivered them to the table.

"Lucy, you can only use one piece," Tam said, gesturing to the game board. "You don't need two."

"But the dog needs to wear the hat," Lucy said cheerfully, adjusting the silver top hat on the dog's head so that it tilted at a jaunty angle. "He's cold."

"He looks like he's headed out on the town," Agnes said. "To the opera, maybe."

"Or to jail," Tam said playfully. "Do not pass go, do not collect two hundred dollars."

"It's Mama's turn," Lucy said.

As Agnes rolled the dice in her palm, the apartment door-bell chimed so loudly that Agnes jumped. Leave it to Wave to install actual doorbells in their underground hideout. Though most people just knocked.

Tam dropped her head into her hand in mock dismay. "Another game night, ruined."

"It's fine," Agnes said, scooting her chair back. "I'll tell them to go."

Tam raised her eyebrows. "What if it's everything's-an-emergency Bradley?"

"Then I'll tell him to..." Agnes glanced at Lucy, who was watching with eager hope of hearing a bad word slip out of her mama's mouth. "Buy some eggs," she finished.

Lucy rolled her eyes. Agnes got up to open the door.

Bradley Archer had made few appearances in the under-water HQ since depositing Agnes here last October. He always checked in on her, made sure she had what she needed, and then flitted off to do... whatever else it was he did.

Tonight, the man actually looked agitated. He stood straighter when she opened the door, his blond hair quivering as though it meant to reach for the ceiling. And he wore his signature orange galoshes, of course. Always.

"Ms. Jenson," he said. "I need your help."

"Buy some eggs?" Lucy's voice said from inside the house. Agnes covered her mouth with her hand, stifling a laugh.

Bradley frowned, but Agnes opened the door wider, gesturing for Bradley to come in. "Just a little family humor," she said. "Would you like some hot chocolate?"

"Only if you've got marshmallows," Bradley said.

"Duh," Lucy said.

Agnes half expected Tam to drag Lucy away under the guise of picking out a movie. Instead Tam watched Bradley enter, arms folded across her chest, chin tilted at an angle that Agnes recognized as trouble. It was true that Bradley tended to sound the alarm for any small concern, but he'd never shown up in person with a problem before.

Agnes handed her boss a mug of cocoa, which he thanked her for and immediately set aside. "I realize I'm interrupting family time," he said. Realized, yet didn't apologize. That was Bradley. "I'm here to ask you to help out on a mission."

Before Agnes could respond, Tam huffed out a breath. "I thought Agnes's mission days were done. That was the deal. Maybe that league should take care if it, whatever it is, if Wave can't."

Bradley sniffed his cocoa. "I wish they would. Unfortunately, they're too preoccupied with their own implosion to remember they're supposed to be heroes."

Lucy's eyes lit up. "A superhero mission?"

Tam whipped her head around. "Luce. Why don't you put the board away and pick out a movie? I'll be right in."

And there it was. Agnes repressed a smile, while Bradley Archer watched their interaction with open curiosity.

Lucy darted off, and Tam said, "I wish you wouldn't fill her head with this superhero stuff."

"Tam," Agnes said, "we're living in an underwater hideout, surrounded by labs that study enhanced abilities. She's got jellyfish swimming past her windows. Trust me, her head is filled."

And in all likelihood, she was also listening from the other room.

"But Tam is right." Agnes turned to Bradley. "You promised I'd never have to go on another mission."

Bradley plucked a half-melted marshmallow out of his cocoa and popped it into his mouth. "And you don't have to go on this one," he said, his words half muffled by puffy sugar. "But you'll probably save like, a lot of people. If you do."

Tam threw up her hands. "How are we supposed to say no to that?"

Agnes's beautiful, kind wife. Of course she'd see it that way. Agnes did, too, but she also believed in keeping her word. And she'd made Tam some pretty hefty promises as Wave had spirited their family into hiding. "We can say no," Agnes said. "It's a family decision, remember?"

Bradley folded his hands on the counter, waiting. If he made a single comment about them being cute, Agnes would use her powers to pummel him with marshmallows.

Tam faced Bradley, scowling the way she did when Lucy was about thirty second from being sent to time out. "Why does it have to be Agnes?"

"Fair question," Bradley said. "We're short on enhanced operatives. I'm having to pull in consultants as it is. And it would really help if we could, you know, drop in from the sky."

"Heard of parachutes?" Tam asked.

Bradley just sighed. "Consider me little more than a messenger. But it's a request. Not an order."

A request. Agnes did believe that, but if she were to refuse? People would get hurt. He'd said as much.

Tam pointed at Bradley. "I don't like you."

He shrugged. "You're not alone. I think there's a club in Wisconsin."

Tam glared harder. "I don't like broken promises."

He didn't look away from her gaze. "Neither do I, trust me. This one, though... it's a code... well, it's a code Agnes."

How bad could it be, that an organization like Wave—even injured as they were—needed Agnes to win a fight? If it was really that bad, she should go. She should help.

"Not without your go-ahead," Agnes said firmly.

Tam sighed. "Fine. I'm in. But Agnes—"

"It's the last time," Agnes said.

Tam looped an arm through Agnes's. "Maybe. I was going to say if you come back dead, I'll kill you."

Agnes tucked a strand of hair behind her wife's ear. "I won't. Promise."

Bradley stood. "Good, good. Thanks for the cocoa. Take the transport to Long Beach. We'll have a car waiting there to take you to Vegas."

Vegas. Great. Well, it wasn't like he'd call her in for a nice, quiet operation, would he? "You're not coming?" she asked.

"I'll meet you there," he said, his galoshes squeaking as he made his way to the door. "I need to call in your partner."

When Nathan had imagined becoming an independent operative, he'd pictured planning and executing the kinds of daring rescues he'd watched in awe on television for years. Flying up to free hijacked airplanes (though he couldn't fly) and saving cars from collapsed bridges (though he wasn't super-strong) and chasing after dangerous criminals (he wasn't super fast, either, and he'd done that much as a cop).

He had not imagined questioning prisoners who had very likely been wrongly incarcerated for years.

"I don't know why you're asking me," the doctor told Nathan for the hundredth time. "I'm sure my story is right there in your files."

It was. A version of it, anyway. Nathan was sitting on the floor outside the doctor's cell, doing everything in his power to look unthreatening as he tried to convince the doctor revisit memories that couldn't be pleasant ones.

Nathan had spent the last few nights digging through every snippet of information the league had collected on the people they'd helped put behind bars in the first place. As with the prison, he'd been granted full access to the files, to the official stories. Police reports, depositions, court transcripts, news reports. The sheer amount of information could bury him in research for years. Still, he'd parsed what he could.

He'd also noticed some gaps. Such as how a healer like Dr. Gordon could have been convicted of aiding and abetting any number of Wave-run crimes without a shred of physical evidence. They'd rounded him up in a hospital, for god's sake.

The way Dr. Gordon—that was the name of the old man that Jo simply called 'doctor'—was twisting his pen cap around, it was almost as if he suspected a trap. Nathan hardly blamed him for that. He'd skipped training yesterday to make his way down the row of cells, to speak to the others. Thirty-three in all, not counting Jenna, their attitudes ranging from hopeful to angry to resentfully silent.

As for their abilities, Nathan had never seen such a collection, had never even known so many Wave operatives were enhanced at all. Teleportation, extra sensory perception, sensory *suppression*, telekinesis, super strength. Flight. Invisibility. Fire.

And the prisoners *were* Wave operatives. He'd checked. Every single one of them, if you counted Jenna before she'd gone rogue.

"I've seen Dolly's side of the story," Nathan said. Because that was what it came down to: Dolly's testimony, Dolly as a key witness, Dolly finding evidence, Dolly giving interviews. Who would doubt the word of the Pearl Knife? Back then, no one. "I want your side now."

Dr. Gordon looked over Nathan's shoulder, presumably for a reading from Jo. She didn't speak, and Nathan didn't look, but she must have given a sign that it was safe to proceed because Dr. Gordon sighed and leaned his elbows on his knees, still squeezing the pen cap.

Nathan didn't like asking him to relive those times. But if he could find evidence that the doctor—and the others, one by one—were here because of Dolly's lies, then he could also procure their freedom.

"I was living in one of the last Wave safe houses," Dr. Gordon said. "I didn't go out in the field much. I was the only healer, so they brought injured operatives to me, and I took care of them. They didn't want to risk my safety."

Nathan nodded. "Where was the safe house?"

"It was a hospital of sorts, one I'd assembled. In St. Louis. Central location, in the U.S., anyway. After the plane, this country became the main battleground between your league and Wave."

That much, at least, aligned with the story in LIO's database. The doctor removed his bifocals and rubbed the lenses on his sleeve before replacing them carefully on his nose. If anything, they looked even more smudged than they had before. Nathan made a note to get the man some cleaning solution.

"And it *was* like a battle back then, Officer," the doctor continued. "It was a war. The operatives they brought me... they suffered horrific injuries. Cuts, burns, claw marks, bites. Poison."

Nathan assembled the old guard in his mind, the roster of supposed heroes who'd worked with Dolly. Her husband, the Inferno; Ranger, who could control animals, and Monster who was part animal himself; the Trap, with her poison-laced fingertips. Rocker, Flick, and Goldi.

The doctor licked his lips. "The night your people found us, our team brought in one man—he was hardly more than a boy—who claimed the Pearl Knife had cut him open just so the Inferno could fry his insides." Dr. Gordon shuddered. "Our boys, they were just trying to get away, you see. I was healing him when your people came."

Nathan nearly flinched at that—*your people*—though he

didn't know how else the doctor could have described them. Dolly and her team had never been his people, and yet... he'd chosen the league, hadn't he?

"They must have tracked the retreating operatives to the safe house," Dr. Gordon said. "They came so fast. I'd barely laid hands on the kid to heal him before they showed up, threw us up against walls, and clapped handcuffs on everyone. All while the boy bled out in agony. To them, my healing made me a war criminal, or so they said. To me..." He swallowed, removed his glasses again. "Well, Officer, I'm sorry to say that to me, your employers are murderers."

Nathan couldn't imagine Eloise attacking someone the way Dr. Gordon described. She was quick to respond to a threat, but she used her abilities with restraint.

According to Dolly, the St. Louis operation had resulted in a dozen arrests, effectively neutralizing a significant number of Wave-planned threats. The file offered little detail, except to say that the threats were to have been carried out in New York, Dublin, and Jerusalem—all cities that had failed to pay Wave for protection.

Nathan shifted on the floor, feeling the ache in his lower back. Recruit training, late nights, stone floors. That would do it. "Our files say that Wave defended the people—and cities— that paid them. And that when they didn't, Wave terrorized them."

"The former's true," the doctor said. "Maybe it was wrong, Officer. Maybe. But do you blame a powerful person for taking a job as a bodyguard? Do you blame them when they defend their client above everyone else in the room?"

No. Nathan supposed not. "What about the terrorism part?"

"It wasn't the way you described it. Wave made dubious choices back then, yes. Choices I argued against."

"Like sending children to bomb terrorists when the city in question did pay up?"

The doctor's hands trembled as he nodded. "It was wrong. It *was* terrorism, and I'm sorry for it. I was never on the ground, but maybe I deserve to be here. I knew about it, after all." He leaned forward, meeting Nathan's gaze with his steady brown eyes. "But, Officer, Wave never attacked cities simply because they didn't pay us. We defended our clients. We ignored the rest. If we'd had more resources, things could have been different."

If they'd coordinated with the league, perhaps, instead of fighting each other. Nathan rubbed his eyes, willing away the beginning of a headache.

His mobile buzzed in his pocket, and he pulled it out, irritated and ready to ignore the call. He wasn't in the mood to talk to his sister, or hear more about the EAEA. Not right now.

But it wasn't Chloe. It was Gail. He took the call. "There's someone aboveground who's asking for you," she said.

Or Chloe had come again in person. "I'm busy right now," he said. "Is it something Ire can help with?"

"No. I mean usually yes, I'd call Ire or El if she were here. But this is a special case."

Nathan's heart skipped double time. It couldn't be Mary, but his treacherous heart wished for her all the same. In the background, he heard Jo sigh sadly. "Who is it?" he asked.

"OK, don't freak out," Gail said. "But it's Jeff Hayes."

―――

Even with his limited knowledge of entertainment personalities, Nathan had known who Jeff Hayes was before they'd ever met in person. Movie posters with his face graced every T-stop in Boston, for a start, and he was the kind of actor who came up over water cooler conversations, even in a police precinct.

As far as Nathan was concerned, the guy should stay stuck in a movie screen and never talk to any real people, ever. To say he and Jeff didn't get along... well, that would be an understatement.

When Nathan met Gail at the recruiting office, Jeff was standing outside, looking unforgivably handsome in his wool cap and black overcoat as he took selfies with tourists who grinned uncontrollably even through their shivers. When he saw Nathan, Jeff gently extricated himself from the crowd and followed Nathan into the office, where Gail turned the sign around, pulled the shades, and promptly vanished into the back.

At least someone around here could manage not to get starstruck. Though he supposed Gail must have years of practice with that, working alongside Mary as she did. Or had.

Jeff turned a slow circle, dropping the cutesy celebrity act while he surveyed the recruitment posters on the walls. "Some of them will wait for me," he said, taking off the hat and flipping it onto the counter. Even rumpled, his hair looked perfect. Nathan stifled the sudden urge to punch him. "I should've worn a ski mask."

"Hurts to be loved." Nathan leaned his elbow on the counter, doing his best to match the movie star's nonchalance. "What are you doing here?"

"You know, you people could use some etiquette lessons. I'm not asking for a full welcome committee or anything like that, but I did get drugged because of you last year. And I helped you after that disastrous fight in the Sea and Stars warehouse. I'd say that earns me the right to a civil audience."

"Fine," Nathan said. "Though I also seem to remember you making untoward comments about my sister."

Jeff pursed his lips. "Hm. That does sound like me. I apologize. I'm not here to insult you, Pearce, much though the instinct does tend to arise as soon as I see your face."

The feeling was entirely mutual. "And still, you haunt me."

"Do you know," Jeff said, as though Nathan hadn't spoken, "that since that whole fiasco, I've had three scripts retracted? And no more on my desk. Not so much as a made-for-TV rom-com."

"You're implying you're out of work because of your connection to the league." Nathan couldn't think of why that might be, even if Jeff had alienated the press somewhat at the time. Maybe his movie pals saw him as complicit in Mary's lies. Seemed like a small-time scandal for the likes of Hollywood.

On the other side of the blinds, shadows moved alarmingly close to the window. Nathan couldn't help but imagine people trying to peer inside, to catch another glimpse of Jeff Hayes.

"Oh, I'm doing more than implying it," Jeff said. "I'm blaming you, to be frank. But if it sounds nicer to say it the other way, sure."

Nathan crossed his arms. "Then why are you here? People know the league operates out of Niagara."

"Yes, well. Some things merit a visit."

"What things? Talk, Hayes. As much as I love therapy time, I've got work to do."

Jeff met Nathan's eyes, briefly, and despite his flippant tone, his expression was serious. "Mary."

Nathan's heart flipped, and he pushed down a wave of panic. He did his best to stay still, to keep from betraying his emotions, until his stillness felt like a reaction in itself. "You've seen her?"

Jeff nodded and picked up a brochure from the rack. "'Bring your enhanced abilities to the next level.' Who writes this drivel? Tell them to use more active verbs." He set the paper down and faced Nathan. "I'm worried about her."

Jealousy spiked through Nathan's chest, and he tamped it down as best he could. He'd surrendered his right to even minor jealousy when he'd chosen the league over Mary. And if Jeff Hayes had extracted his head from his own backside for long enough to be worried, then Nathan was worried, too. Where was she?

"She's on some kind of mission, or crusade," Jeff said.

Of that, Nathan was well aware. He and Steve had spent a few nights trying to catch a lead, before Steve had run off with Eloise and Nathan got distracted by the prisoners. Beyond the one cameo in Malibu, she hadn't left a trail. "A crusade that involves kidnapping retired superheroes and stashing them... where, exactly? Do you know?"

Jeff's lips parted in surprise. "You know about this? You and your pristine moral code *know* about this, and you're not doing anything about it?"

Nathan shrugged. He wasn't doing anything because he couldn't *find* her, but Jeff didn't need to know that.

The part of Nathan that had spent half a lifetime wanting to be an independent operative—two-thirds of a lifetime, really —balked at the idea that incarcerating anyone outside a court of law could ever serve as justice.

She might still see herself as a vigilante. But it wasn't like the Mary he knew.

Then again, LIO had a stash of dubiously guilty prisoners in their basement, too, and they *had* been processed through a court of law. Black and white were getting hard to distinguish.

But no; right and wrong were always clear. It was who did right, and who did wrong, that threw his entire life into upheaval. Nathan had known about Dolly's crimes when he'd joined up with LIO. As much as he'd idealized her, he'd understood that she was not the hero he'd spent his life wanting to be. But he'd believed—rather foolishly, he supposed—that LIO's crimes would be simple to rectify. Right was right. Wrong was wrong.

It was Nathan who seemed to be veering off course. The beginnings of a headache needled at his temples as Jeff waited for him to respond, to defend himself somehow. But Nathan couldn't, because he had no defense to offer.

Jeff flipped his thumb along a stack of brochures. "She's not well. I mean really, Pearce, you ought to see her. She's practically a skeleton. A very tired, very stressed out skeleton."

Nathan swallowed, wishing he could imitate Jeff's casual attitude. His conflicted emotions had to be pasted across his face. But then, the movie star wasn't actually casual, was he? A good actor, but the man could barely stop moving. He ran his hands along the brochure stands, flicked the edges of the posters. He didn't want to be here, and he'd come anyway.

"So help her," Nathan said.

Jeff made a frustrated noise in the back of his throat. "I'm trying. She's not exactly keen on collaboration as I'm sure you can attest. And even as a skeleton she can kick my ass without trying."

"I've no doubt."

Jeff unbuttoned his coat, though the cold leaking under the door made Nathan want to stuff his hands in his pockets. "That's it? I came all the way out here so you could tell me to help her? Me? Your mortal enemy?"

"You're not important enough to be my mortal enemy."

Jeff clutched his heart. "You wound me."

Nathan thought of how Mary had asked him to come with her last year. If he'd gone, would he have tried to stop her from this crusade—essentially arresting LIO's old guard, holding them accountable for their crimes—or would he be right there beside her?

Had she planned even then to go after them? Or was it a thought that had arisen later?

"Mary doesn't want my help," Nathan said.

"She doesn't want anyone's help. That's the problem." Jeff picked his hat up off the counter and bunched it in his hands. "I'm here because she's off the deep end, friend. She's going to sink, and I'm not sure I can pull her up."

Nathan sighed. He didn't want to trust Jeff, or be nice to him. But somehow, he couldn't help the urge to calm the man's nerves. "She's been doing this on her own for a long time."

"Except she had you, for a while."

And LIO. For a long time, she'd had LIO.

Jeff pointed a finger at him, and Nathan had the urge to bat him away. So much for being nice. "But you abandoned her. She hasn't said as much, but I can see it on your face. You did. My god, you're a complete idiot. What were you thinking?"

Nathan ran a hand through his hair. No one else had said it out loud. Not Eloise, certainly; personal matters were personal, and besides, his choice had been to her benefit. He wondered whether she thought that. She and Mary had been raised as sisters, after all.

And it just *had* to be Jeff Hayes who finally voiced the truth. Nathan wanted to be sick. "I'm not sure I was thinking at all."

Jeff held out a scrap of paper and shook it in Nathan's direction. "She's going to New York. I don't know why. But if you lose her again..." He took a breath, as if he wasn't sure he should share the information. "There's a reporter named Dawn Kimble who's got enhanced abilities. She can track Mary."

Nathan took the paper, and scanned the address scrawled across it in hurried blue ink. Jeff's handwriting, maybe, copying

something Mary had written. A reporter with enhanced abilities that let her track people? That could be... complicated.

Nathan *was* supposed to be working on the disappearing
old guard situation, even with Steve off on a side quest with
Eloise. Even with the prison revelations. Nathan worried the
paper between his fingers, thinking. "Is it true your work's dried
up because of us?"

Jeff shrugged. "Seems so. But if you see Mary, don't tell her,
will you? I've got an image to maintain."

As soon as the plane's wheels hit the tarmac in Sacramento, the Pearl Knife began pushing Eloise toward the coast. She felt it tugging at her gut as she and Steve made their way through the terminal, and she wouldn't have needed to consult her GPS or the setting sun to point due west.

To the familiar patch of redwoods, the Knife now added flashes of a cabin. A house, with a porch and a gravel drive, rusty trees rising all around it.

If you know where we're going, send us there. Cut us a portal, Eloise thought, doing her best to beam a vision of the vendor stand the Knife had made her skip last fall. That was how the Pearl Knife communicated, wasn't it? But the Knife didn't respond. For the first time, Eloise wondered if it even knew how it had cut the portal back in Santa Monica.

Maybe the blade wasn't being stubborn. Maybe it was as clueless as she was.

With portals a no-go, Eloise led Steve to the airport garage, where she took the driver's seat of the sedan LIO kept there. As they kept cars in most major airports. Steve slid into the passenger seat without comment, one elbow propped against the window. It gave him a casual look, like they were out here for a vacation.

The further west they drove, the clearer the Knife's pictures became, until Eloise found herself exiting the highway and following a detailed map in her head through a small town and along a secluded country road, which led to a more secluded dirt road and up a switchback driveway. She was glad for the late afternoon light; this would have been impossible to navigate in the darkness.

The Knife guided her up the drive to the cabin that had kept her mind company for the last two hours, a compact house surrounded by sun-filtering redwoods.

"Doesn't look like anyone's home," Steve said as they pulled up in front of the house. "Shall we?"

No cars in the drive, at least. Dirt crunched under her feet, the car door closing with an echoing thud, and she paused to look up at the house. It was a small wooden cabin with a wide front porch and a bay window looking out from the second floor. No curtains twitched at the sound of the car.

"Feels almost balmy after Niagara," Steve said, but Eloise didn't agree. Maybe it was the humidity, or the feeling of dread that welled in her gut when she looked at the house, but the cool air seemed to slice into her lungs with a vicious clarity.

Eloise drew the blade out of its sheath as they made their way up the front steps, as much to keep a hold on it as to prepare herself. No one answered the door when she knocked. Before she could ask him to help, Steve ran the perimeter, returning with a puff of dust and a shake of his head. Nothing.

A flick of the Knife's tip singed the lock into compliance, and Eloise pushed the front door open.

The cabin smelled of apple spice and tomato sauce and wool, the scents enveloping Eloise as she stepped out of the chilly afternoon. Afghans lounged colorfully on neat sofas, and a gray cat shuffled down a narrow staircase to welcome her, spiraling around her ankles as if greeting an old friend. Why would the Knife have brought them here?

Steve blurred into motion, checking the cabin for occupants while Eloise waited for the Knife to tell her something. Anything. It had taken up a stuttering sort of resonance, a buzzing burn that felt like a perpetually dissonant chord sounding in her head. Oddly, it reminded her almost of the way it rattled when she brought it too close to Dolly.

Steve rematerialized at her side. "No one."

The Knife pushed an image into her mind, and Eloise followed it to the kitchen island, where a stack of articles had been printed with a streaky printer cartridge. With Steve watching over her shoulder, she thumbed through the headlines.

Police Suspect Enhanced Criminals in Chicago Heist
No Sign of Forced Entry in Tulsa Bank Robbery
Enhanced Thieves Strike Minneapolis

"These are the problems Travis Bertram was talking about," she said. "The enhanced criminals he wants us to check out."

Steve nodded, leaning over to read the articles. "Do you think we've found them?"

"Maybe?" It felt like such a warm, pleasant hideout for robbers. Either she'd been watching too many movies, or she'd forgotten how varied criminal hideouts could be. She hadn't exactly gone on many missions in the last few months.

Maybe that had been a mistake.

Eloise began opening kitchen cabinets as Steve took a seat at the desktop computer in the corner, an older machine that nonetheless booted up with a sleepy whir of its fans.

There was nothing in the cabinets but dishes. Eloise

ducked into the bathroom to check the medicine cabinet, but it held only the usual stock of bandaids and minor painkillers.

When she returned, Steve was printing a document. "They logged out of email, and I'm not a hacker," he said. "But they didn't think to clear the last thing they printed."

"Which was?"

Steve pulled the paper out of the tray and held it up. "Driving directions," he said.

"Who still prints driving directions?"

Steve shrugged. "I don't know. But it looks like our criminal's headed to Vegas."

Mary had avoided New York as long as she could—too many people, too many eyes. But she'd been desperate to get out of California, and Goldi had been hiding in the city for years.

The lights of Times Square hawked their wares without shame in a rush of gaudy glamour that made Mary shudder. The eyes she'd been so worried about noticing her were drawn to the frenzy of billboards and taxis, taking in the winter smells of roasting nuts and avoiding the mysterious billows of subway steam.

Mary bypassed the clattering distractions and cut through the theater district to the marquee advertising the sensational Broadway magic show that had made international headlines over the past year or so. A magician who put new spins on old tricks, they claimed. A genius.

Or, Mary thought, an illusionist adept at tampering with her audience's perception of reality.

The theater district buzzed with electricity, lights hideously bright after her months of creeping through the darkness. She'd braided her hair and tucked it into a baseball cap, and the weather was blissfully cold, allowing her to hide inside an oversized parka. She liked winter, really, as long as she was adequately dressed for it.

Disguised as she was, she couldn't help looking over her shoulder every block or so. Her run-in with Diana and the others had her spooked. Did they expect her to come here next? Was Goldi in league with them, too?

More importantly—had Dawn Kimble decided to follow her here? That would be ten kinds of stupid, but Mary wouldn't put it past the OperativeWatch reporter.

Mary hurried, breathing her way through the crowd with her eyes lowered. When she reached the Magic Box Theater, she practically shoved her ticket into the usher's hands and paused to allow the security guard to scan her with his metal detector before slipping into her left-aisle seat in one of the flashiest theaters she'd ever been in. And Mary O'Sullivan had attended more gaudy award ceremonies than she could even remember.

Here, lights played along the rippled silver walls, giving the impression of waves, with projected fish swimming across at a leisurely pace. As if that weren't enough, holographic sea creatures patrolled the center of the theater, jellyfish clouds dipping through the waiting crowd, sharks circling the chandeliers.

It was as if Goldi wanted to announce her true identity to the world. Maybe she did. She'd always liked playing games. The minute someone actually made the connection, she'd vanish. But Mary was here because she wanted to see the face the retiree wore now, and remind herself of the power of Goldi's illusions.

The lights dimmed, the fish fading to outlines before blinking away.

And the show truly was impressive. Mary had half expected Goldi to wear the proof of her power with something obvious, like a skirt made of live birds or a tiger companion, but the magician demonstrated a dedication to restraint that had allowed her to remain hidden.

Certainly she'd made adjustments to her face; her nose molded into a smaller shape, lips widened, jaw pulled to a stronger point. She'd fashioned her hair into a tower of flame with a golden circlet perched at its base, and Mary felt certain that her dress shimmered too much for reality.

But for the most part, Goldi saved her power for the show. Entire flocks of doves vanished and reappeared among the chandeliers. Members of the audience reached for butterflies and hummingbirds that hovered just above their heads and marveled at how Goldi escaped from a water tank by stepping straight through the glass.

During the climax of the show, Goldi led the handsome young man who worked as her assistant through a series of traditional magic tricks, all impressive but mundane acts. Until, as Goldi levitated the prone young man three feet above the stage, a heckler stood up in the back of the theater, cupped his hands to his mouth, and yelled, "We know how this trick works. Fake!"

Goldi squinted into the audience, lifting a hand to her brow as if that would let her see through the blinding lights—which, Mary knew from experience, it certainly would not. She then passed a hand over the floating assistant—no wires—and another under him.

"Perspex box," the heckler yelled, and Mary would have bet her fortune that the man had been planted in the audience. She'd have liked to come back another night, to test that theory. Unfortunately, tonight would be Goldi's final performance, at least for a time. The magician just didn't know it yet.

Goldi flashed the heckler a coy smile and looked back to her assistant—who was surely an illusion himself, for he began to float upwards, higher and higher, until he soared above her head. She motioned with her hands, and the assistant tilted into a standing position.

"There's gotta be a wire," the man beside Mary muttered to his companion, his voice tinged with awe. But as if she could read his mind, Goldi sent a pair of the blades spinning in a crisscrossing formation above the assistant's head, as if to prove there were none.

The audience erupted with applause, Goldi took a million bows, and Mary left the theater with everyone else. Originally, she had considered manipulating the show somehow. Taking Goldi away through one of her tricks, or something like that. But that option, though satisfying, would have been far too public. Especially now that the others were hunting her.

Instead, Mary made use of the shadows. New York certainly had enough of those. She managed to find an unwatched corner outside the stage door, an exit Goldi had used to leave the theater for the past few nights. When a stage-hand exited, Mary flicked a door-holding chip into the frame and waited until he'd disappeared before slipping in after him.

The corridor was a jungle. Oh, it smelled like sweaty polyester and cleaning solution, as any backstage area might, but the walls dripped with leaves. A snake spiraled among the vines, hissing, and beetles carpeted the floor. As Mary paused, a fine mist drifted in from the ceiling.

Because the genius of Goldi's illusions was not only that they looked real, but that they *felt* real. No doubt her sham of an assistant shook hands with producers, too.

And then there was Goldi's voice, honey-toned and drifting through the corridor, her projecting power an offshoot of the illusions she created. "I've been expecting you," she said. "Whoever you are."

Either she wasn't in contact with Diana, or she was lying.

Mary crept forward, ignoring the vines that pretended to pull at her arms. The illusions couldn't stop her. They could only pretend.

"People are easily distinguished by their fears," Goldi said, conversational, and a swarm of buzzing insects followed the wave of her voice down the hall, swirling along the ceiling and whirlpooling into Mary's path.

Mary ignored the skin-crawling buzz of their wings, and even the prods of false stings, reminding herself that she wore long sleeves. No gloves, but Goldi didn't know that, and Mary pushed forward. Not for the first time, she wondered if Goldi's powers somehow drugged people into believing what they saw.

She'd have loved to get Agnes's input on that.

"That rules out Diana," Goldi said, and Mary filed away that slice of information; she hadn't known the Trap feared bees.

Goldi sent a trio of dogs barking along the corridor, huge drooling mastiffs with their jaws snapping audibly. One of them leapt at Mary's arm and hung there, a feeling of pressure on her elbow that she couldn't shake off. Goldi did expect retirees, then. Bees for the Trap, and now dogs—and everyone knew that Monster was terrified of dogs.

But here, Mary paused. Because if Goldi had been expecting her, it had to be because she knew the others had disappeared. And if she knew they'd disappeared, then she shouldn't be expecting one of them to attack her.

As the thought crystalized, the vines fell away from the walls and the dogs vanished, their barking replaced by the roar of a jet engine. And suddenly Mary was standing in the aisle of an airplane, the midwest rolling by outside the windows.

Mary stopped, fear coating the inside of her throat. She handled airplanes because she had to, because jaunting back and forth between New York and Los Angeles for LIO had required it. But this was not just any plane. It was the mirror image of the small private jet her parents had used upon occasion.

It was the plane that had crashed, with all of them on it.

"Ah," Goldi said, "Mary. I thought perhaps."

If she hadn't known all along. Goldi loved to play games. And whether Goldi knew it somehow or simply guessed it, Mary's flashbacks had grown far more frequent of late. She hardly needed illusions to feel off balance, but with the plane closed around her like a coffin, she fought to draw breath.

Mary realized she'd been standing there, breathing raggedly, hands clenched at her sides, for several seconds. She took a step forward.

Her mother materialized in the seat to her left, long blonde hair glistening as she smiled up at her daughter. Mary's heart seized, pain blasting through her chest at the unimaginable cruelty of it. She actually felt herself reaching out to touch her mother's face, her lips half parted to call out a warning.

The floor lurched, the engines whining in protest. Mary stumbled, her gaze falling on a sticker on the cockpit door—it was all so real—a seashell decal with the family motto scripted over the shape: *adventure doesn't wait.*

And the sight of that sticker, that little detail, brought her vision into focus. Mary set her hand firmly against the wall and steadied herself, breathing deeply. She could confirm, then, that Goldi had been involved in the crash. Because she still didn't know which of the retirees had had a hand in her parents' deaths, aside from Dolly, and who had only known of the plan. She just knew that Eloise was unlikely to pursue the truth, and that someone had to.

But there was no reason that Goldi should know about the seashell decal. Unless she'd seen the inside of the plane.

The walls tilted, smoke raging outside the fake windows,

and Mary clamped her jaw shut, pasting her gaze to the floor. The illusion lurched around her, and she punched an arm through the failing walls of the plane and onto the rough cement that ran beneath.

She was not on a plane. Her mother was not here, nor her father, whose iconic silhouette Goldi had placed near the cockpit, his face horrifically stoic as the plane contorted around them.

Footsteps pounded ahead of her, and Mary anchored her mind to the sound, to the wrongness of her father's face. Eyes on the floor—the aisle lit with strips of emergency lighting, the seashell pattern stamped in the carpet—Mary pushed through the illusion to where Goldi hurried along the passageway.

Mary didn't know how far the magician could get before the illusion would fade on its own, but she'd have been willing to bet it was a long way. The plane tableau strobed as Mary unclipped the syringe from its spot on her tool belt and forced her body into a run.

Cursing herself for relying on the needle rather than loading darts with the serum, Mary reached blindly for her stunner, drawing the weapon from her belt and shooting it in the direction of Goldi's retreat.

A scream tore through the cement hallway as though ripped out of Goldi's throat, a ragged cry of pain. No telltale electric sparks cut through the illusion, and panic took hold of Mary's throat as Goldi wailed. She'd clearly been hit by something. Pulse pounding in her ears, Mary tried to retract the stunner, but something foreign returned to her hand, its sharp ends wet with blood.

She hadn't shot the stunner. She'd shot the grapple hook. Horrified, off balance, Mary braced herself against the wall. She couldn't have killed the illusionist. She couldn't have.

Goldi's sobs wracked the darkness, and relief flooded

Mary's chest with warmth—at least she was alive—as the hallway changed again. In a blink, Mary was standing in the wreckage, twisted metal penning her in, black smoke obscuring the sky. A pale hand lay among the blades of frosted grass. She made herself look away.

Pain arched through her hand and she dropped the syringe as blood trickled down her wrist—the *feeling* of blood, she insisted. But her brain was lost to the illusion.

The world blinked black, and Mary felt herself hit the concrete. She squeezed her eyes shut, trying to tell herself it was false, trying not to imagine Goldi laughing at her from the end of the hall through her injuries. Trying to bring herself to get up.

Slowly, the illusion faded. Still trapped within her own memory, Mary crawled into a supply closet and locked the door.

Images wavered across Mary's half-conscious mind, the flickering flames of birthday candles lit by Will's powers; the tick of her first watch, a gift from Monster; the uncontrollable laugher of a three-legged race, her ankle tied to Eloise's; the clear skies Carlisle had arranged for a rare beach excursion.

And overtop it all, a soundtrack of her mother's dying sobs, screaming metal, the taste of blood.

Voices woke her hours later, or perhaps only minutes. The visions had faded, replaced by darkness and the smell of cleaning solution. Mary used the supply shelves to pull herself to her feet, wiping her mouth on her sleeve. She didn't think she'd been sick, but the inside of her mouth tasted bitter.

She stepped forward and inched the door open. Had Goldi

lived through her attack? If so, Mary had to—what? Help the woman who'd terrorized her?

Yes. Mary would take her to El if she had to. She hadn't meant to shoot her grapple hook at a person. God help her, she hadn't.

The hallway lighting was dim, the visions completely gone. Just normal backstage walls, with concrete and cheaply framed posters of various shows the theater had hosted.

Goldi sat at the end of the corridor, her head propped back against the wall. Guilt surged through Mary's body at the sight of the bandages wrapped around the magician's shoulder. It looked serious.

Goldi looked toward the end of the hall. "No whiskey?"

Mary squinted, trying to see who Goldi was talking to. She didn't dare stick her head out further.

When Nathan stepped out of the shadows to hand Goldi a bottle of water, Mary's knees nearly gave out again. She clutched the edge of the door frame, disbelief pounding through her body. How could Nathan be here? How had he found her?

"Drink water," he said. The sound of his voice shook something loose inside her, something jagged and painful. Mary edged back into the shadows, resting her forehead against the doorframe so she could still see them. She couldn't look away.

"Bossy," Goldi said, sulking, but she drank the water.

Nathan crouched beside her. "If you're feeling better, we should move," he said. "You don't know where she went?"

Goldi sipped the water, prim. "I only know she tried to kill me."

Nathan ran a hand through his hair, and longing catapulted across Mary's ribcage before she could even attempt to stop it. It would be so easy to open the door, to give herself up.

But Nathan wasn't on her side. And in her weakened state,

he might just manage to arrest her. He'd bring her back to El, throw her into that fancy jail next to Jenna. If she was lucky.

Treacherous tears pricked at her eyes, and she batted them away savagely. Nathan couldn't be here by accident. Either LIO was setting a watch on the retirees, or Jeff Hayes had betrayed her. Aside from Dawn Kimble, a permanent caveat, Jeff was the only person who knew where she'd gone.

Mary retreated back into the closet, inching the door closed and turning the lock as quietly as she could. She tucked herself beneath the lowest shelf in the corner and waited until they were gone.

And then she did what she did best. She ran.

Mary had to have been here.

With Goldi's shoulder bandaged and water delivered, Nathan had left the illusionist alone in the cramped corridor—against her protests—while he checked each dressing room. With those clear, he'd moved up to the stage. Nothing. Not so much as a late custodian.

"I told you," Goldi said as he helped her to her feet, "she tried to kill me. She wouldn't stay around."

Goldi was certainly hurt, unless the injury was a trick of some kind. He'd seen the plane illusion, or the tail end of it; the woman was capable of strong deception. But the way she gasped as she walked toward the stage door, half supported on his shoulder, he doubted it was an act.

Why would Mary shoot a weapon at her like that? Mary worked with darts, stun guns, shockdisks. She didn't shoot people in the back. She didn't shoot them in the *front,* not with a weapon like this. From the shape of the wound, it looked like she'd hit the woman with her grapple hook. Like she'd been trying to harpoon a whale.

It wasn't like her. Was someone out there pretending to be Mary? Nathan hadn't been completely on her side when he'd just thought she was incarcerating the old guard somewhere. If she really was trying to kill them... he didn't know how he'd handle that. He'd have to try and stop her, somehow.

Nathan spotted a door he'd missed before and paused to try the doorknob. "Locked."

He started to put her down, but Goldi clung to his shoulder. "What do you think you're doing?"

"I can open the door. It'll only take a moment."

Goldi sighed dramatically. "Just get me out of here. Can't you see I'm in pain? I could bleed out any moment."

Nathan supposed they should get her to HQ and check for internal bleeding, or more serious damage. He nodded and helped Goldi toward the door.

There wasn't any point in staying anyway. Mary was gone.

M ARY WAS GETTING tired of crisscrossing the country. After New York, she'd have liked to crash in Malibu, to fly into LAX and climb through Jeff Hayes's guest room window.

Maybe he hadn't turned her in. But maybe he had. She couldn't trust him. She couldn't trust anyone.

So with blood on her clothes, Goldi's screams echoing in her ears, Mary drove Grandma through the mountains to Aries, keeping herself awake with coffee, music, and sheer force of will.

It wouldn't last forever. One miscalculation, one too many overconfident choices, and she'd doze off for a moment to find herself careening off a cliff.

Maybe that would be fitting.

Mary was still a mile out from Aries when she smelled the smoke. Smoke in the forest could have a thousand innocent sources. A campfire, or a wood stove. But it wasn't. She knew it wasn't. With dread welling in her gut, she stepped on the gas, gunning it until she reached the spot where the perimeter should have alerted her to Aries's proximity.

The perimeter was down, and Aries was on fire, flames

licking at the sky with startling intensity. Even outside, the air was thick with rancid smoke.

Mary drew the car up as close as she dared. The garage door gaped open, and she knew the dangers—she knew—but she had to check. She had to make sure the prisoners had escaped. No matter who they were, no matter what they'd done, she couldn't leave them to die.

She couldn't stop to think about it, either. Mary poured a bottle of water over a spare shirt and held it over her face as she ran inside to check the prison. Maybe it was madness, but if it came to the worst, this would make a better death that careening off a cliff.

Crouching as low as she could, Mary jumped through the unfixed hole Monster had left in the back door of the garage, and heat assaulted her from all sides. Fire climbed up the walls, eating away at the house's supports. Any minute, the place would cave in completely.

Mary rounded the corner to find the cells gaping open, the forcefields deactivated. Empty. Sobbing in relief, she staggered back for the exit. Whatever they'd done—*this*, probably—the retirees were alive. She wasn't responsible for them burning alive. She lurched aside as the nearest cell wall came down, nearly crashing onto her head.

She was climbing back through the hole before she realized: her Diana trap. Her prototype. What would she do without that? She had no way to recreate it, and no other way to beat Diana.

And she had no time to hesitate over a decision. Already coughing, smoke burning into her lungs, Mary ran back through the prison, dodging the crumbling cells in a desperate bid to reach the stairs. "System," she said as she threw herself toward the steps. "Are you OK?"

No answer. Sirens called from a distance, practically

obscured by the roar of the fire, and Mary forced herself up out of the prison inferno and into the kitchen. The curtains were like streamers of fire, throwing flames out the heat-shattered windows. She had seconds. If she was lucky.

"System," she said, "the prototype dumbwaiter. I need it."

The System didn't reply. Cursing, Mary lifted the dumbwaiter manually as smoke poured up the stairs from the garage. This was madness, but Mary was desperate.

The prototype clicked into place, and Mary grabbed the tray, nearly dropping it when heat seared her hands. She pulled her sleeves over her palms and held it gingerly in front of her.

She didn't dare go back out through the prison, and the deck was engulfed in fire. Throat burning, Mary ducked low to the ground and made for the front door of the house, an entrance she'd never used before. The frame was warped with heat, and she threw her body against the door to get it open, falling out onto her front step and stumbling down the driveway to get back to the van.

The sirens were getting louder. Still coughing, gasping for fresh air, Mary leapt into Grandma's driver seat and tossed the prototype aside, hands smarting when she wrapped them around the steering wheel. She realized, vaguely, that they were burned. From the tray.

Well. She'd been burned before. She wheeled the car back down the dirt road, before her addled body could betray her into stopping. So close to Aries, she'd surely be caught.

As soon as she was back on the main road, Mary pulled the car over and leaned her head on the steering wheel, letting herself weep until she had to open the car door and stumble into the trees to be sick.

She had nothing but the sweatshirt and jeans she wore, and her Coral getup rolled in a ball in her duffel bag. No tools beyond the few she'd brought to New York, and the prototype she'd just risked her life to save. No tech, no System, no friends.

She didn't know how the retirees could have found her. And it had to have been them; who else? Maybe Dawn had tracked her here at some point after all. Maybe Monster had simply escaped again.

It didn't matter. Mary rinsed her mouth with stale water from a bottle in the back seat and got back into the car. She needed to drive. She'd been hunting the LIO retirees for months, dragging them back here—or trying to. She'd hunted them. And now they'd smoked her out. They could be watching her, waiting to ambush her.

And if they weren't? If they weren't, they would be.

They were hunting her now.

AGNES HELD LIGHTLY to the edge of the helicopter, ducking her head out to watch the blue and red lights of the police cars that raced along the Vegas strip below. They stood out to her like beacons amidst the blur of come-hither neon that defined the strip, because she was looking for them.

She hoped the arrival of law enforcement didn't mean her team had come too late. Once upon a time, Wave would have pinpointed these enhanced criminals within days of their first attack, or so Bradley claimed. Recent events had badly hampered their resources.

Well, they were here now. And Tam was right; people were in danger. How could they say no? Still, her heart thumped in her chest at the idea of diving into a mission. She'd never much liked being in the field.

Agnes's mysterious partner ducked in beside her to peer out at the strip. He'd worn a dark-visored helmet from the time of their introduction on the tarmac and all the way through the flight, keeping his features entirely obscured, and he hadn't said much. He was tall. That was about all she could say.

He seemed polite enough, but Agnes didn't like this

element of the mission, didn't like partnering with someone whose face she couldn't see.

But she was here now. She'd just have to be cautious.

"See anything noteworthy?" he asked.

"I think we'll need to get closer."

He gave a brisk nod and leapt out of the helicopter, his parachute activating several seconds later.

Agnes didn't need one of those. She let herself fall into the sky, relishing the rush of air around her as the helicopter veered away. Savoring the freefall for a glorious moment, Agnes called the air molecules to her service.

The air hardened, and she built it into waves that carried her easily after her partner. She'd focused on her similar abilities with water molecules and dust in the air for so long that she'd nearly forgotten how powerful the atmosphere could be in all its force. She needed to spend more time on that in the lab. See what uses might benefit society as a whole.

The lights swelled closer, and Agnes accelerated to land at her partner's side on the roof of the Vegas Lights Hotel. The sign glittered on the side of the building, essentially beneath their feet.

"If we're going in together," she said, "I at least need to know what to call you."

Her partner unclipped his parachute, letting it drop down behind him. "Fair enough. Call me the consultant."

"So if we get separated I'm supposed to yell 'where are you, the consultant'?"

"How about Joe?" he said. "Just call me Joe."

Agnes couldn't help wondering why it mattered whether she knew his identity. Was 'Joe' someone she'd recognize?

In this moment, it didn't matter. Agnes's air molecules picked the roof-door lock with a quick flick of her mind, and then she and Joe were inside, bypassing the elevator to hurry down a set of metal steps and into the top floor of the hotel. They burst into a more guest-worthy stairwell, and Agnes could practically feel her partner listening as they paused at each landing.

Who were these enhanced criminals, anyway, that they'd come to cause trouble in Las Vegas? Their previous targets had been noteworthy, yes, but not so flashy. But Wave knew their faces, had tracked them here. There hadn't been any doubt. Maybe they were just looking to hide.

As Agnes reached the fifth floor, an explosive *bang!* filled her ears, and she dove after Joe and into the corridor just in time to see the door to a hotel room fly from its hinges and straight into the police officer who stood outside it preparing to knock. The door exploded into the wall, trapping him as a pair of figures rolled out from behind it.

They were hitting each other. For a moment, Agnes's heart leapt—maybe the league had made it here, after all—but then they stilled for long enough for her to catch sight of their faces. Familiar, from the briefing she'd gotten. Not LIO. Wave didn't know what their powers were, but they knew the faces of the enhanced criminals who'd been causing trouble across the country.

The thieves were fighting each other, one of them all shaggy black hair and muscles, the other thin and bald, his body masked in a too-large overcoat.

And they were more than thieves, now. The police officer they'd hit with the door wasn't moving. As the second cop moved toward them, gun drawn, the skinny thief—who'd somehow pinned the other guy to the floor—stopped slugging his partner to slap a hand against the wall. It shattered, wood and drywall splintering into a million pieces. Agnes threw up a shield, hardening the air around the cop, and the shards fell uselessly to the floor.

Joe strode forward to pull the exploding criminal off the black-haired thief, lifting him by the collar like a misbehaving kitten.

Casino security guards rushed the hall, every one of them wearing a three-piece suit, followed by three more police officers. The second thief scrambled to his feet, bolting for the part of the wall that still stood. His fingers disappeared into it, and his arm made to follow. Agnes wrapped him in air, pulling him back out of the wall and hardening his molecules back to their proper shape before slipping a syringe out of her pocket to dose him with power suppressant.

She'd like to know how this man's powers worked. They reminded her vaguely of her own, though she hadn't worked out how to walk through walls. Yet. Seeing him shift his molecules that way gave her an idea or two, but this was hardly the time to plan her next lab project.

The thief succumbed to the sedative, and Agnes laid him gently on the floor. Joe still held the Exploder in the air, waiting for Agnes to dose him. The man was struggling, but not to get loose. He was pointing his toe, straining to reach the floor.

"Joe," Agnes said, "be careful, he's trying to—"

The man just barely touched the carpet, and the floor exploded beneath them. Agnes wrapped Joe in a flow of air before he could fall, lifting him back to the corridor. They were going to need to evacuate the rooms on this floor, and the one below it, immediately.

Screams echoed up from the rooms below, sparks fizzling through sprays of water that spilled from ruined pipes, and another loud crack announced the Exploder's intention to bash his way through to the ground.

"Go," Joe said, "right behind you."

"No, I've got it," Agnes called back. "Get the people out."

This was exactly the kind of situation Agnes had been

trying to avoid when she'd joined up with Wave. She wanted to focus on lab work, on harnessing the power that came with enhanced abilities and using it to make the world a better place. Not chase destructive criminals around.

Agnes dove into the hole, following the Exploder as he cracked his way through the building and calling for people to run. Not that they needed her instruction; screams followed her descent through the building.

She'd reached the second floor, nearly caught up with the Exploder—he was getting tired, she thought, lagging—when he opened up a larger hole than before, and only a quickly woven flow of air stopped a robe-clad woman from tumbling into the hole after him, narrowly saving her from electrocution. Agnes lifted the sobbing woman back into the room and called for her to run.

Agnes landed in the lobby of the hotel half expecting to find the Exploder had disappeared. The lobby shared its floor with cheery rows of slot machines, all jangling with music and lights. The place smelled like dust and drywall. And fire, though there wasn't one of those. Not yet.

The Exploder was still there, making a break for it across the entryway, his wet shoes sending him into a slide. The hotel staff ducked behind the counters as the Exploder tried to make his escape, security guards pushing patrons out of the way as he ran. But he didn't appear to be looking to explode anything, just to get out.

Agnes wrapped air around him, but it only stopped him for a second before he blasted through her hold, bashing her hardened air molecules back into their previous state. She shuddered as her body took in the aftershocks, like absorbing recoil from a gun.

Agnes hesitated, unsure of how to proceed, and the Exploder set his hand on a slot machine, effectively transforming the coins inside into bullets. Agnes threw up a shield, but several people still fell, screams of pain echoing in her mind as she failed to save them all.

Joe landed beside her as the Exploder burst toward the doors, and together they ran after him.

Agnes felt the rush of wind before she saw the streak that raced in from behind her and zoomed through the lobby to cut off the Exploder, materializing into a man in a pinstriped hat. He placed himself between the Exploder and the doors. He was vaguely familiar, and her frantic mind tried to place him. Was he another threat? Or another partner?

Before Agnes could figure out what to say to him, the Pearl Knife sailed through the open doors like a late hotel guest, with Eloise a few steps behind.

ELOISE FOUND the hotel lobby in chaos. People ran for the exits, avoiding the water—and occasional sparks—that gushed from a huge hole in the ceiling by the check-in desks. Coins lay scattered across the floor, which was apparently half hotel, half casino. And while no one looked seriously hurt, many of the guests who flashed across her line of sight sported gashes on cheeks and arms. A woman in a cocktail dress with beads along the hem crouched behind a slot machine in the far corner, cradling her wrist to her chest.

Eloise took it all in as best she could, even as she kept her eyes on Agnes. The former LIO scientist stood with her mouth open in surprise, a helmeted operative at her side. She couldn't see the other person's face, only that they were tall and broad, their general largeness making Agnes look even smaller than she was.

Steve remained frozen at Eloise's side, as though waiting for her word. A standoff. Perfect. Eloise had hoped to deal with this quickly and get back to the mystery of the Knife—and why it seemed to have led her here so abruptly, after she and Steve had spent three days bumbling through Las Vegas trying to figure out where exactly their alleged criminals were holed up.

In all the pandemonium, it actually took Eloise a moment to notice the fifth man. He stood between the two pairs of operatives with his hands stretched over his head. Skinny and bald, with a long tan coat, his eyes darted around, looking for an exit, and he'd inched his way to the edge of the tile as though to make a break through the maze of slot machines. He looked hunted.

Well, if he ran then Steve would catch him.

"Please tell me that's the enhanced criminal we're chasing," Eloise said, eyes locked on Agnes.

Agnes set her fists on her hips. "You mean as opposed to me?"

Eloise motioned to the person beside her. "Or your friend."

Agnes tipped her chin up, and her glasses slipped down her nose a tick. "I refuse to dignify that with a response."

"Right. Because you don't work with criminals."

She didn't mean for it to sound as bitter as it did. LIO and Wave both had crimes under their belts. LIO and Wave were both trying to do better. Supposedly. Still, Eloise couldn't bring herself to trust an organization that used mind control serums to demonstrate their power, or blew up buildings to stop other people from blowing up buildings. She wouldn't.

"El," Steve said, "I don't think Agnes is the one robbing banks."

Agnes gave him a shrewd look, tilting her head like a bird until her eyes finally widened in recognition. She and Steve would have only crossed paths a few times before the old LIO fell apart, but she did know him.

The skinny man standing in the center of it all licked his lips, looking back and forth between Eloise and Agnes like he was watching a tennis match.

Eloise would deal with him in a minute.

"What are you doing here?" Eloise asked Agnes. "I thought you wanted to stay in your lab."

"And I would have, if you'd dealt with this guy sooner."

"Because everything dealing with enhanced abilities falls on me now?"

Not that she'd seen any evidence of enhanced abilities yet. Judging by the level of damage down here, though, he could certainly have them.

Agnes crossed her arms. "The government seems to think so."

The skinny guy darted another look at Agnes. Just as Eloise realized her mistake—letting herself be distracted by politics and personal drama—he lifted his foot.

Agnes saw him and started forward, but the guy stomped down with a victorious smile stretched across his face. The floor exploded beneath his feet, rippling out from his epicenter in a circle of destruction. Chipped tile burst into the air in dangerous projectiles, and Steve blurred, knocking Eloise to the ground.

The enhanced guy ran for the doors as Eloise staggered to her feet, ears ringing. The woman behind the slot machine was crying now.

Eloise ran after the destructor as he cut across the half-moon driveway in front of the Vegas Lights Hotel, dodging around the valet stand where more frightened guests and employees huddled. She drew the Pearl Knife from its sheath, trying to think of a way to stop the man without killing him.

Across the street, the Bellagio fountains sparkled.

As Agnes fell in beside Eloise, the air thickened. Water rushed across the street, abandoning the Bellagio fountains to the tune of surprised shouts and even a smattering of applause from people who appeared to think the airborne wave was an upgraded trick of some kind. Had to love Vegas. Hands raised,

Agnes pulled the water into a bridge, pausing traffic on the strip below before organizing it around the escaping destructor—exploder? what *was* he?—like a cage.

The guy plunged his hand into the water, trying to blast it away, but for whatever reason, he couldn't explode it; the water simply fell back into place. He backed up, frustrated, turning a frantic circle.

The water allowed Agnes through, and Eloise followed, with Steve and Agnes's silent partner right behind. Looking more confident than ever, if a bit strained—it was a lot of water, even for Agnes's significant powers—Agnes plunged a syringe into the guy's neck and kept him from falling with a gentle weave of air.

Given the destruction inside the casino, Eloise thought she might have let him fall. Agnes leaned over him, checking his breathing. Finally, she rose, nodding.

"Thank you," Eloise said. "We'll take it from here."

Agnes laughed. Water still rushed around them, and to Eloise it felt like being trapped in a backwards waterfall. It smelled faintly of chlorine.

"Excuse me?" Agnes said. "You think you can show up in the eleventh hour and just cart away our hard work?"

Eloise planted her fists on her hips. "LIO is tasked with handling enhanced criminals," Eloise said. "I can let my contacts know you assisted."

Impressive as that display had been, she couldn't allow Wave to take the prisoners. God only knew what they'd do to them. They might even turn them into recruits.

"Oh, great," Agnes said. "You'll let your contacts know. Thank you, El, that's lovely. You're not taking him."

Like hell. Apparently, Steve had exactly the same line of thought. He started toward the passed out destructor, and Agnes's partner moved as if to block his way.

Eloise unleashed the Knife.

Or at least, she tried to. The Knife flew a foot before stopping in midair, hanging between Eloise and the anonymous Wave operative. Eloise pushed, and the Knife pushed back, vibrating with that rattling hum she recognized from the cabin.

Eloise dropped her hands, and the blade clattered to the ground. Hands shaking, she wiped her palms on her pants. The chlorine smell was starting to get to her, but she hardly wanted Agnes to drop their wall of privacy. The moment she did, their faces would be all over social media. And soon after that, the news.

Eloise had to control the situation. She had to control the story.

"You were in Santa Monica," Eloise said, facing the operative. It was like trying to talk to an oversized bug, with that visor locked over their face. The distorted reflection of her own face made her feel self conscious somehow.

The operative nodded.

"Who are you?"

They hesitated, the moment extending. Eloise was aware of crowds gathering at the fringes of the conversation, but hidden as they were behind the curtain of water, no one could see them. Soon, though, someone would dare to breach their hideout—an angry hotel manager, maybe. Or a cop.

"Let them take the exploder," the operative said to Agnes. "The other one, too. Fifth floor."

Steve looked to Eloise for confirmation, a move she appreciated more than she could say. She nodded. "Get them to HQ."

"And the Knife?" Steve asked.

She couldn't help feeling glad for his discretion, and his concern. He wanted her to prioritize it—to prioritize herself. She'd have to make sure to tell him that by staying behind, she was doing just that. This person, whoever they were, could potentially unlock one question about the Knife. And that wasn't nothing.

"I'll call you," she said. "Thank you."

Agnes frowned, but Steve just nodded as if he understood, then shouldered the criminal and streaked away.

Eloise could really use him on her team.

She looked back to the helmeted operative. They hesitated a moment, then unclipped the straps and eased the helmet off. Eloise lifted a hand to her mouth, unable to make so much as a sound.

The anonymous operative was her father.

POLICE CARS FILLED the circular driveway outside the Vegas Lights Hotel, blue and red emergency lights adding to the glare of the Vegas strip beyond, all-too-human reflections on the ghost before her, as Eloise did her best to hold it together. She was a professional. She had to be.

She was the leader of LIO, and she was going to fix this mess.

She'd never had a problem taking care of the things that needed doing, no matter how tedious or distasteful. So now, even with her heart cracked open, Eloise made phone calls. She conferred with law enforcement personnel, politicians. She barely registered the distraught hotel-casino managers who thanked her, their expressions stony. So much destruction. So little control.

And before her stood a man she'd buried long ago. Her father was here. *Alive.* He followed her around the destroyed hotel lobby, silent, wearing that helmet to hide his identity from everyone else—he'd donned it the minute Agnes had dropped her water shield. And the way Agnes kept casting him disbelieving glances, Eloise guessed she hadn't known who she was working with, either.

Eloise kept her back straight, her expression and tone calm. The picture, she hoped, of a reassuring presence.

On the inside, her muscles felt as weak as water, as if they might give out at any moment and drop her on the curb. On the inside, she felt undone.

By the time Agnes had returned the water to its rightful fountain—no applause now, the audience having caught on to the nature of the situation—and Eloise had calmed the hotel manager enough to place a call to a frantic Travis Bertram, an hour had passed. An hour in which she knew no more about how her father could be alive, and why he hadn't contacted her, and what he was doing working with Wave.

She'd imagined having him back, more than once, though not since the revelations about the part he'd played in crashing Mary's plane. Dread tampered her joy, making it hard to breathe. Was it traitorous to feel some measure of relief? Was it traitorous to hope that Dad's partnership with Wave meant he hadn't participated in the deaths of their two celebrity members?

And if it turned out he had... what would she do then? Shun him, as she had Dolly?

When there were no more pressing issues at hand, Eloise requested a private meeting space from the assistant manager. The poor man had a deep gash across his cheek, and he gave them directions while Agnes hung back to find him help.

Dad followed Eloise through the wrecked hotel lobby, and the thought occurred to her that they probably shouldn't stay here until someone had checked the structural integrity of the building. But Eloise needed answers. And she needed them now.

As they passed into the hotel's abandoned function area, a tall woman with a bright red ponytail fell into step beside Eloise. She had a lanyard around her neck identifying her as press, though it seemed to be there to allow her backstage access to something called the Gargantuan Extravaganza. Whatever that was.

"I promise I'll do a press conference as soon as I know enough to satisfy the public," Eloise said, before the woman could speak.

The woman stayed with her, matching her step for step. "Will you also comment on New York?"

Eloise missed a step. "I'm sorry? New York?"

The reporter nodded, her ponytail bouncing. "Rumor has it a former league operative was injured there last night. Apparently she's been starring on Broadway, and no one knew it."

That was Goldi, unless someone else had become a headliner in the last day or so. But she'd been injured? That couldn't have been Mary, surely. Could Eloise have been wrong about her? Maybe someone else was after the old guard. In which case she truly had no idea what Mary had been up to. She wasn't sure which to hope for.

"Thank you," Eloise said. "I'll comment on both incidents as soon as I can give you satisfactory information. Excuse me."

As she continued down the hall, her father ducked into a meeting space at the end. She gave him a wave, lingering in the hall to call Ire from her ear com.

"We have a situation here," he said, by way of a greeting. "But judging by the news, you've got one, too."

Eloise rubbed her temples. How many catastrophes could pile into one day? "What kind of situation?"

He should have called her. Except he'd known she was busy. There were too damn few of them.

Ire cleared his throat. "Like all the retirees screaming at me in your office. That kind of situation."

The retirees? *All* of them? She almost asked if that included Diana, but she bit her tongue just in time. Eloise could deal with the Trap, if need be. "Give them some liquor and tell them I'll be there in a few hours. I sent Steve on ahead of me, so hopefully he can help in the meantime."

"Liquor? That's your answer?"

"Slip in a sedative if you need to. I'll be there."

Eloise ended the call, took a deep breath, and stepped into the meeting room.

The room looked shockingly normal, given everything that had occurred in the building tonight. Round tables with blindingly white tablecloths dotted the space, faux gold chairs arranged around them as if someone had been prepping for a wedding reception when the chaos began. Or a business seminar, or whatever people rented a Vegas casino function room for.

Her father had pulled a chair out from one of the tables so he could sit with his legs extended. A casual pose, at first glance, except for the way he jumped to his feet when Eloise entered. Nervous or not, he seemed to dominate the whole space. Tall and broad-shouldered, his dark complexion a match to hers, he looked the way she remembered. More tentative, perhaps, and with a few more tendrils of gray curling through his black hair.

She shut the door, wondering what on Earth she was supposed to say. For a moment, they just stared at each other.

"I don't want to make excuses," Dad said.

He had tears in his eyes. Eloise wondered if she had tears in hers. She felt numb, from her fingertips to her ice-heavy stomach. "But I want to hear them," she said. "You wielded the Knife. Didn't you?"

In all her dreams of seeing her father again, that was not the sentence she'd imagined herself saying. But it poured out of her mouth, as if the words carried a will of their own. Because it was the only thing that made sense. Because if he had wielded the Knife, it meant there was an expert in the world that wasn't Dolly. If he had wielded the Knife, even briefly, he might be able to teach her how.

Dad pulled a chair out at his table, inviting her to sit. Eloise chose one at the table beside his, and he gave her a rueful smile before dropping heavily back into his chair. "I wielded it once."

His voice was deep, smooth as butter. She remembered him singing lullabies to get her to sleep. Or at least she'd thought they were lullabies until she got older and recognized them as slowed-down Supremes tunes, and a few Elvis songs.

"I held it for about an hour," he said. "Mostly, it was wielded against me."

Eloise realized the Knife was humming a soothing rhythm into her mind, trying to calm her. She sent a wave of anger back at it, distress that it had kept this from her.

It had, though, led her to him. Unable to move, Eloise at least tried to breathe. "The Knife sent me to the cabin."

With a weary nod, Dad leaned one arm on the spotless tablecloth. "I had to go. She used the Knife against me. My own danger, I could have endured. But El…" He swallowed, looked at the floor. "She could control my powers through that thing. Completely. And she did."

Eloise sucked in a breath and almost choked on it. She couldn't shake the numbness, couldn't bring her sluggish mind to work out a response. Dad watched her almost anxiously, his brows drawn together as if he doubted she'd believe his word. And no wonder. Dolly had controlled Dad's powers through the Pearl Knife? Truly? The Knife's melodic dirge seemed to confirm it, a wave of grief mixed with regret. Questions crowded into Eloise's dumbfounded mind, implications piling up faster than she could acknowledge them. Had Dolly controlled the others, too?

Perhaps not. Perhaps the others hadn't resisted her will.

While Dad had? Eloise licked her lips, trying in vain to tease some semblance of feeling back into her hands by digging her nails into her palms. Her fingers tingled in response. "So you... what, you found a way to transfer the Knife to me?"

Dad bobbed his head, as though in rhythm to a tune she couldn't hear. "It was tied to me through my powers. I figured it out. I used that."

And yet the Knife's proximity didn't hurt him the way it hurt Dolly.

A spark of hope bloomed in Eloise's stomach, and she tamped it down. It was too early to assume her father could help solve her problems, help her gain control. He'd held the thing for an hour. How much could he know?

Still, it was easier to focus on the Knife than her own hurt. Dolly may have held him captive, but he'd still left Eloise to fend for herself. Not to mention Mary. How in the world was she going to tell Mary?

No. Better to focus on the Knife. "Does that mean you understand how it works?" she asked.

He lifted a shoulder, tilted his head. She'd forgotten that gesture. The familiarity of it hurt. "A bit."

"What is it?"

"The Knife? I don't know. I believe it may not be terrestrial."

Eloise pictured a pearl-white comet falling to Earth, explorers harvesting its power from the arctic or the Pacific Rim. Somehow, she didn't think that was what he meant. "You think the material is alien."

"I think the engineering is."

Eloise clutched the now happily humming Knife, her palms dewy with sweat. "You were there the day of the bike chase. The Knife refused to hurt you."

He nodded. Waited.

"Did you tell Wave that LIO took the plane down?" She pointed to the decal on his outfit, though the gesture wasn't exactly necessary. He'd been among the van's escort when it'd stolen Agnes. He was here now. "Are you with them?"

He rested his arm on the table briefly, then moved it back to his lap. "Not even Bradley Archer knew about the plane, until Mange. He certainly didn't know I was alive until recently. But Wave did save my life, El. They faked my death. So I help them, when they need a consult."

A consult. A strong arm. A fiery ally. Sure. Eloise's com chimed in her ear. She imagined chaos breaking out at HQ, the retirees wreaking havoc, trying to take over. She needed to get back.

Still, she silenced the call, eyes on the gleaming Knife in her hand. "I can't control it," she heard herself say. "It disobeys me. Not just with you, I... I've had this feeling it can do so much more than I know."

And clearly, she'd been right. It could *control* someone else's *powers?* Eloise had a sudden, laughable urge to launch the thing back into space—whether it had come from there or not—and the Knife pulsed insulted indignation into her mind.

Dad leaned his elbows on his knees, his eyes bright with hope. "I can help," he said. "Come back to the cabin with me. Maybe I know something, and if I don't, I can... we can figure it out together."

Eloise's com chimed again. Sighing, she slipped the Knife into the sheath at her hip. "I have to go back to HQ. Everything is exploding without me."

"Let them handle it. El, the Knife is... it's worth figuring out."

Of course it was. Perhaps more than ever. But LIO needed her at HQ. They needed her now, and she couldn't shirk her responsibilities, not even for the Knife. Certainly not for someone who'd abandoned her. Dad could have told her the truth, left a letter. He could have done *something*. Instead, he'd run away.

Maybe it was unfair. Maybe she didn't care.

Eloise stood. "Then you should have stayed to help me with it instead of running away. I have responsibilities. I can't abandon them."

With her heart on fire, she turned and left him behind.

Eloise was halfway back to HQ, the country passing too slowly beneath the plane while she ran disastrous scenarios in her head for her return to Niagara, before she realized: throughout the fight, the chase, and the chaos that had followed, her father hadn't used his powers a single time.

THE PARSE GALAXY, SECTOR 43.448

Sloane had always been able to sleep just about anywhere. Once, as a kid, her father had taken her to Tronan for a brass-band parade, and she'd passed out in the middle of a seventy-seven trumpet serenade.

He'd taken her to a doctor to get her hearing checked.

Neither trumpets nor blaring alarms nor earbuds blasting screaming metal could keep her from falling asleep, on air trains, crowded transports, and more than one elevator.

But Archimedes Sol could.

With their two days spent, the *Moneymaker* and its crew had meandered at the edges of the Torrent system, playing around in the planet's orbit and dancing a gravity-assisted waltz around its four moons while Sloane tried to think of a suitably criminal plan.

And the process of thinking about such a plan severely interrupted her attempts at beauty sleep. Finally, she got up and went to the galley to rummage for some liquor, where she found Oliver already there. He was playing a solo card game against a Holo Friend, a lizard-esque cartoon character Sloane vaguely recognized from an old kids' show. Black bruises still covered his jaw after the beating courtesy of Archimedes Sol, though the swelling around his eye had thankfully gone down.

"Couldn't sleep?" she said.

Oliver flipped a card onto the table, and the cartoon lizard cackled, the sound calling to mind a hundred wrestling fights with her little brother over the remote, the crunching of sugary-sweet cereal as they watched *Reese and the Reptiles Rock the Galaxy* for hours on a holiday.

And of course, there was the sound of her father yelling at them to turn off the entertainment mods and go out for some fresh air. Which had been easier said than done, given that they'd grown up in a domed colony.

Sloane poured herself a shot, then sat on top of the holo, which yelped in consternation and vanished.

"He doesn't like that," Oliver said. "You made me forfeit."

Sloane slid across the bench and onto his lap. "Poor baby."

He pouted, and she kissed him, and for about thirty seconds, she thought she might turn tonight around after all.

And then the ship lurched, tossing Sloane onto the floor. She picked herself up, swearing. Oliver was already leaping for the nav-deck ladder—chivalry was second to ship-lurching emergencies, she got it—and she clambered up after him.

Hilda was fighting the controls in navigation. That was the best word for what the older woman was doing, anyway, punching the console and swearing. "Shield's half down," she said. "I didn't see them coming."

Sloane cursed. "What were you doing, sleeping up here?"

"Even a pilot's gotta catch some Z's sometime, girl. It's past autopilot o'clock."

Sloane leaned over the pilot's shoulder to look at the screen, Oliver peering in from the other side. "Archimedes Sol?"

"Fleet ships," Hilda said. "Three of them."

Sloane didn't know how the pilot could tell just by looking at the blobs on the screen. Up until recently, the biggest difference she could have pointed out between various spaceship models would have been whether their amenities offered private sleeping accommodations or cattle-call seating areas.

This ship, she'd have called a piece of crap.

"Archimedes Sol ratted on us to the fleet," Sloane said, offended. "That asshole."

Hilda shot her a sideways glance. "You tried to steal a million tokens from him."

"Only half a million, and he said he'd come after us himself. I don't like a liar."

Oliver laughed. Hilda swerved. Sloane stumbled, landing on her butt and narrowly missing cracking her head on the dash. Why couldn't her uncle have sprung for a ship with a bigger deck? She felt like she was another major swerve from landing in the pilot's lap. She didn't know how Oliver had managed to stay on his feet, but the man looked positively unconcerned.

"Warn us before you do that," Sloane said, belting herself into place.

"Oh, I'm sorry, would you rather have been obliterated by the missile they just launched at us?"

Sloane cursed, rubbing her hip. "How does Archimedes Sol expect to get his money if he blows us up?"

Hilda shrugged. "Not like he needs it. You didn't actually steal anything from him."

"He's playing with us," Sloane said. Playing for keeps, though.

"Or," Oliver said, "the fleet ships are after me."

Hilda and Sloane both stared at him.

He shrugged, though neither of them had asked a question.

"I might've pissed them off a little bit before I joined up with you."

Sloane raised an eyebrow.

Oliver licked his lips, finally sinking into an auxiliary seat to strap himself in. "They might be, uh, under the impression that I'm supposed to be, I don't know, still working for them."

Great. *Now* he told them. Even with all Hilda's button-pushing and ship-maneuvering, she gave a start, her scowl deepening. So she hadn't known, either. As if sensing her distress, Hilda's parrot hopped onto the dash. The pilot swiped the bird away, and it flew an indignant circle above her head before darting out of the room.

Sloane sighed. "You deserted."

Oliver shrugged. "And sold some of their secrets."

Hilda looked up at him, every hint of the absent-minded matronly pilot wiped away from her face. "To?"

He sniffed. "I'd rather not say."

Sloane began to question her taste in men. She checked her straps, making sure everything was secure. "OK," she said. "OK. Any chance Alex has that wormhole perfected?"

Hilda snorted.

Well, it had been a long shot. Sloane looked at the screen, pretending she could make some sense out of it. "Right. So we're going to have to evade them."

"Good," Hilda said, hooking a thumb over her shoulder at Oliver. "Let's turn that one over."

One of the blobs on the screen spit out a smaller blob, which arched straight toward the *Moneymaker*.

"I don't think they're in a mood to negotiate," Sloane said, as Hilda swung the ship around. "What are you doing?"

"Getting them to call off the missile," Hilda said. "Watch and learn, baby. Not every ship could pull this maneuver."

As the *Moneymaker* blob on the screen zipped closer to the

fleet blobs, Sloane questioned whether their ship could do it, either. The *Moneymaker* zoomed over the blobs on the screen, the shields shuddering as they bumped against the Fleet ship's shields.

The Fleet ship tried to hail them. Hilda just zipped on past.

Sloane turned around to face Oliver, who looked a little green. He probably understood what was happening better than she did. Looking at him, she had to wonder: did he have a secret stash of tokens lying around in his account? Because if he did, that would help. A lot. She'd even try to pay him back, probably.

"Hey," she said, "how much money did you get? For the secrets?"

He leaned his head back and swallowed hard. "Nothing. I traded for something else."

Sloane thought of the X-Lux after hours trip, how she'd never thought to ask how Oliver had paid for whatever tech he'd purchased from the Wringer guy. She swallowed, her mouth suddenly dry. "Something valuable?"

"Magic beans," he muttered.

Sloane frowned. She didn't understand what that meant, except that he didn't have any money to help them out. Or to turn in to the fleet.

"Hold on to your hats," Hilda said, and the *Moneymaker* screamed away.

Nathan knew his body needed sleep after tonight's whirl-wind of a trip to New York City, but his mind craved action. He had to have missed Mary by mere minutes tonight. Goldi's plane illusion in that backstage corridor could have been meant for no one else, and even so he cringed thinking of the woman's injury. Goldi's shoulder had been dislocated, with a nasty gash to go with it.

Nathan had seen Mary withhold help to preserve her iden-tity—he'd fought with her over it, in fact—and he'd seen her defend herself by knocking out guys twice her size. But he'd never seen her throw a weapon like that. She could have killed the woman.

When he thought back to the plane illusion, part of him couldn't blame her.

Still, Nathan had transported Goldi to HQ without trou-ble, leaving her with the medical team before attempting to get some rest. He had a feeling he'd need it; he'd barely made it to his room before the rest of LIO's old guard had shown up at the league's door—the Casino entrance, though unlike Steve they'd used the bell that Nathan had assumed was a joke.

Rocker, Ranger, the twins. And the Trap, wearing her

signature red gloves. Legends walking, every one of them was bursting with rage. They wanted answers.

So Nathan settled for a bare hour of sleep before dragging himself to Ire's door. The strongman was awake and dressed, his red hair askew, eyes bloodshot. It was a mark of his fatigue that the man didn't order Nathan back to bed. There was too much to do.

"Steve's halfway here with the enhanced suspects from Vegas," Ire said, shaking Nathan out of his thoughts. "Eloise says she'll be back in a few hours. I think the retirees accepted it."

Nathan doubted they'd be willing to wait long.

"Right," Nathan said. "What do you need from me?"

Ire sighed and leaned against the door frame, the metal apparently designed to take his weight. He rubbed a hand over his face. "I need you to go up to the academy," he said. "There's a situation."

"Related to one of the current situations, or separate?"

Ire shook his head. "That's what I need you to find out."

Nathan selected Mary's silver smart car from the LIO garage and took the quietest route out to the academy warehouse. He could have chosen any car in the collection, and she'd probably kick his ass if she ever caught him driving hers. In fact, he thought he might be able to lure her back here just by somehow leaking the information to her.

He probably shouldn't have chosen it at all. It wasn't as if they'd ever driven in the smart car together. If he'd expected it to make him feel closer to her, or supply some answer about her intentions—or her whereabouts—he was sorely mistaken. The car was just a car, and Mary was still gone.

The streets were quiet at this hour, and cold. Probably a correlation there. No one wanted to go out for a frigid pre-dawn stroll. He passed only a few cars on his way, and no pedestrians.

Until he reached the academy.

The first thing Nathan saw, as he turned onto the street, was the line of protestors. Not five or six, as he sometimes saw outside Gail's liaison office. Dozens. Fifty or more. They carried painted signs and marched with determined strides, bundled in parkas and hats and sturdy boots.

Nathan parked the car and got out, with every intention of calmly surveying the situation. People were allowed to protest. But the first sign he saw read: *EAEA has it right: control enhanced humans!*

Biting back a curse, Nathan pushed his way through the line, where he found his sister standing in the middle of the marching circle. She was holding a bullhorn and leading a chant he couldn't quite make out through the rushing rage in his ears.

Chloe greeted him with a tilt of her chin. "We're not on your property," she said, her breath fogging between them in angry bursts.

Nathan raised his eyebrows. "We rent, anyway."

Chloe clutched the bullhorn like it was a life preserver and she was about to go over the falls. "You can't make us leave."

Nathan held both palms out at waist level, immediately regretting his lack of gloves. "Relax. I just want to talk." He set a hand on her elbow and started to draw her away toward the empty street, where they could have some privacy.

But Chloe pulled away from him as though he'd hurt her. "Whatever you want to say, you'll say in front of everyone. We know what happened in New York."

Nathan blinked at her. The cold must be fuzzing his brain, because he didn't understand the connection. "You think you have some inside knowledge because a few news stations reported an attack on a Broadway star? You don't know what you know." It took a strong effort to keep his voice calm. He wanted to yell at her, to shake her.

The march had slowed around them, the protestors inclining their heads to hear their conversation. Chloe actually shook the bullhorn at him. "We know you let them escape."

Nathan threw up his hands. He hated confusion, hated subtext. Why didn't anyone just say what they meant? "Who?"

"Mary O'Sullivan," she spat. "*Coral.* Whatever she's calling herself now. She might not have enhanced abilities, but she's a vigilante, Nathan. She can't be allowed to roam free."

How did she know Mary had been there? He wanted to ask, but he couldn't stand to picture the triumph on her face. Chloe had connections? The league—and by extension, Nathan—had more.

With an effort, Nathan folded his arms across his chest, tucking his throbbing hands into his armpits. "All right. You think I let Mary escape. And who else? You said 'them.'"

"The illusionist, of course. Goldi. She's even more dangerous, Nathan. How could you?"

Nathan nearly let out a breath of relief. Goldi was safe at HQ, which meant Chloe didn't know everything. That was good. He'd been half ready to initiate a mission to find a mole at HQ. It wasn't impossible, with such a large team, that someone could be leaking information.

But the team knew about Goldi, not Mary.

Nathan realized with a start that Chloe was still yelling at him. "...trusted you to take care of this, to handle people with enhanced abilities. You can't just let them roam free."

Nathan stamped his feet, unable to restrain his shivers. It was so damn *cold* here. "Our job is to keep enhanced *criminals* behind bars," he said. And they weren't even doing that. He was sure the doctor hadn't committed any crimes, nor had Jo. Nathan was still working on the rest, or he would as soon as he could catch a moment. There were too many problems vying for his attention, too many things to fear. "We're not here to round up innocent enhanced humans who are just living their lives."

Chloe stuck her nose in the air, lips twisted in disdain, and Nathan found that he didn't even care. She wanted to live a close-minded life, run by bigotry? Let her.

"You can't make us leave," Chloe said.

"I wouldn't dream of it. Nice signs. You'll probably have an audience in a few more hours. Try to hold out til then."

With that, Nathan turned his back on his sister and pushed through the line of protestors to make his way back to the car.

"Do your job," Chloe called after him, her friends chiming in with murmurs of agreement. "If you don't, we're going to do it for you."

MARY MADE it fifteen miles from Aries before her stomach rebelled again, forcing her to stop Grandma in the narrowest stretch of road. She flung the door open and wretched into the trees, her whole body shaking. Smoke inhalation, excessive exertion, lack of sleep. Name a problem, she had it.

Wiping her mouth on the cuff of her shirt, she climbed back into the driver's seat, stomach still roiling. At this rate, she'd swerve off a cliff. She needed rest.

Cautiously, Mary drove another five miles to the entrance of a tiny trail. Its mouth was hidden, but she'd checked it out when she'd first come to Aries after studying hiking maps of the area; vigilantes with super-secret estates had to know when outdoor enthusiasts might accidentally stumble on their hideouts.

The trail wasn't made for a car like Grandma, or any kind of vehicle. Mary made silent apologies to whatever mountain club maintained these paths as she maneuvered the van between the trees, hoping the branches would spring back to hide her presence.

It was the best she could do. Mary turned off the ignition

and reclined her seat, closing her eyes. The flames from the fire still burned behind her eyelids, and her mouth tasted like ash. She could almost imagine the System calling for her help. Ridiculous though it was, the System had been a friend to her these past few months. A colleague.

Apparently she could lose her sister, her lover, and her entire life—both public and secret—without dissolving the crust of ice she'd frozen over her heart. And yet somehow the loss of a computer was the thing that finally unleashed the tears from the back of her throat. She was powerless to stop them.

A sorry excuse for a vigilante, she told herself. It didn't help. Goldi's visions had worn her defenses to shreds, even before she'd seen Nathan or dealt with the fire. Mary tried to breathe, tried to will her body toward sleep—at least a doze—but her arms were shaking, her stomach still turning uncomfortably. She wondered vaguely if she might be in shock.

When a knock sounded on the window, Mary was almost relieved. Oh, she couldn't fight anyone; she'd definitely die. But at least she wouldn't have to try and force sleep.

Thankfully, though, the pale face on the other side of the window didn't belong to any of the retirees. Mary rolled down the window, letting a burst of sharp mountain air into the car. It smelled sweet and fresh. A small relief. "Lois Lane," she said. "I'd ask how you found me, but I guess I know."

Dawn Kimble wrinkled her nose. She had on a dark jacket, the hood pulled over her blonde hair. "You're a mess," she said. "Come with me."

Mary popped the seat back to driving position. "Nope. But thanks."

The reporter yanked the car door open. Mary really should have had that locked. She wasn't thinking clearly. "Move over," Dawn said. "I'm driving."

When Mary didn't budge, Dawn shoved her. "Move. Over."

Mary stared at her. This woman had guts. Eloise should really be trying to recruit her. "There's a cupholder in the way."

Dawn pushed her again, and Mary held up her hands in surrender. She was too exhausted to resist, and despite Dawn's annoying tendency to show up—again and again—she hadn't tried to kill Mary yet. "OK, OK," Mary said. "Moving over."

Dawn took her time driving, brights on, slowing on the curves. Mary tended to whip around the twists, but then she did know this road. When Dawn took an unfamiliar turn up a steep rise, Mary clenched her fists, refusing to ask where the reporter was going—or where she'd left her own car, or whether she'd sold Mary out to the retirees and planned to serve her up on a platter.

Mary wasn't used to the passenger seat.

After half an hour or so, Dawn pulled off the road and into the parking lot of a mountain motel. Small but neat, with a vacancy sign burning by the road and a cheerful red roof.

"Checking in?" Mary asked.

The reporter held up a keychain in the shape of a pine tree, the number 5 stamped clearly in chipping white paint. "I've been here a while," she said.

Mary blinked, surprised. "Staking me out?"

"Yup."

Well. One point to Dawn Kimble for honesty.

Once inside, Dawn shoved Mary toward the bathroom with a pile of clean clothes and strict instructions to take the hottest shower she could manage. Mary wasn't completely sure if she was being mothered or insulted, but she figured it didn't really matter.

A couple of hours ago, Mary had been battling the flames at Aries. Several hours before that, she'd been hiding in a broom closet, trying to recover from Goldi's plane flashbacks and the shock of seeing Nathan again.

At the very least, she owed herself a shower.

When she came out, dressed in Dawn's Kansas University sweatshirt and a pair of yoga pants that were several inches too short for her, Mary half expected Dawn to try and tuck her into bed. Mary's head still felt foggy, but the shower had cleared some of the cobwebs. She could drive tonight, to... well, she hadn't quite decided where. Long Beach, maybe. Somewhere near the ocean.

"Thanks for the shower," Mary said, squeezing her hair in a towel before tossing it onto the back of a desk chair. "I'd better go."

Dawn planted her hands on her hips. "You might smell better now, but you're still a mess. You need help."

Why did people keep saying that to her? All the wrong people, too. Mary laughed. "In exchange for what? An exclusive interview? All my secrets? No thanks."

Dawn's eyes widened in exasperation. "I'm not evil, Mary. I'm not cruel. And neither is the media as a whole entity."

"Could've fooled me."

"We just want to help you."

"Oh? All those reporters waiting in Malibu just want to help me? How magnanimous of them."

Dawn sat on the end of the bed, clasping her hands together until her knuckles turned white. "Most of us just want the truth."

Mary thought of the reporter who'd ambushed her in the bathroom, the mob Diana had called down on her at her parents' funeral. They'd only wanted the lurid details, no matter the cost to a little girl. "But not all of you. Can I keep the clothes?"

Dawn nodded, and Mary started for the door. The reporter

stayed where she was, apparently resigned. "Where are you even going to go?"

Mary grabbed the keys from where Dawn had set them on the bureau. "I've still got a few options. I'm sure I'll be seeing you soon."

Nathan couldn't help wondering how Mary would see the mismatched band of LIO retirees who'd assembled in Eloise's office. These people had been her family, once upon a time. Oh, he knew Will had been her mentor before he'd passed away, and that Dolly had been like a second mother to her. But they weren't the only enhanced independent operatives who'd helped to train Mary, partnered with her on missions, raised her.

No matter which way he turned it, he knew how she'd see them now. Murderers. She'd see them as murderers.

Eloise stood behind her desk, the view of the falls behind her crusted in a new layer of snow and ice. With the room full of people, her eyes stayed locked on the most dangerous one.

The Trap—or Diana Morton, an identity Nathan hadn't known before today—paced furiously behind the two chairs in front of the desk, her expression so sour that Nathan half expected her fingers to begin dripping with their infamous poison, even through her red gloves. She had her hair, dark with streaks of silver, pulled into a bun at the nape of her neck.

As for Nathan, he'd taken a position beside the door next to Ire. With the rest of the old guard clustered by Eloise's bar across the room, Nathan got the distinct impression of a grade school dance and nervous children too shy to talk to the ones they fancied.

Not that the old guard fancied him. If anything, they were entirely indifferent. Rocker leaned back against the wall with a scowl to match Diana's, his eyes darting frequently to the bourbon at his elbow, arms flickering back and forth between the silver-toned color of the walls and the tanned flesh of his skin. Brown hair receded from his forehead, falling well past his shoulders.

Beside Rocker, the twins watched Nathan and Ire with eerie stillness. Petite and light haired, Brenda and Donny were legends when it came to hand-to-hand combat.

There were more of them, too. Ranger, Goldi, Monster, and Carlisle were all recovering from injuries in the infirmary. Injuries for which Mary was responsible, according to Diana.

Nathan wasn't sure he could believe it. Or maybe he simply didn't want to.

Flick was the only LIO retiree who hadn't returned to HQ. Steve stood in the back of the room, directly opposite Eloise, shifting his feet uncomfortably every few minutes. Stuck firmly in the middle—retirees versus LIO—or so it would seem. Nathan still had trouble reconciling his friend's presence here. It felt like worlds clashing together.

Steve probably felt the same way. Only he had three worlds clashing, instead of just two.

"Let me try to understand this," Eloise said. She stood tall behind her desk, arms folded across her chest. At her waist, the Knife glittered like a threat. "Mary tried to kill Goldi in New York, after which you tracked her to a hidden estate out west where she was hiding Carlisle and Monster."

"And Flick," Diana said. Steve shifted his feet again, clearly uneasy. What was his father's part in all of this? Nathan wanted to trust his friend, but he couldn't say which side Steve might choose if it came down to a fight.

Eloise nodded. "And you arrived just in time to save the prisoners from a fire that Mary set to murder them?"

Diana stared at Eloise, her expression stony. "That's right."

Nathan shook his head. He'd seen the aftermath of the Goldi situation, and it horrified him. But he couldn't believe that Mary would collect LIO retirees just to kill them like that. And by burning down an entire house? One she apparently owned? It didn't add up.

It just wasn't Mary. But none of it was. Kidnapping people, drugging them, dragging them away to hidden estates. Where was the line?

No matter their legendary reputations, these people had killed Mary's parents. For all that Nathan questioned some of her choices, he wouldn't trust them above her. What if Mary had been forced to injure Goldi in self defense?

The more these people spoke against Mary, the more he wanted to side with her.

The Trap—Diana—stopped pacing and leaned her palms on the back of a leather-cushioned chair. She carried the edge of a vinegar scent, probably related to the poison, though certainly it fit her personality. "You could have stopped Mary early on," she said. "You chose to ignore her."

"The retirees left LIO of their own accord," Ire said. "You forfeited the right to comment."

Diana grunted. She didn't even bother to look Ire's way. "Retirees. You make us sound like a washed-up crew of old farts, fighting over the best bingo stamps and watching *Jeopardy* reruns all day."

"If the shoe fits," Ire said. Nathan could feel anger radiating off the strongman, his muscles practically quivering with restrained rage. He wondered how many of the retirees Ire could take down on his own.

"Old guard, then," Steve said, placating.

"First wave," Rocker muttered.

Diana pounded the back of the chair. "Originals."

Across the room, the twins exchanged pale-eyed glances. Their power, as Nathan understood it, was the ability to read one another's minds, to communicate telepathically. If they had an opinion on what they wanted to be called, they didn't voice it.

Eloise raised a hand. "This is beside the point. We need to prioritize your safety."

"Safety?" Diana scoffed. "I don't want to be safe. I want that girl's head on a pike."

"No," Nathan said, before he could stop himself. Eloise shot him a look he couldn't interpret—why, when the others were allowed to speak, he didn't know—but he couldn't help it.

Mary was a force to be reckoned with, no doubt, but there was no way she could fight off all these angry retirees, or whatever they wanted to be called. And what if Eloise decided she needed to bring Mary in? Cold fear settled across his chest, as if someone had locked a vice around his body.

In the back of the room, Steve stood up straighter and untucked his hands from his pockets. "I assume you mean that figuratively, Di."

Diana twisted, still half facing Eloise, and blinked at him, assessing. "No," she said, drawing the word out as though speaking to a child, "I mean we find her and slit her throat before she slits any more of ours."

"She didn't kill anyone," Steve said.

"She tried," Diana replied. "And she'll try again."

Nathan shook his head. No matter what he'd seen in New York, he couldn't believe that.

Ire pulled himself up to his full height, which most people would find intimidating. The man had to be close to seven feet tall. "It doesn't matter what she did. We don't slit throats."

Nathan shot him a look of gratitude, but Ire's attention was locked on Diana. She turned her back on Eloise and crossed her arms at the wrist, exercising her fingers loosely as though to remind them of who she was. As if they could forget.

He remembered the whispers about what she'd done to the celebrity doctor who'd accidentally created her powers while testing energy drinks. Supposedly, she'd ambushed him by hiding in the fountain at his fancy office building in New York—aquatic respiration had let her stay there all day—and forcing her poison down his throat from one of his own energy drink bottles.

Even after IOs had gained so much popularity, people tended to skirt around the subject of the Trap. They were never really sure if the woman was a hero—she did save people, sometimes—or a villain.

Standing with her here now, Nathan knew how he'd vote.

"Flick's son," the Trap said, ignoring Ire's comment. "Good boy, coming all this way to help us. If she didn't kill anyone, then where's your illustrious father?"

"On the run, I'm sure," Steve said, smiling slightly. "He's good like that."

Diana sighed, twisting her lips into an approximation of regret. "I wish I could have your optimism, Flick's son. Perhaps you're right, and your father is alive. But I don't trust it." She rounded on Eloise again. "Do you know where she is? Where she'd go?"

Don't tell her, Nathan thought, though Eloise didn't seem to know where to find Mary, either. They couldn't let Diana find her. That much was clear.

"We are pursuing the matter," Eloise said. How she could

stay so calm, with so many angry eyes on her, Nathan didn't know. It was impressive.

"You have to know." Diana gripped the back of the chair until Nathan thought the wood might crack under her hands. "You *do* know. You're keeping it a secret. Why? To protect the person who's destroying us?"

"We're pursuing the matter," Eloise repeated. "We've assigned a team, and—"

"Your 'team' consists of baby Flick and an un-enhanced cop," Diana interrupted. "Sorry, boys, but it's the truth. What can they possibly accomplish?"

Nathan glanced around the room, considering which items he'd throw at her first if this devolved into a fight. Should have stationed himself next to the bar, with all those bottles. He might be un-enhanced, but he certainly wasn't useless. And he wasn't a cop anymore, either.

Eloise said, "We're the same age you were when you—"

"These children are exhausting," Diana said, turning to Rocker and the twins, and Rocker nodded in agreement. "Eloise, go fetch your mother. It's time the adults took over."

Every word out of the woman's mouth undermined Eloise, condescended to the rest of them. What did Diana want here, really? He couldn't believe this was just about Mary. Diana acted like she was in charge.

Or like she wanted to be.

Eloise came slowly around the desk, footsteps landing solidly in the carpet, the Pearl Knife unsheathed and hovering above her palm. "Enough," she said, and Diana went still, eyes trained on the glittering blade. "Interrupt me again, and I'll put you on the prison level until you're ready for a civil conversation."

Diana's eyes bulged, but Eloise raised a hand, and the woman held her tongue.

"I'm in charge here," Eloise said softly, so softly that Nathan could have sworn Rocker leaned forward an inch to hear. "I assign teams. I decide who's ready. And I say that we absolutely do not slit throats. Ever."

Diana waited a beat, as if to ensure that Eloise had finished speaking. She then waited an extra beat, which drew a respectful moment into a mocking one. Eloise just smiled, until finally Diana said, "Sometimes, Eloise, throats need slitting."

That, Nathan thought, was exactly the attitude Eloise had been attempting to reverse. Murder, betrayal, conspiracies. And the world saw LIO as the heroes. How could Mary ever forgive him for choosing them over her?

"I disagree," Eloise said smoothly. "Now, you must be tired. You seem overwrought from your experience, and no wonder. Gail's waiting outside to take you to your guest rooms. She'll radio me if you cause trouble. One foot out of line, any of you, and you'll be on the prison block. Am I understood?"

Diana lifted an eyebrow before dipping a short bow. "Completely."

The retirees filed out of the room—Rocker casting a last glance back at the drink cart—and the tension in the room dissipated.

Unfortunately, Nathan had a feeling the discussion around Mary's fate had only just begun.

Eloise waited for the door to close before sitting down on the edge of her desk, shaking her head. Nathan hoped she had extra guards—and surveillance teams—watching the retirees' every move. No doubt she did, plus three other contingencies as well. Eloise knew what she was doing.

Still. They couldn't let these people get out. Diana couldn't be allowed to find Mary.

"Well done," Steve said, but Eloise just looked at him, appraising. Nathan half expected Ire to excuse himself, as he usually did the moment a meeting finished. But he stayed where he was. Waiting.

Eloise sheathed the Knife and took a shaky breath. "I need to tell you all something."

Steve straightened. "League secrets? I should go."

"You're welcome to, if you like. But this concerns... the mission you were helping me with. You should stay." She looked around at all of them, meeting their gazes individually. "Needless to say, there's a reason I asked the others to go. This conversation has to remain in this room."

Given that Nathan wouldn't have trusted the retirees with so much as the access code to the cafeteria, that made sense.

Steve pursed his lips, but he leaned back against the wall, apparently deciding to stay. Nathan couldn't help wondering what it was about Steve's history with the league that made him distrust this place so much. Was it just the overall secretiveness—something Eloise clearly wanted to combat—or was it something more personal?

"Should we sit down for this?" Ire asked.

Eloise looked at the desk. "Maybe. My father is alive."

Stunned silence answered her. Nathan glanced at Steve, who was blinking in disbelief. Ire actually moved away from the wall to take one of the chairs by the desk.

Nathan didn't know what to think. He was probably the most emotionally detached from this particular announcement. Certainly the public knew the Inferno had died, but Nathan had never known the man personally. Just the legend.

And the crimes. Were they supposed to rejoice that the Inferno—Will, he reminded himself—was back? Or lock him up?

Steve folded his arms, unfolded them again. "The helmeted operative in Vegas?"

Eloise nodded. "Wave helped him fake his death because

Mom was using the Knife..." She trailed off, gave her shoulders a shake. She didn't look relieved, or happy. She looked... burdened. All at once, Nathan wondered if Eloise had added her father to LIO's prison roster.

"Mom used the Knife to control his powers," Eloise said.

And, Nathan assumed, to help take down certain airplanes. Probably not in a cell, then. That certainly put Dr. Gordon's story about the Inferno into a new light. It felt like a confirmation.

Nathan's gaze drifted to the moon-like light of the blade at Eloise's hip. "It can do that? Control other people's abilities?"

The thought was... for once, it made him glad he didn't have enhanced abilities of his own. Though when it came to good and evil, black and white, Nathan could at least trust Eloise's intentions.

Eloise lifted a shoulder. "Apparently. Dad used his link with it to transfer its power to me."

And then he left. Questions rolled through Nathan's mind —why leave, if the Knife had been transferred? Why lean on Wave, of all things?—but one thought floated over and above everything else.

Mary's mentor was alive, and he was innocent. She needed to know.

Steve opened his mouth like he wanted to say something, then closed it.

"How do we know it's true?" Ire asked quietly. "He could be lying to you."

Eloise circled a finger around the hilt of the blade. "The Knife resonates when he's in the room. It led me to him, and it refuses to hurt him."

"And we trust the Knife?" Ire asked.

Steve shifted against the wall, clearly uncomfortable. What did he know?

"Well enough." Eloise furrowed her brow. "It doesn't hurt him the way it hurts Dolly. I wonder..."

Nathan shook his head, not following her train of thought, but Steve said, "You wonder if the Knife hurts her on purpose."

Eloise sat in her desk chair and leaned her head against her hand. "Exactly."

Mary had described the way the Pearl Knife's presence caused Dolly physical pain. Eloise's grandmother had died before severing the Knife from her consciousness, but Dolly had supposedly passed it on intentionally. Perhaps Will's intervention had done something to hurt her in the process.

All at once, Nathan felt the urge to sit down beside Ire. He was in over his head, with all these league secrets and enhanced abilities. What did he know about any of it? What could he even do? He pressed his palm against the wall, searching for some kind of an anchor and wishing, wishing that Mary were here.

"We know too little about it," Steve said. "Maybe Will can—"

Eloise held up a hand. "That is a conversation I'd rather have between the two of us," she said.

"Secrets?" Ire grunted.

Eloise sighed. "Personal ones."

Nathan wasn't sure Ire would accept that—wasn't quite sure he should accept it himself—but the strongman simply nodded and rose from the chair. "I need to check on the academy," he said. "Make sure the protestors don't recruit any of our recruits."

Nathan cringed. He should probably go along, but he wasn't exactly eager to face Chloe again. More than anything, he needed sleep. If it would come, after all this.

Eloise nodded, her face drawn with fatigue, and Nathan thought he'd never seen her look so exhausted. Retirees, protestors, Mary, and now Will's return? The woman deserved a monthlong vacation.

"What about the retirees?" Nathan asked.

Eloise leaned back on the desk. "We'll just have to keep an eye on them. Don't worry, Nathan. Mary can handle herself."

Nathan nodded, but Eloise didn't understand. Mary handled herself a little too well, and she knew it. That was what scared him. She might keep going until she collapsed, and none of them would know how to help her.

Or she might cling to this crusade until the shadows consumed her.

STEVE STAYED where he was when the others had gone, leaning against the wall as though it alone could keep him standing. Eloise's office stretched between them like a gaping wound. She considered asking him if he wanted a drink, just to break the tension, but thought better of it. Instead, she stayed where she was in her chair behind the desk.

They shouldn't have let the retirees into HQ, not that Eloise would have done anything differently. But she was all too aware that there were eight pissed-off enhanced humans on the premises, while she had four independent operatives on her side, one of whom was un-enhanced, and another who didn't want to be here.

Not to mention her own troubles controlling her powers.

"I thought you were going to prioritize the Knife," Steve said finally.

Eloise wanted to say something biting about the size of her to-do list, but she breathed through the impulse instead. Steve only wanted to help her. "I am," she said. "Right after I deal with the old guard, or whatever it is they want to be called."

"It sounds like your father could help with the Knife."

"And I know where to find him."

Steve gave her a long look, and she found herself missing the hint of mischief in his eyes. He looked so disapproving. Maybe they'd been spending too much time together. Her seriousness was rubbing off on him.

"I don't need you to tell me how to run this place," she said. Diana's input was more than enough criticism for one day.

Steve crossed the room and came around the desk, sitting on the edge to look down at her. He'd come around the desk before, when she'd collapsed—how many days ago? She was losing track of time—but the movement felt surprisingly intimate. Eloise sat up in her chair, as if she could combat the closeness by remaining stiff. Professional.

"I'm just saying you don't prioritize yourself," he said gently. "This place needs you, and it needs you at full capacity. Understanding your powers."

"Before I kill everyone by mistake?"

He smiled, acknowledging the joke—had she meant it as one? She wasn't sure—but his eyes still lacked that mischievous streak. When had she started liking that?

"Possibly," he said.

Eloise pressed a fingertip to her temple, wishing there were a way to think this situation away. "I'm not sure if you heard Diana just now, but she wants to kill Mary. And we're sorely outnumbered here."

Steve nodded and stood up, as if he knew better than to expect her to budge. He headed for the door, where he paused to look back over his shoulder, and for a brief moment Eloise considered asking him to stay. "Just... don't wait too long, El," he said. "This is important."

Eloise watched him go, missing Mary of all people. Mary would tell her to send everyone to hell, and say nothing helpful at all. But she'd be on Eloise's side—Eloise thought she would, anyway—which would make Eloise feel better.

Not that Steve *wasn't* on her side. Just that Mary would... get it? But since when had Mary understood any decision Eloise made, ever? Eloise was starting to romanticize their relationship. It wasn't good.

If nothing else, Mary would understand why Eloise hadn't been to see Dolly in months. That thought, more than anything, was what made Eloise decide it was past time she paid her mother a visit. Dolly might not tell her anything about the Knife intentionally, but she might give something away. And Eloise certainly gained nothing by keeping her distance.

Sighing, Eloise got up and closed the Pearl Knife in its cabinet. The blade responded by sending a twisted wave of dislike and understanding through Eloise's thoughts. It didn't like to be left behind, and Eloise didn't like leaving it. She sent back her own feeling of regret before heading out of her office.

Eloise had assigned a pair of guards to her mother's door, not that it was really necessary; Dolly's severance from the Knife had resulted in an early-aging process that had transformed her body into that of a frail, ninety-year-old woman.

Dolly could no longer see anything except for the brightest lights. And she absolutely, positively, could not come near the Pearl Knife.

In contrast, Eloise hadn't been without the Knife since... She tried to remember, and decided it must have been the last time she'd seen her mother. In the fall.

Eloise took her time approaching Dolly's darkened corridor. Mary would object to the arrangement, Dolly keeping her same quarters after admitting to awful crimes—but what was Eloise supposed to do? Put her on the prison block with Jenna?

Perhaps she should. She didn't know. She knew for a fact that it was foolish to come to her mother for advice, but she needed... information, at least, about how Dolly had kept everyone following orders.

Perhaps Eloise would simply enact the opposite tactic to whatever Dolly suggested.

She could hear the guards chatting as she approached, and they greeted her with smiles, Greg to one side—blond and freckled, cheerful—and Natalie on the other, her long hair pulled back in a fishtail braid.

"Good, you're here," Natalie said when Eloise paused at the door. One more thing to add to her to-do list? But Natalie was smiling. "You can settle an argument for us. Does frozen yogurt count as ice cream?"

Greg shot Nat a look of false affront. "It totally does. You can top it with chocolate chips and sprinkles, and hot fudge."

"Health food in disguise," Nat said, giving her braid a flip.

Greg scoffed, but Eloise noted the way he watched Nat out of the corner of his eye. "Hot fudge is health food?" he said.

"Why are you talking about ice cream in January?" Eloise asked, smiling. It felt good to smile. "You're making me cold."

Natalie set her hand on her hip. "Greg wants me to try the new frozen yogurt place up top, and when I try to tell him I'd rather eat my shoe than frozen yogurt, he tries to tell me it's the same as ice cream."

Eloise blinked. "Oh. Got it. Greg, frozen yogurt isn't ice cream. If you want to ask Natalie out, take her for real ice cream. Or hey, try dinner."

Leaving the shocked guards behind—and probably about five seconds from setting a date—Eloise opened the door to her mother's room, still smiling to herself. It was nice to see that people could still be happy around here, once in a while.

One step into Dolly's room sobered Eloise's mood. It was almost shocking how little had changed in here. There was the slit of a window that looked out at a slice of the falls, shining as white as the Knife—which Eloise could feel pulsing gently from her office. The soft music, the little bowl of potpourri, the carefully made bed.

And her mother. Sitting in the rocker, looking fragile enough to disintegrate, her skin so white it seemed a shade short of translucent. Dolly was in her mid-fifties, and she looked for all the world like she was a month from the grave.

Dolly nudged a toe against the carpet, tipping her rocking chair into a gentle rhythm. "So I do have a daughter," she said. "I thought only soft guards were left running this place. You need to be harder on them, or they'll never last."

Not an auspicious start for a mother-daughter heart-to-heart. She'd stayed away too long. Eloise glanced toward the door. "Maybe this place could use a little softness."

Dolly chuckled, a dry rasp. "Give it six months, El, and see what kind of choices you face. You call what I did corruption. I call it survival."

"Those things are hardly mutually exclusive," Eloise murmured. So they were going to get right to it, then. No preludes. Perhaps her mother had been waiting for this conversation. Planning. Eloise should have come here with intention rather than desperation, but she was here now, and she wouldn't run.

She made herself move further into the room, made herself breathe in the heady scent of dried flowers, the menthol tang of medicine. "I'd rather LIO disband than that I resort to murder and kidnapping. And framing innocent organizations for terrorism."

"Spare me," Dolly said, still sounding amused. Eloise squinted at her, searching for a hint of the woman who'd raised her. Which was the lie? Or was this version of Dolly just an evolution, perhaps even a glimpse at Eloise's own future?

"Wave is hardly innocent," Dolly said, "and neither is

Mary. She's the one who's out there sweeping my friends out of their homes for a crime I committed. Isn't she?"

"Your friends were involved," Eloise said. "They knew."

"Then she should let the law take care of it, like we did back then." After framing the hell out of everyone who'd disagreed with them. Dolly rocked her chair, keeping that infuriating smile on her face. "Is that why you're here, Eloise? To discuss right and wrong?"

"No," Eloise said. "I'm here about the Knife."

Dolly stilled, and Eloise felt a shock of pleasure at having surprised her. Unless it was an act. "What about it?"

Eloise made herself answer calmly. Sensibly. "It has more powers than you've told me about. I want to know more."

"And spoil the adventure of learning about it yourself? Why? Can't you control it, Eloise?" Dolly spat the words out like a curse, cruel mockery meant to wound her daughter.

But Eloise had been through too much to trust her mother's version of who she was; if nothing else, she knew her own strength. She laced her hands together over her stomach, as if that would help her hold back the rage that had been simmering inside her since October. Dolly couldn't control her, so she jabbed straight for Eloise's heart. But Eloise could not be wounded that way, and she wouldn't let her mother break her calm. "It's funny, Mom, that your mind would go there. Why would you think that?"

"Because I had trouble with it," Dolly said, shifting her tone. Placating. Even kind. Eloise had the sudden feeling that she was the one being interrogated here. "It's natural. Come, Eloise, talk to me. I can't help you if you don't tell me."

Eloise rolled her eyes. "Far be it from me to spoil the adventure."

There was a beat of silence, in which Dolly rocked her

chair, her expression unreadable. Had she wanted Eloise to admit she had trouble controlling the Knife? To what end?

"In that case," Dolly said, "I think I'd better be going."

It was Eloise's turn to be surprised. She blinked, confused. Where could Dolly possibly go?

A movement flashed in the corner of the room as Rocker's body shifted suddenly from bedpost to flesh. Startled by his presence here, Eloise actually took a half step back. How could he have gotten in?

On the other side of the door, Natalie's braid dropped out of sight, as a stream of ashy steam hit the glass. Steam? Or poison? Eloise called to the Pearl Knife as Rocker slid toward Dolly, felt its frantic response as it sliced through the cabinet latch and sailed across her office.

Now would be a good time for that thing where you skip from place to place, she thought, but the Knife made directly for the door.

Rocker reached Dolly, and Eloise ran for him, knocking the camouflage artist aside. He stumbled, a brief stutter in his goal. When Eloise place herself between Rocker and her mother, he bared his teeth. He wasn't bulky like Ire, but he was tall; between the darkness and the way his body changed colors in flickering shifts, he was hard to see.

And hard to avoid. Eloise tried to hit him, but his body flickered, and her knuckles hit solid wood instead of flesh, as if she'd punched the bed frame instead of the man. Something slammed against the door, but she couldn't turn to see what it was as she tried to keep Rocker from locking his fingers around her throat.

Eloise was a competent fighter, no question. Against someone who could shift his body into any material in the room? That was somewhat different. She rebuffed his attacks, barely, her hands smarting as he pummeled her defenses. If she gave him a chance, he'd lift her like a rag doll. She could feel it.

The Knife careened closer, and Dolly dropped her head into her hands, crying out in pain as the door crashed open. Diana stepped over the two fallen guards, moving into the room with a twin on each side. Her hands were bare, oily poison staining her fingertips.

Rocker shifted toward Dolly, but Eloise hooked her arm through the crook of his elbow and pulled him back around, managing to land a punch before he realized she was aiming for his jaw. He flinched, face melting into solid rock—the ceiling, she realized dimly, the ceilings were rock—and then he knocked her to the side. She fell, her hand radiating pain up her arm as it hit the floor.

Rocker lifted Dolly into his arms, and the old guard marched out of the room. As easy as that.

With her hand shooting pain, Eloise jumped up and ran for the door, lifting her left hand—throbbing but not broken—to catch the Knife in midair as she reached the corridor, where Greg and Natalie lay facedown on the floor.

Diana couldn't have killed them. Not before they'd had their date. It was a ridiculous thought, and Eloise tamped it down before she could sob with frustration.

Steve rushed past her as she started down the hall, stirring the air around them with a breath of wind as he blurred to a stop. "What happened?"

"Check the guards," Eloise said without stopping. She ran to the end of the corridor, where the hall ended in a T. *Which way?* she asked the Knife, flustered at how quickly the retirees had disappeared. It shouldn't have been possible for them to get so far so fast. Usually the Pearl Knife anticipated her need to track someone. And usually, it tracked them without any trouble, at least over short distances. Certainly, it should know where to find Dolly.

This time, the blade answered with confusion. Its communications jumbled into her mind in feelings and half-images, and even through its panic—mixing with her own, reflecting the feeling back to her—Eloise understood the message.

The retirees were gone. Vanished.

And Goldi? Monster?

The Knife quivered like a dissonant chord, disquieted by its inability to track them. The infirmary-bound retirees were gone, too. Eloise tried to soothe the Knife, as it so often soothed her, but her own thoughts were too jangled to do it much good. Still, the blade seemed to appreciate the effort.

It didn't know where they'd gone. It couldn't feel them. *How?* she thought, but the Knife didn't know.

With a final fruitless glance down the hall, Eloise turned back to Steve, who was crouched over the fallen guards. Black poison dripped across their throats, opening gaping holes in their flesh that rotted as she watched, the smell of vinegar and decay mixing in the air. Their eyes were already staring, unseeing.

Diana could have spared them, had she wanted to. She hadn't bothered. Tears welled in Eloise's eyes, and this time she let them fall. She dropped to her knees beside the fallen guards. With the poison everywhere, she couldn't even risk closing their eyes. "Don't touch it," she said, unnecessarily—Steve had grown up around the Trap, too—but she appreciated his nod of acknowledgement. "How did you know to come?"

"I followed the Knife," he said. "I was coming back to... I left so abruptly, I just... It passed me in the hall. It seemed.... frantic?"

Eloise clutched the Knife's handle, feeling numb. Two team members were dead. She'd assigned them to guard Dolly's door, and she hadn't considered, for even a moment, that the retirees would come for her mother. For all their harsh words in Eloise's office earlier, she hadn't imagined they'd actually kill anyone.

"It's my fault," she said. "I underestimated Dolly. I underestimated them all."

"El," Steve said. When she didn't look up, he touched a gentle index finger under her chin, lifting her eyes to his. "El. It's my fault. I should have watched them. I should have... I never thought they'd respond this way. My father couldn't possibly approve of this."

"Not even with his life on the line?"

Steve dropped his hand back to his knee, and Eloise felt the loss of his touch, a pang in her stomach. "I don't think Flick would want to murder Mary."

Eloise could hope that Flick hadn't come back here because he'd disagreed with Diana's intentions. She could hope that they hadn't let him die in the fire, if that story was even true. "They're going after Mary," she said, straightening slowly. "We have to go. I'd better get Nathan. Can you call Ire? He'll want..." She swallowed, motioning to the bodies.

Bodies. In LIO HQ. She felt like a fool.

Steve caught her arm, holding her hand gingerly. "You're hurt."

"Barely." The hand was swelling, though, and would continue to do so.

He turned her hand gently over in his. "El. You need to get patched up."

"I'll take a steroid shot. We need to go to Mary."

"Go where? You don't know where she is."

Eloise sighed. "I don't. But I think Nathan knows someone who can help."

This time, Mary used a false ID and cash from her emergency envelope to rent a studio apartment in Long Beach. She should break free of L.A., she knew that, but she couldn't bring herself to cross the country again, to drive for endless hours, or worse, get on another plane.

No matter where she went, there was a chance that reporter-slash-crusader Dawn Kimble would accidentally lead Mary's enemies straight to her door, though maybe Dawn would take a hint and stay out of Mary's way from now on. Not that Mary was ungrateful for the help, or the shower. She just couldn't risk trusting a reporter, couldn't risk drawing the retirees to her.

The apartment wasn't exactly dirty, though Mary certainly wouldn't have invited any of her celebrity ex-friends for tea. She didn't think she was applying extraneously high, heiress-level standards by wishing the countertops in the galley kitchen lacked their seemingly permanent layer of sticky something. The kitchen was so small the stove only had two burners—not that Mary knew how to cook anything, anyway—and dusty cobwebs dangled from the corners as if their owners, too, had evacuated in favor of cleaner accommodations. The corners were dingy, the carpet frayed. Mold spotted the lining of the shower curtain.

On the plus side, the place only smelled a little bit musty.

Mary stretched out on the green-covered futon without bothering to change her clothes and shut her eyes, her head still ringing from hours on the plane, on the road. She didn't know what would happen once the authorities stamped out the fire. Would they try to contact her? Or was she a fugitive? She hoped it hadn't spread into the woods. Perhaps she should have stayed.

Even in the best case scenario, Mary could hardly hope to rebuild the place under the current circumstances. She'd considered buying an apartment in Paris, back when Will had been on that whole 'get your own private assets' kick. Not for superhero activities. Just because she liked Paris. Something overseas sounded pretty good right about now, the long plane journey aside.

Mary didn't realize she was dozing until a sound startled her awake. She lay in the darkness, grasping for orientation in the orange glow of the streetlights that leaked in from outside, struggling to register the sound in her mind. Something she should recognize.

The door clicked shut.

Mary leapt to her feet as shadows poured into the room, her only advantage a beat of surprise as her attackers found her awake and standing. A pair, their movements fluidly coordinated. The twins.

Mary dove straight for them. "It's you guys," she said as she batted the first twin aside. "How sweet of you, to come to me. You have no idea how much time this is going to save."

To spin one twin away was to invite the other. Donny twisted toward her as Brenda attacked again. It was like fighting a pair of angry blond elves, and unfortunately, they were good.

They'd have claimed Mary's full concentration on a good day, and her muscles were still strained, her head throbbing.

Brenda or Donny landed a blow to her face—she couldn't really see which one—and she ignored the blood that welled into her mouth as she threw a blind punch back in their direction.

And hit a metal wall. Because Rocker was here, too, and he'd transformed his arms into metal, like the pipes that made up the futon frame. It wasn't tire-iron level stuff—more like IKEA-kitsch aluminum—but still. Metal on flesh had an obvious winner and loser.

Hand smarting, Mary righted herself and twisted out of Donny's grip, his nails scraping her wrist as he tried to catch hold.

She'd beaten worse odds than three-on-one, but not against fighters like this, who knew how to attack all at once without stepping on each others' toes. Not among enhanced humans.

And they knew it. Brenda and Donny fought like a coordinated dream, choreographing their moves in their collective minds—she'd never quite understood how the mind-reading worked—and grabbing her arms from each side. Mary struggled, landing a kick to Rocker's un-metaled shin that hardly made him pause. He hit her across the face, the blow smarting through her skull. Part of her felt like he'd been toying with her this whole time, and the little girl who'd wanted to prove her worth so badly came rushing back in full force as she tried to kick her way free.

"Where is he?" Rocker growled. He had his long hair tied back, accentuating the granite-like lines of his face.

"Go fuck yourself," she said.

And then, Diana's voice. "Now, now," she said, and Mary struggled harder.

The old Mary—no, *Coral*—never would have allowed

herself to be cornered like this. How had they found her? Was Dawn lurking outside after all? They could have followed Mary's stop-and-start path from Aries without too much trouble. She'd watched for a tail after her stop at the motel, but her concentration had been shredded, her hands stinging from the fire. Maybe Monster had clung to the roof. Maybe Flick had simply run after the car.

The twins held Mary as Diana crossed the room, her poison fingertips hidden beneath those crimson gloves of hers. They looked orange in the streetlight, and the blind-shaped shadows stamped across her face only highlighted her smug smile.

Poison fingers. What the hell. The doctor who'd done that was a freak, that much was known. He'd been trying to create some kind of an energy drink, or so they said, and Diana had willingly submitted to testing in exchange for a pittance—and while she hadn't exactly complained about the results of the experiment, she hadn't exactly let the doctor live, either.

And Diana had other talents, too.

"Diana," Mary said. "I was saving you for last."

Rocker hit her again, and she bit back a grunt, letting her chin touch her chest for a second. "I'd love to ask if that's all you've got," Mary said, heart beating a rhythm of pain in her gums, "but it just seems so cliché."

"Among the three of us," Diana said, eyes glittering, "you know we've got more. It'd be fun to draw this out, Coral, but you're only the top item on a long to-do list."

"Coral's gone," Mary said. She needed to free one of her hands, to get to the Diana trap prototype—only the one, dammit, but she'd take it over nothing—and secure it over Diana's hand, needles and all. Somehow.

She hadn't thought this out. But then, there was a reason a

prototype was a prototype. Not that she had a way to make anything better now. If this didn't work, she'd be out of options.

Diana tugged at her left glove, drawing out the moment despite her supposed hurry. Dolly might have pretended to be sweet, and Will might have played the mentor, but the Trap had always been a bitch.

Even if Diana had played no role in the murder of Mary's parents, she still needed to be taken out. Mary tested Brenda's grip on her right wrist, but the twin responded with a crushing pressure that felt like it cut to the bone. Where did these people train? After LIO, anyway. Clearly they'd kept up.

"Mary, then," Diana said. "Tell us where he is, and we'll make this easy."

Mary had no idea who 'he' was, but she also had no intention of letting Diana know that. "Like let me go easy, or kill me fast easy?"

A car alarm blared to life outside, and Brenda flinched. The movement was all Mary needed to twist her hand so hard that the joints cracked audibly, dislodging Brenda's grip to reach into the wide pocket of Dawn's sweatshirt to draw out the robo-glove. As Brenda flailed to get Mary back in her grasp, she aimed the glove desperately for Diana.

But it was just that, a desperate move. Desperation made her clumsy, and the glove wasn't up to the task. She had no free hand to hold Diana, no chance. Not against so many. Rocker pulled Mary's arm so hard her shoulder flared in pain, and the glove clattered harmlessly to the floor.

Diana picked up the prototype, turned it over in her hands. "Needles? Is this meant to harm me, Mary?" She tsked. "Not your style."

"More yours," Mary said, clenching her teeth against the pain.

Diana smiled. "Where did you hide Flick? We got Monster. We got Carlisle. But Flick is gone."

Mary swallowed, hoping Monster wasn't waiting out there in the hall. "He probably ran off. He does that."

"Is he dead?"

Mary might not survive this, but the longer she drew it out, the better chance she had. And if she did escape, she intended to find out why Diana wanted Flick so badly. Was it because she wanted to locate another of her allies? Or because of something else?

It could mean nothing. It could mean everything. Eloise would file it away, a thin voice said. Eloise would remember. So would Nathan. It was a fragment of a thought, a shred of regret buried in molten fear.

"I thought you had a hot date," Mary said. "Don't be late on my account. Feel free to show yourselves out."

Diana stepped in close, Rocker moving aside to let her in. Diana hovered a bare finger over Mary's cheek, and Mary flinched, immediately wishing she could call the movement back; it only made the Trap smile wider. Diana dropped her hand and lifted Mary's right one, which Rocker released so the Trap could touch a finger to the scar that ran across Mary's palm.

Pain seared through her hand, like a line of acid eating at her skin and twisting through the flesh until even the bones felt as if they'd crack with the pain. Her fist tried to curl in, to protect itself from the attack, but Diana held it open. Savoring. Mary pressed her tongue to the roof of her mouth. The tears that tried to flood her eyes were just her body's response to pain. She knew that, but she didn't want to show this woman a single one.

"Your parents were like this," Diana said. "So... annoying."

Mary bit her lip, already swelling from where the twin had hit it, her cheek throbbing from Rocker's multiple hits.

But it was Diana, ultimately, who would kill her. Mary's hand burned, blood pooling in the still-upturned palm, and it was only the beginning. She didn't know if a small wound from the Trap's poison could kill her on its own—probably not, though perhaps if Diana let it go long enough to seep into her bloodstream—but the pain was intense.

Diana would keep pushing. Diana was patient. Diana *enjoyed* this. But Mary had nothing to tell her.

Mary wondered, vaguely, whether she'd committed to this crusade because she'd known it would come to this. The Trap was among the most dangerous of them, and Mary had saved her for last.

Mistakes. Nothing but mistakes, for miles.

Mary kicked, but Rocker protected Diana from the blow, taking the hit with a grunt. The twins held her fast, fingers digging into her shoulders. Four enhanced humans against one regular nobody. No contest.

Diana pressed Mary's palm, almost with a lover's care, and this time Mary couldn't keep the sob from escaping her lips. The poison would sear holes in her hand. And no matter what she said, or didn't say, Diana wouldn't stop there.

"Last chance," Diana said. "Tell me where you're hiding my family."

Nathan spent the whole journey to Los Angeles with anxiety lancing through his stomach, the country passing below in strings of lights. No one knew how the old guard had disappeared from HQ, or how far ahead they might be. Mary could be dead.

And Nathan had abandoned her.

Steve paced the aisle as they flew, which only made Nathan's anxiety worse. Eloise sat across from him, the Pearl Knife on her lap. She was staring at it as if it had betrayed her, or failed her somehow. He knew she could feel it, that it communicated with her, but he didn't quite understand the mechanics of the relationship. He wondered if she was talking to it now. He wouldn't have been all that surprised to suddenly hear her muttering to it out loud. For that matter, he wouldn't have been all that surprised to hear it respond.

They landed in Long Beach. They drove, with Nathan's heart beating a panicked rhythm of fear: they were going to get there too late to help her.

The door to the apartment, the one Dawn Kimble had sent them to find, stood wide open when they arrived on the second floor of the complex. It was the first sign of trouble, a door standing ajar in the middle of an urban apartment building. The rest were shut fast, neighbors either ignoring the trouble or oblivious to it.

Because there was definitely trouble. The vinegary scent of Diana's poison hung rancid in the air, and the tense rumble of voices rolled across his awareness. Call it instinct from years on the force, honed by a few months with LIO. Nathan knew trouble.

Mary was strong. On her own against a posse of enhanced former league members? He didn't know who could beat that.

Before Nathan could burst through the door, the Knife blinked through his peripheral vision, shooting by his ear and into the room ahead of him. He still wasn't used to that. A seemingly sentient blade, whirling around his head.

He didn't need Steve's hand on his shoulder to make him pause. Whatever the Knife scouted in there, though, it made Eloise shout, and Nathan pushed into the room before he could think that letting the enhanced humans go ahead of him might be wise.

A stumpy bottleneck of an entryway brought him into a dimly lit studio apartment, shadows and streetlights mottling the room in strange patterns.

They had her surrounded at the window, the twins pinning her on either side, Rocker and the Trap standing before her like a pair of mafia thugs. Diana's fingertips dripped with black fluid. Nathan could only just make out Mary's silhouette between them, but even in the dark, he knew it was her. How could he not? She'd haunted his dreams, his every thought, for months. She was slumped back against the window, her hair unbound, her chin dropped low against her chest.

If the twins let go of her, he thought she might fall.

Panic surging, Nathan bolted toward them, with Steve whirling in behind him and El on their heels. The twins let go of Mary's arms and she fell back against the wall, head smashing against the window frame. When she righted herself, albeit unsteadily, Nathan let himself breathe.

And then the battle was crashing around him, and into him. Steve blurred for Rocker, using his momentum to knock the camouflage artist to the floor. Eloise pointed, and the Knife caught Brenda's shirt by the collar, lifting her toward the ceiling and away from Mary.

Nathan tried to make it to her, but Donny came at him. Nathan blocked the first blow easily and feinted left, but Donny didn't bite. He deflected Nathan's attempted hit easily, and Nathan half expected Mary to yell at him for telegraphing his moves. She didn't, and he'd lost sight of her in the melee. Was she fighting? Fleeing? Was she dying?

Pushing the thought away, Nathan narrowly avoided a stumble as Donny surprised him by leaping onto the coffee table, which shuddered under the twin's slight weight. Nathan tried to kick out his legs, but Donny sidestepped easily, landing a kick of his own squarely to Nathan's unprotected forearm.

Nathan's training kicked in, and he let his body move with the hit, whirling back around to distract Donny as Mary appeared at his side. She kicked the leg out from under the table and it split through the middle with a loud crack, sending Donny sliding for the floor.

Nathan went after him as Donny darted for the door. Diana had stationed herself at the bottleneck, hands outstretched as she allowed Donny to run past her. She could shoot her poison, Nathan thought.

She didn't. Maybe she was running out, after torturing Mary. Maybe she was saving it.

Maybe she didn't want to risk harming Eloise. Or the Knife. With the blade still pinning her shirt to the wall, Brenda kicked uselessly. In a smooth movement, she tore through the fabric and fell to the ground with a grunt. She ran after her brother as the Knife quivered in the wall for a moment before ripping free with a spray of drywall.

Steve was still battling an ever-changing Rocker as he transformed his limbs from protective pillow to hard metal from second to second. But Steve was fast—that was his thing—and he caught several punches to Rocker's core as the shapeshifter struggled to keep up. Diana was shouting for them to abort—why?—and Rocker extricated himself from the battle with a roll, diving toward the doorway.

Face masked, Eloise appeared beside Nathan and pressed a tube into Mary's hand. The antidote to Diana's poison. "Get out of here," Eloise said, but though Mary took the tube, she shook her head, sitting down hard on the floor. Her sweatshirt hung in tatters, the blackened evidence of Diana's poison dissolving the fabric even further as he watched, oily residue mixing with Mary's blood.

In the seconds that had taken, Diana had disappeared down the hall. Eloise and Steve streaked after her.

In the wake of the fight, the coffee table tilted drunkenly, and cracks splintered the TV screen. If anything, those details seemed to fit this dingy place. More than Mary did.

Nathan knelt beside her, heart stuttering with fear for her, of her. He offered her a hand. "Are you all right?"

She wasn't all right. He could see that, feel it. She took his hand, and as he helped her to her feet, he thought she'd accept his help.

And then, before Nathan realized what was happening, Mary attacked.

MARY TWISTED Nathan's arm and dropped into a roll, body screaming as she flipped him over her back and threw him to the floor. Poison sang through her core, her limbs shaking as it inundated her cells. Still, she had time to take El's antidote, time to live.

She had time for this.

Nathan pushed to his feet, faster than he'd been the last time they'd come face-to-face—even after fighting the twins—and raised his hands. "I deserved that," he said, though he didn't look as if he really thought so. In this light, his eyes were bitter black. "But Mary—"

She couldn't let him finish. She threw herself at him, fury and fire, and he blocked her blows without trouble. She was frayed, moving too slowly to mask her intentions. The pain made her feel drunk, the world tipping, or maybe it was the poison. Or the smoke she'd inhaled earlier. Or the blows to her skull.

There were so many options.

A small voice inside her called her ridiculous, a child willing die for her foolishness, but she couldn't stop. She tried to slap him, and he sidestepped.

"Fight me," she said, allowing herself to step back. "Fight back."

"You know I won't. You're hurt."

She knew he wouldn't, anyway. But on her best day, she'd be standing on his chest by now. Rage thrummed through her, mixed with grief and the unimaginable shame at having trusted this man. "You sided with my enemies."

"Eloise isn't your enemy."

She knew that. "How did you know they were coming for me?"

He pressed his lips together, sucked a breath in through his teeth. She knew the answer. She waited for him to say it. "They said as much. They took Dolly."

Which meant that Eloise had let them into HQ. "And I take it they did not peel this information out of Dolly as she sat rotting in the cell she deserves?"

He hesitated. Gave his head a minuscule shake. She gave him a moment to speak against that decision, but he didn't. "Toeing the LIO line already?"

He didn't move. He just stood there and took it, looking worried. Looking like Nathan. Mary was breathing hard, spots invading her vision, and she realized her cheeks were wet.

Again she pushed her body, demanding its best performance as she swung again, as he dodged again, hands raised in protection.

With hurt coursing through her—pick a kind, any kind—she only knew she had to hurt him, too. Reckless, impulsive, it didn't matter. Her jaw throbbed where Rocker had hit her, a dozen strips of pain burning across her torso as the poison did its work, but she didn't care.

"Mary," Nathan said, dodging another hit. "I need to tell you something."

"I don't want to hear anything you have to say."

"Mary—"

"Stop. Stop saying my name."

"But—"

She leapt at him, fists flying, wishing for her tool belt, wishing for her dart gun, wishing for anything that could hurt him. She swung, like molasses this time, and he caught her wrist. She tried to twist away, but he held on. Not hard, like the twins, but firm, fingers pressing lightly against her pulse. He could have tugged her closer—their bodies were a step from flush against each other—but he didn't.

Nathan glanced at her palm, at the scar that was again a wound—no coincidence, that, and thank you Diana—at the blood pouring out of the cut and down her wrist. He let his gaze rest on hers. "Mary," he said. "It's about Will. He had nothing to do with the plane. And he's alive."

Will? Her mind spun, confused, while Nathan just stared at her. Concerned. Frightened, even. Mary shook him off, and he let her go.

Ragged and bloody, Mary pushed past Nathan and ran.

ELOISE BOUNDED after the Pearl Knife as the blade chased Diana and the others down the stairwell in a fit of rage and shame, as though the blade meant to take full responsibility for losing track of them back at HQ. Shaken as Eloise was by Mary's appearance upstairs, by the blood and the poison—the torture, damn it—she knew she had to focus.

Nathan would take care of Mary, and there would be time for explanations. As long as Mary dropped the stubborn act and swallowed the antidote. The street was quiet, but curtains twitched in a window across the street, and Eloise had a feeling they might have police to contend with before too long.

On the other hand, this seemed like the kind of street that might avoid calling the cops. One could hope. Protecting cops against Diana and the others would add a level of difficulty, as would the inevitable red tape afterward.

Steve rushed past Eloise and leapt over the building's concrete stairs, falling in a step behind the Knife, which led him around the corner faster than Eloise could follow. At least the blade appeared to recognize him as an ally.

Eloise followed them anyway, as best she could. The Knife

beamed a thread of warning into her mind and she slowed, taking the corner with care.

Diana and the others stood in a line across the street, with Monster hulking behind them, Carlisle clinging to the pole of a streetlamp and clearly ready to leap on them if necessary.

An ambush. Sure, why not. It explained why they'd run away so fast.

The Knife shuddered a strange resonance through her mind, and Eloise saw that Goldi stood at the back of the group, hovering protectively beside Dolly. It had been so long since Eloise had seen her mother anywhere but her room, and the corridor outside of it, that she nearly missed a step. Dolly was cradling her head between her hands, Goldi glaring daggers at the Knife.

"Well?" Eloise said, keeping a strong mental hold on the Knife as it bobbed beside Steve. She could protect him, if they attacked. Maybe not from all of them, but the Knife was powerful. And Steve was fast. "Ready for round two?"

Diana tugged her gloves out of her waistband and replaced them on her hands, as if Eloise were nothing more than a slight annoyance. "Nope," she said. "Dolly dear?"

Eloise's mother straightened, Goldi's metallically manicured fingers holding her by the elbow for support as Dolly slashed a hand above her head.

A silver thread rent the air, and Eloise started forward, but the retirees were already leaping through the portal as the Knife quivered uncontrollably in Eloise's mind.

Diana disappeared last, and the portal blinked out of sight.

Eloise sent the Knife straight to the spot where the portal had been, slashing uselessly at the air. It beamed frustration back to her, and she pushed it harder, imagining the exact line of silver, the exact shape. It was burned on the inside of her eyelids.

The Knife tried, and failed, and Eloise grabbed the hilt and punched it into the air herself, as though she could use it to rent the universe apart.

"Eloise," Steve called, but his voice sounded far away, underwater.

The tip of the blade caught on nothing, on something, and Eloise pulled. Silver light peeled away from her hand, and she pushed the Knife through the gap to the tune of wrenching metal. She ignored the off-key screeches, the Knife's alarms, ready to force this blade to do her bidding once and for all, to retrieve her mother and these villains who'd come after Mary, who had once been part of Eloise's family.

Pain exploded through her head as the portal pushed her backward with a rush of stale air. Eloise fell back, tasting blood as she hit the pavement, the Knife clattering to the street. She could feel it smarting.

Steve knelt by her side, dabbing gently under her nose with a tissue. It came away wet with blood. "What the hell was that, Eloise?"

Pain blistered through her mind. She tried to sit up, but nausea forced her back down. "My mother made a portal," she said. "On her own."

Without the Knife. Or had she been using it somehow? Tapping into its power? Questions whirled through Eloise's head, making the pain worse.

"I saw. And then you responded by trying to implode the universe?"

That was certainly how it had felt. "I forced the Knife to copy her," Eloise said, and the Knife moaned into her mind, pained. "It worked. For a second."

Steve glanced down the street in the direction of the vanished portal. "I don't think it did what she did, El. I caught a glimpse through there. It looked like a lab or something."

"Maybe that's where they went."

Steve pursed his lips as if he disagreed, but he didn't argue. He helped her to sit up, and the nausea abated slightly.

Eloise took a shuddering breath, not yet ready to pick up the Knife. It pulsed angry agreement, and she had a feeling that if the blade were capable of storming off in a huff right now, it would.

If Eloise continued to ignore the problems with the Pearl Knife, to shuffle them to the back of her priority list, someone was going to get killed. And it might just be her.

"I need you to go back to HQ," she said, voice shaky, as Steve helped her to her feet. "Take Nathan. Take Mary, if she's still up there."

Open concern flooded his eyes, and for a moment she thought he might protest. Insist she go to a hospital, as if a doctor could help her. But he just looked at his hands. "And you will be?"

Eloise took a deep breath, still half tasting blood and metal and stale portal air. "I need to find my father. I need to know what he can tell me about the Knife."

PARSE GALAXY, SECTOR... SOMEWHERE

SLOANE SAT on the counter in Alex's lab, thumping her heels on the cabinet below in rhythm to Cartie Oh's new single. Unfortunately, Sloane had no sense of rhythm, so the whole thing just sounded like a confused band of elesloths.

"Can you please stop that?" Alex said, her goggled face about one inch from a machine that Sloane would not have put her own face near for any number of galactic tokens. Alex had been assembling the thing, whatever it was, since the *Moneymaker* had cruised out of the casino bay. Not even the fight with the fleet ships had stopped her from toying with the complex array of belts and gears and humming engines, all leading to a huge glass fishbowl-looking thing that occasionally sputtered a couple of blue sparks. The whole thing smelled like an overexerted egg beater.

"Sorry," Sloane said. "I'm stressed."

"And your answer to being stressed is to annoy me?"

"Hey. I'm the one who gets to be annoyed around here."

That comment actually earned a glance from Alex, and a pair of insultingly raised eyebrows. "You're kidding, right?"

"No. I kid a lot, but that was serious."

Alex returned to screwing whatever dangerous thing needed screwing on the table, and Sloane wished she'd had that thought out loud so she could've made a dirty joke. Had Oliver been here, she'd have made it anyway, but he was up on the nav deck with Hilda trying to figure out how far they could coast on the fuel they had left without getting stranded in the middle of random space.

At which point Archimedes Sol's casino thugs would be wiping the ship off the bottom of their boots. Sloane was still trying to decide whether she was angry with Oliver for failing to inform her of his history with the fleet.

"Vincent left the ship with you because he trusted you to get it back to him," Alex said. "And us, too. But all you've done so far is get us further into debt."

"Not true."

"Right. You also slept with the security officer."

A little bit true. "Maybe if Uncle Vin had a properly trained crew, they could've gotten his ship back to him all by themselves."

"You accepted the job," Alex said.

How could she not? Alex, Hilda, and Oliver had shown up on Sloane's college planet looking for all the world like a band of lost orphans. Nerdy, old, and hot orphans, respectively, but still. And no matter how much these second-rate criminals acted like they all trusted each other, and that Sloane's uncle had treated them as family, Vincent had DNA-locked the ship's controls to Sloane and Sloane alone.

She didn't like them, but what was she supposed to do? Make them hitchhike across the galaxy while she stashed the *Moneymaker* in a parking garage for fifty tokens a month?

"My father is going to kill me," Sloane grumbled.

"Given the information currently available to us, there's at least a fifty percent chance that Archimedes Sol will kill us first," Alex said. "Or possibly the fleet."

Before Sloane could form a comeback—if that had even been intended as a joke; she wasn't sure—the machine on the table kicked on. Alex stumbled back as the thing issued forth a grinding hum that made Sloane clap her hands over her ears.

"What's happening?" she shouted, but Alex wasn't looking at her, nor did Sloane think Alex could hear her as the grinding slipped into a squeal that made her think of feedback at a club with a shitty beat-jockey.

The glass ball at the center of Alex's machine was vibrating so hard Sloane wished she'd put on the goggles, after all, in case the thing shattered. And because she was watching it with her full attention—though any of the belts or gears on the thing could certainly fly off and ninja-star a hole through her skull—Sloane saw the instant the slit appeared.

First it just looked like an ocular migraine, a cut of light across her cornea. She blinked, and the slit opened wider, stretching until it was like looking through a window. Forgetting her fear, Sloane leaned closer.

On the other side of the window was a knife. A dagger? It was long, the blade so white it might have been made of bone. The tip of it actually pierced through the sliver of light, hanging inside the ship for a bare moment as if pulled this way by forces unknown.

Then the slit snapped shut and Alex's machine shuddered to a stop, the room falling silent so suddenly that Sloane felt the physical absence of the sound in the ringing of her ears.

Oliver crashed into the room, weapons drawn, with Hilda on his heels as Alex whipped the goggles off of her head and tossed them into the air. At which point the goggles smacked into the ceiling and fell back down, because this was a spaceship and the ceiling was like two inches away.

"I did it!" Alex cried, and Oliver relaxed like she'd pressed a button, returning his weapons to their various pouches. To Sloane's surprise, he kept his focus on Alex as though he very much wanted to hear her big announcement.

"Did what?" Hilda said, bracing a hand on the door frame. "Crashed the ship? Because you almost crashed the ship."

"We're in space," Sloane said. "What's to crash?"

Hilda rolled her eyes. "Fine, it almost vibrated apart. Equally bad." Possibly worse, Sloane thought. "What was that?"

Alex stopped dancing and dove for her computer, typing madly. "It was a resonance," she said. "That was a wormhole."

Oliver took a step toward the table, his brows drawn together in concentration, then paused. What *was* his deal with Alex and her work? Sloane frowned at the crystal-ball thing. "It was really small. And it showed us, what? A kitchen knife?"

"It was a *wormhole*," Alex said.

It really seemed very unlikely. "Maybe you tuned into a holo channel by accident," Sloane said. "A cooking show."

Hilda sighed. "I'm going back up to the pilot's deck. Try not to get us sucked through space and time, will you?"

"No promises," Alex said. "It was a wormhole, and it wasn't a kitchen knife. It actually looked kind of like the Blade of Starlight."

Oliver barked a laugh, but Sloane just looked at him in confusion. Hilda just stood by the door with her arms crossed, so presumably all the various criminals had heard of this thing. "The Blade of Starlight," Sloane said. "Sounds like something from a bad epic elf vid. 'For sooth, I hath contorted the blade of starlight from the tablet of doom.'"

No one laughed. Not even Oliver, and Oliver laughed at everything.

"Don't worry," Oliver said, though Sloane wasn't particularly worried. She simply didn't like to be the only ignorant one in the room. "It couldn't have been the Blade of Starlight. The Blade of Starlight is like—" He held out his hands, clenched them into fists, and wiggled his fingers.

"An octopus?" Sloane asked, scrolling through her search feed.

"I don't understand how you two work," Alex muttered.

They didn't do a whole lot of talking, that was how. Not that Alex needed to know that. Sloane scrolled through the search feeds and picked up the first article she saw from a marginally reputable source.

"Uh," Sloane said, "this says there's a seven-million-token reward for your Blade of Starlight."

Oliver dropped his hands and pulled himself up on the counter, earning a glare from Alex. "Uh, yeah," he said. "Oldest bounty in the galaxy."

"It's famous," Alex added.

Of course her uncle's crims would know about a bounty like that. Sloane kept conveniently forgetting that Oliver was one of them—a criminal. Or maybe she remembered it too much and that was why she thought he was cute.

When Sloane had the money to swing by planet Urshuk for a therapy session, she'd try to unpack that. Maybe.

"Who set the bounty?" Sloane asked.

"No one knows," Oliver said. "It's a big fat mystery that no one's ever going to solve, because the thing's been missing for like fifty central-gal years. No one's ever going to find it."

Alex nodded in agreement.

Sloane just blinked at them. "But we just found it."

"Through a wormhole," Alex said.

Sloane tapped the crystal ball, and Alex slapped her hand away. "So open up that window thing again," Sloane said. "Just make it bigger this time."

Alex was looking at her like she'd lost her marbles, or maybe like she'd never had any marbles to begin with. "That slit of a wormhole that just opened? That's my life's work."

"And it's worth seven million tokens."

Alex shook her head. "It's worth billions of tokens, Sloane. *Billions.*"

"As I see it, that's an argument in my favor."

Alex propped her hands on her hips, giving Sloane the impression of an annoyed gnome. She was really in epic-elf-vid mode today. "It took the span of my life up until this point to get a resonance that created a wormhole the size of a small water pipe. I have no idea how it happened. I have to analyze the data to figure out—"

"Then analyze the data," Sloane interrupted. "Do it again. We need the tokens, Alex. We can get this starlight sword thing and use the bounty to pay Archimedes Sol. And get to my uncle. And then you'll have money left over to fund the rest of your research."

"Even if that were theoretically possible," Alex said, "I don't think it's a good idea."

"Why the hells not?"

Oliver slipped off his counter and sidled over to where Sloane stood, leaning into her side. "Alex is right. You don't take a job when you don't know who's running it. Who's powerful enough to offer that many tokens, and then who's powerful enough to *steal* the thing from that person?

"Maybe it's not stolen. Maybe Alex just showed us a... magic sword lost and found."

Alex shook her head. "We'll be up to our ears in trouble."

"We're already past our ears," Sloane said. "We're about to be casino thug chew toys. Or fleet chew toys, thank you, Oliver."

Oliver didn't even have the grace to look ashamed. Instead,

he and Alex exchanged a glance that made Sloane want to whack them both over their heads. But unfortunately, Sloane had no chance of opening her own wormhole to steal some elven sword thing from... Well, she didn't know who, and she didn't care. Whoever they were, they probably didn't have wormholes. And Sloane did.

Or she would. Very soon.

Mary had nowhere to go.

She found herself staggering west along streets she could hardly see, inebriated with poison and pain. She should have stayed behind to talk to Eloise at least, or to dose herself with the antidote to Diana's poison, which felt like it was eating its way through her veins. She couldn't convince herself she was safe enough to stop moving, not even for a moment. Maybe the paranoia was a part of it. Or maybe it would save her life. She couldn't tell the difference.

Just a few blocks to the water. She could make it that far.

Will was alive. He was alive, and he'd had nothing to do with the crash. How could Nathan know that? How could he believe it? Mary wasn't sure she could.

She'd been aiming for the beach—what better place to die, if she had to?—but she made it as far as Long Beach's fancy glass-walled library before she collapsed, barely managing to disable the paltry security system on the back door before her legs gave out.

Hands shaking, Mary withdrew Eloise's antidote and squeezed the gel into her mouth. She shouldn't have let herself get distracted fighting Nathan.

She should, perhaps, have let him help her.

▭

Mary woke hours later, her mouth dry, her head cricked at the same angle she'd dropped it in against the wall when she'd passed out. Last night? An hour ago? She couldn't be sure. Not longer, surely. Someone would have found her. Friend, foe, librarian. At this point she wasn't sure she cared.

Head pounding, she found a water fountain and drank.

By the time the fluorescent overhead lights scattered on, signaling the beginning of the work day, Mary was hiding in a broom closet. And hoping against hope that no one would need to mop a floor today. She locked the door from the inside, barricading it with a chair, and squeezed around the cart to fold herself beneath the lowest shelf while voices rose and fell outside the door.

She didn't know what day it was. She didn't have her tablet to check the library's hours; she didn't have Coral's getup, or even Grandma to help her mount an escape. Had Diana and others left the van alone? Or had they torched it?

She couldn't risk finding it, not now. They had to have followed her to the apartment, which meant they knew what her car looked like. Had she lost them? Or were they biding their time?

It was dark when Mary woke again. Stomach growling, she raided the librarians' break room and their stash of frozen burritos. She hydrated. The cuts across her body still stung, her hand burning every time she flexed it, but at least she felt clearheaded now, the poison neutralized from her system. Plus, the bleeding had slowed significantly. So that was a plus.

She couldn't hide here forever. Aside from the fact that kids eventually vomited in story rooms, requiring the use of cleaning supplies, the retirees were no doubt still after her. She'd rejected her only potential allies—Nathan's iron grip still echoed against her wrist, the depth of emotion in his eyes threatening to call her home—and antidote or no, her body was striped with injuries.

She could only think of one person she could still force to help her. So she hot-wired a motorcycle and drove up the coast to Malibu.

Bloody and broken, Mary hauled herself up Jeff Hayes's trellis and into his bedroom, where the movie star lay in bed beside a woman with bright red hair. Mary had never seen her before, at least from what she could tell. One of her feet dipped out from under the covers, the moonlight illuminating a fuchsia manicure.

Mary crept to Jeff's side of the bed and pressed a hand over his mouth. He breathed in sharply, eyes wide, and a spike of guilt lanced through the rest of Mary's pain. Frightening one of the only people who'd been willing to help her. Great. Well, it was done now. She'd just have to add it to her list of sins.

Jeff followed her into the hall, rubbing his face with a shaking hand. He looked her over, and Mary was fully, desperately aware of the bloodstains on her shredded sweatshirt, the bruises on her face. Her whole body felt tender. Raw.

"Don't take this the wrong way," Jeff said, "but I'm getting mixed signals from you."

Mary leaned against the wall. "I need your help."

"You need a doctor."

She shook her head, skull throbbing. "I need you to take me to North Dakota."

▭

Mary wasn't sure what she'd been expecting to see when Jeff's plane touched down in the middle of the flat expanse of land in North Dakota where her parents had breathed their last, fourteen years ago. Without exact coordinates, she'd never have found this place; she'd never have distinguished it from its surroundings, from the miles of plain that stretched across the state.

Though perhaps the ghosts might have led her here.

A thin layer of snow crunched under her boots as she crossed to the heart of the field, memories rushing around her like ghosts. With a few hours yet before dawn, aurora borealis painted the sky with shuddering towers of brilliant color. It felt inappropriately beautiful, almost mocking, in such a wasted place. A sacred place. She let the freezing air wash over her, let it sting her cheeks. The air smelled cold, dry. Like oncoming snow.

The wreckage had been cleared away fourteen years ago, and Mary couldn't imagine the league would have left so much as a dime-sized piece of evidence. Certainly no note of innocence from Will, no echoes of her parents' screams. Those lived only in her mind.

She'd mourned her mentor for two years. She'd hated him for what, three months? Four? And with Nathan's news came a whole new level of confusion. No need to mourn. No need to hate. She wasn't sure she'd ever been so lost.

Wrapped in a parka, Jeff left the plane and trudged over to her, his face hidden by a hood that was probably lined in fur. He tucked his hands in his pockets. "Please tell me you didn't drag me out here just to be with your feelings. That girl charged about a thousand dollars an hour."

How could it be that it was Nathan she fought now, and Jeff Hayes who stood by her side? Nathan had done wrong—she still thought he had—but her treacherous heart missed him, more than she could have possibly imagined.

And at the first possible opportunity, even with her trying to beat him up, he'd made it a priority to tell her the truth. At least, something he saw as truth.

Out loud, Mary said, "You can afford her."

Jeff shivered, casting a glance around at the sky. "I don't know what you hope to find out here," he said, wrinkling his nose. "Or why your plane couldn't have gone down in Baja or Hawaii."

Mary ignored him and paced a circle, her boots cracking the icy snow. She wished for a parka, but something in her felt she deserved the pain of the cold, the way it stripped her bare. Even with her right hand throbbing, and the striped wounds Diana had etched across her abdomen, the cold pierced deeper. This *place* pierced deeper.

"I don't know how to win this," she said. "There are reporters and villains around every corner."

"And some of them are the same people."

Once upon a time, she'd have said they all were. At the moment, she wasn't so sure.

"As far as winning," Jeff said. "It depends. What's the prize?"

Justice for her parents, or so she'd told herself. But if Nathan was right, if Will was innocent, then packing the retirees off indiscriminately might not be justice at all. Oh, some of them were guilty—some of them had told her as much. But they deserved what they themselves had never offered her parents. They deserved someone who would sort things out. Fair trials, and all that. And in that moment, as much as she missed Nathan, the person Mary wanted most was Eloise.

El was a fixer. El approached situations with clarity, logic, and leadership. El had a magic Knife that could kick butts—or slice through them. Because Diana and Rocker and Goldi were still out there. And Monster, and Carlisle. They still wanted to kill Mary. They might want to kill Flick, too.

"They won't stop," Mary said softly, and the northern lights surged in agreement, a reckless streak of red breaking in among the green. "I hunted them. Now they'll hunt me. It never ends."

"Unless you end it."

Mary had nearly forgotten Jeff was there. And he *was* there, shivering and stamping his feet, his face hidden in the hood. He could have gone back to the plane. Hell, he could have refused to fly her out here. "What do you mean?" she asked.

"Bring them to you, but on your terms. Bait them."

"How?"

Jeff tsked. "Darling, you're forgetting your superpower."

She shook her head. It felt unreasonably cruel, even from him. "I don't have any enhanced abilities, Hayes."

Jeff lay his hands on her shoulders, forcing her to look him directly in the eye. "You do. You, Mary O'Sullivan, are a celebrity."

A burst of wind sliced across the field, vicious as it slashed through her clothes. "You've got that power, too."

"Surely. But yours puts mine to shame."

"You're drunk."

But Jeff refused to be silenced. Once the man started talking, there was no hope for anyone who craved peace and quiet. "You're good with all the fighty-fighty krav-ma-jitsu or whatever," he said, letting go of her shoulders, "but you're also a celebrity. And in times of trouble, you know, it's possible to work *with* the press, rather than against them."

She'd spent years trying to protect her secret identity from everyone, from the press. But Jeff wasn't wrong that she'd also manipulated them. She'd known when cameras pointed at her, and she'd used them to her advantage. She'd lived in a glass-walled house, for crying out loud, because she'd known the world could see in.

She'd built her life around a circle of illusions.

Now, reporters like Dawn Kimble knew all that, and they wanted the full story. It wasn't celebrity hunting any longer; it wasn't voyeur, and they weren't paparazzi.

They wouldn't give up the quest merely because she'd temporarily disappeared. It was too big. And maybe Dawn had the right of it; maybe the world deserved answers.

Mary tapped a finger to her lips, thinking. Maybe, if she told Dawn what she planned, she could manipulate the situation with everyone's best interests in mind.

A private meeting for the media. A public one for Diana and the others.

Maybe it was time to square with the new normal. "Jeff," she said, "I think you're finally right about something."

"It does happen occasionally. I blame the medication."

Mary hugged her arms around herself, stuffing her hands into her armpits. At least they weren't numb yet. It wasn't exactly easy to win a fight with frostbitten fingertips. "I'm going to call a press conference."

"Are you going to call it here?"

Mary blinked at him. "No."

"Excellent," he said, taking her arm and pulling her back toward the waiting plane, "let's get back to SoCal before my testicles go on strike."

Nathan couldn't bring himself to leave L.A.

Eloise had left to find Will, and Steve had left to support Ire at HQ. Eloise had wanted Nathan to go, too, but how could he choose LIO with Mary out there alone? When he didn't know if she'd taken the antidote, or if she was curled up somewhere, succumbing to some other, greater injury?

In his mind, Mary was too hurt to move. Too hurt to ask for help. He'd abandoned her once, chosen LIO over her because of some insane desire to please a sister, a family, who'd never deserved his loyalty. He'd abandoned her because he hadn't been able to see past his own ridiculous versions of right and wrong.

So instead of returning to HQ after the disaster of a fight in Long Beach, Nathan combed the streets around the apartment for any sign of Mary while the surveillance team worked the cameras in the area. Between widespread outages—too widespread to be anything but the retirees' doing—and Mary's ability to disappear when she wanted to, he found nothing. He widened his search, sweeping toward the beach.

Nothing. No dropped seashells to follow this time.

With the sun sending its long, golden legs across the sand,

and Long Beach well and truly scoured, Nathan turned his attention to Malibu.

"You're not going to try her house, are you?" the surveillance tech, Pete, said into his ear. "It's crawling with reporters. I don't see how she could have gotten in without making the evening news. Or at least Twitter."

Nathan watched the last of the sun's rays glinting off the water. He didn't know if Mary could have made it as far as Malibu, though it was only about an hour away. He didn't think she'd have gone back to the house.

Nathan sighed. "No," he said, "there's no point in trying the house. If she's in Malibu, she's with Jeff Hayes."

Between renting the car and stopping to eat—and ignoring Chloe's incessant calls, which had begun sometime between the beach and the drive to Malibu—then stashing the car a few miles away from Jeff Hayes's house, it was late by the time Nathan scaled the fence to the movie star's backyard.

Backyard. It was more like an amusement park, with its elaborate swimming pool and elegant bridges. Like he'd designed it as his own mini resort or something. Standing on the Hayes side of the fence, Nathan couldn't help thinking back to the party that had brought everything tumbling down last year.

He remembered how Mary had stood frozen on one of those bridges, a blue drink in her hand, pretending to be under the spell of Wave's mind control serum. He'd been so angry at her deception, pretending to be a victim to preserve her secret identity while people were in danger. While her friend died, even.

Heroes did good. Villains did bad. But Nathan himself had

carried a bomb into an office building at thirteen and killed dozens of people. That he hadn't known, that they'd turned out to be terrorists themselves, that his family had essentially disowned him... Those details merely added to the spiral, the confusion. He couldn't make up for it by enforcing some imaginary moral code on every other person who hoped to make the world a better place.

Good and evil, heroes and villains. Those were terms for comic books.

Real life made a tangle of light and dark.

Nathan climbed the trellis that led up to Jeff Hayes's second floor hallway, but the window was locked. Afraid of setting off an alarm, he peered inside, then knocked on the window.

All was quiet. No lights, no sound. No one home.

As Nathan dropped back to the patio, wondering if he ought to wait for a while, his mobile once again buzzed in his pocket. This time, looking out at the darkly reflective water of Jeff Hayes's pool, Nathan picked up the call.

"You were supposed to *win* in Las Vegas," Chloe said. Her voice sounded prim and far away. "What the hell happened?"

Nathan frowned. He hadn't slept in a while, but he didn't think rest would help him to understand his sister's outburst. "Las Vegas," he repeated. "I wasn't even there. And I thought we did win. How did you know—"

"You didn't win before those men caused massive amounts of damage," Chloe said. "They killed a cop, Nathan. How could you let that happen?"

Nathan felt, somehow, as though he were about to be fired from a job he'd never accepted in the first place. And still, something tugged at his stomach, telling him he ought to have done better. That she was right to be disappointed in him, that he ought to be disappointed in himself.

"That hotel is in shambles," she continued. "And you let Wave show up first!"

"Chloe," Nathan said.

But his sister was on a roll. "We set that up for you," she said. He assumed he meant the EAEA, though that made no sense. "The whole thing. And you wasted it. If you don't do your job—"

"Then you'll do it for us?" Nathan interrupted, anger surging through his chest, twining with his fear for Mary, his feelings of regret. How could the EAEA have set up the situation in Vegas? And why? In hopes of making LIO look good? The idea was laughable. "You already said that, and I'm still not sure what it means. You're lobbyists. How could you have set up what happened in Las Vegas?"

There was a pause, and he could hear her breathing. He could practically hear her thinking, trying to arrange the right words. The right lies.

"You know what," Nathan said before her thoughts could gel, "never mind. I don't really care what you have to say."

Chloe huffed out a breath. "After all Dad and I endured from you, Nathan? I would have thought you'd be grateful that we talk to you at all."

They didn't talk to him, though. They hadn't, not for years. And his association with the league was the only reason she was sniffing around now. Her interest had nothing to do with their past, with trusting him, with understanding a goddamn thing he'd been through.

Part of him wanted to tell her off, to scream into the phone until Jeff's important celebrity neighbors called the cops on him.

"If you want to be one of the heroes," Chloe said, "then stop messing around and *be* one."

He'd taken one step in the right direction, coming here. But it was only the beginning. Maybe Mary had made a mistake, protecting her identity that night. Or maybe she'd been right all along.

There wasn't a right answer, because it wasn't black and white. That was the point. Nathan thought about Dr. Gordon and the other Wave prisoners, rotting away in a cell because of Dolly. And he knew what he had to do.

He'd have to go back to HQ. But he'd return to L.A. as soon as he could manage it.

"You know," Nathan said, "I think that's the smartest thing you've ever said to me. Goodbye, Chloe."

ELOISE'S BREATH made little clouds of steam as she breathed into the cold mountain air, but it turned out that Steve had been right after all; the place did feel balmy in comparison to Niagara. She gripped the Pearl Knife, fingers wrapped tightly around the hilt, and tried to imagine a portal like the one she'd seen Dolly make. On her own. Without the Knife.

Several paces away, her father leaned back against a tree, watching. He wore a hunter green vest over a thick black sweater, a wool cap pulled tight over his head. He looked casual, but his eyes were sharp and alert, his attention laser-focused on watching her practice.

Eloise's heart beat to a conflicting tune of relief and regret —*alive, alive, alive*—and yet she couldn't help but feel her mother's presence lingering between them like a curse.

They'd been out here for hours. She'd made absolutely no progress.

"It doesn't know how," she said, feeling as though sweat should be pouring down her forehead. That was how strained she felt, pushing the Knife like this. It wasn't that it pushed back, exactly, just that it... resisted. "I keep showing it what I want, and it just... can't."

The Pearl Knife buzzed, practically a growl. Eloise interpreted frustration, though whether with her or with its own inability, she didn't know.

"We can't expect to learn everything we need to know in the blink of an eye," Dad said, as if they hadn't been standing in the woods since dawn. How patient did a person have to be? At the moment, Ire, Nathan, and Steve were holding down the fort at HQ. She trusted them, she really did, but Steve didn't even want to be there at all, Ire was focused on his academy, and after Long Beach, she kept half expecting Nathan to call and resign in favor of chasing after Mary.

Eloise took a deep breath, trying to steady her racing thoughts. She couldn't do anything about them right now. She could only focus on the Knife. And on her father.

"Dolly made a portal on her own." If Eloise hadn't seen it happen with her own eyes, she wouldn't have believed it. But then again, a year ago she wouldn't have believed the blade could make a portal like that, either. "Is she somehow still linked to the Knife? Could she have stolen its power?"

The Knife stirred in indignation, but Eloise thought it was still a question worth asking.

Dad just shook his head. "I don't know. We're in unchartered waters here. But from what you told me about the way the Knife's proximity hurts your mother, I'd say it's a reasonable guess."

Eloise flung the Knife at a tree a few paces off, and the blade sliced straight through the trunk, leaving a slender hole through the center. She stared at it, wondering how hard she'd thrown the thing. All her years of target practice, and she'd never seen that before.

The Knife spiraled around the trunk a few times before returning. In its silence, Eloise interpreted chastisement.

"Where did they go?" Eloise said, resisting the urge to

throw the Knife again. "How can we find them? They could be anywhere."

Dad pushed away from his tree and came to stand with her, rubbing his hand on his pants. "El, my brilliant daughter, you can't do everything. That's why we formed the league in the first place. It's just too much for one person's shoulders."

Easy for him to say. He'd had a whole team of colleagues. Evil ones, as it turned out, but still.

Eloise flipped the Knife over her fingers, the blade impossibly warm against her skin. "I can't run the league any more than I can control the Knife. They run from me. They don't trust me. Steve won't stay, and Mary..." Eloise swallowed. The thought of Mary's absence stung, more than usual. Even poisoned, even after hours of torture—in Eloise's imagination it was hours, though it might have been minutes—Mary had chosen to run away instead of coming home.

She couldn't possibly believe Eloise could have had a hand in what Diana had done. She wouldn't.

Dad squeezed shoulder, and all at once the past rushed back to her with such force that she nearly sobbed: Dad's hand on her shoulder after she'd landed a particularly good throw with a knife; Dad's hand on her shoulder after she'd helped Mary acclimate to HQ; Dad's hand on her shoulder when Steve had left, when she'd been worried about a mission, when he'd shared his cancer diagnosis.

"It's not about holding tight," Dad said, his voice soft and somehow still resonant among the trees. Almost like a prayer. Almost like a song—like the Knife, when it was comforting her instead of sulking. "It's about loosening your grip. It's about letting go, and letting the league be better for all your differences. If you hold too tightly, the others can't bring their best to the table."

She thought of the way he'd spent every spare moment in

the training rooms at HQ, leading by example while Dolly controlled him—controlled his powers—the whole time. He'd injected his love into the place, regardless of his circumstances. It made Eloise want to weep.

"You lead," Dad said. "You don't force anyone to follow. And maybe it's the same with the Knife. I spent years fighting that thing, El, pushing back against every chain it tightened across my mind."

The Knife shuddered, huddling into her head like a scared thing. Or a guilty thing. *It wasn't your fault*, Eloise thought, but the Knife only let out a keening cry—feeling?—in response.

"But once I surrendered to it..." Dad lifted his hands, tipping a small smile. "The Knife let me handle it. It let me transfer control of those threads to you."

She wanted to know exactly how he'd done it, every step. But Eloise should know by now that the Knife communicated in feelings, in images, in song. It wasn't bound by the logic, or the protocol, that guided Eloise's life.

The Pearl Knife didn't work based on step-by-step, how-to instructions. No, the blade relied on instinct. She didn't know how it knew the things it knew—how it could draw maps into her mind, or answer her call from half a mile away, or cut through space. She only knew it did those things best when she didn't ask. Before she even knew *what* to ask.

"Maybe the Knife needs a partner rather than a master," Eloise said. She could almost feel the blade sitting up in interest, in hope.

The skin around her father's eyes crinkled when he smiled. He stepped back over to his tree and folded his arms across his chest. "Maybe so."

Eloise breathed deep, inviting the cold air to clear out her lungs. Her hands trembled as she let the hilt go, willing the Pearl Knife to do what it would.

It was terror. But it was also... freedom.

The Knife sighed, looking light as a leaf as it floated out of her hand and twirled across the clearing, gentle and free. Eloise didn't call to it. She didn't issue a command, or an image, or a question as to what it intended. Dad watched its gravity-defying dance, too, and Eloise thought she saw fear shadow his features for a moment. But the expression disappeared so quickly that she might have imagined it altogether.

As she looked away from her father and back to the Knife, the blade spun a figure eight before slashing an elegant silver line in midair.

A portal. A smaller one than she'd seen before, but she had a strong sense that the Knife was performing a demonstration. Steve had been able to see through the portal Eloise had forced back in Long Beach, and Eloise squinted, trying to see what lay on the other side.

"It's the inside of the cabin," Dad whispered, wonder lacing through his tone, and Eloise could see he was right. The gray cat was curled up on the rainbow afghan, the sun streaking across the wooden floorboards. "Incredible."

Eloise's phone vibrated in her pocket, and she remembered to breathe. She pulled out the phone, hands shaking, eyes locked on the portal. It didn't disappear. It stayed, the Knife dancing proudly around it.

The call was coming from an unregistered number. Probably Travis Bertram. Eloise picked up, figuring she might as well face the fallout from Las Vegas right after a miracle had occurred. She was unlikely to ever be in a better mood than this. "Hello?"

There was a brief pause, and Eloise wondered if she'd lost the call. And then a familiar voice spoke from the other end of the phone. "Eloise? It's Mary."

IT FELT unreal to have LIO's resources at Mary's fingertips again. To have the team in her ear to tell her exactly where Dawn Kimble lived in downtown L.A., and that the third landing of the fire escape led straight to the reporter's bedroom window.

She'd expected to have to wake the reporter, to have to scare her the way she'd scared Jeff the other night. Instead, when Mary peered through the window, Dawn was on the edge of her bed. Waiting. As soon as she saw Mary, the reporter got up to let her in.

"I felt you coming," she said.

Mary threw a leg over the windowsill. "I thought it was like a scent thing."

Dawn still stood between Mary and the rest of the room, blocking her from entry. Mary could make out the reflections of framed photos on the walls, though she couldn't see the images themselves. She thought the bed skirt might have ruffles. The curtains certainly did.

"I'm not a hound," Dawn said. "What are you doing here?"

"How does it work, then?" Mary asked, still perched on the windowsill.

Dawn flicked a strand of hair back over her shoulder. She had on pink plaid pajamas. "It's like a map in my head. Once I meet a person, they have a sort of signature on the map and I can find them again."

Mary nodded. "You'd make a fair independent operative, you know."

Dawn shrugged. "I like my job."

"How did you get your powers? Chemical accident? Product testing? Wrong place, wrong time?" Mary knew she was stalling, but she couldn't help herself.

Dawn folded her arms across her chest. "What. Are you doing. Here."

Mary wasn't good at the whole mea culpa thing. Never had been. Still, she held her hands up in surrender. "I'm here to apologize. And to take you up on your offer. I could use your help."

Mary sat in the back seat of Dawn's red compact Toyota, trying to see what the reporter was texting to her OperativeWatch colleague.

"Tim shares information with his friends from the U.S. Post, CNN, and the L.A. Times," Dawn said as she texted. "The U.S. Post guy, he'll share anything with anyone just to look cool. And the L.A. Times woman is dating someone at the Washington Post."

"Handy to know where people are at all times," Mary said, peering over Dawn's shoulder. "Creepy, too. But handy."

Dawn shot her a side glance, then rolled her eyes. "If I tell Tim I saw you on the beach again, the secret passage into your house will clear up in five minutes. If three of them leave, everyone else will follow for fear of missing a story."

Mary shook her head, imagining the flood of reporters high-tailing it down to the beach. "I can't believe they're still here."

"News has been slow. You're the country's biggest scandal. And half of them are interns at this point."

"Still."

Dawn sent her text, and ten minutes later Mary was directing the reporter into the third parking spot of a beach viewpoint down the road—a viewpoint the league had built overnight many years ago, to the great dismay of some of Mary's neighbors. She hopped out to find the hidden panel under the pavement, where she entered the access code.

"Is this off the record?" Dawn asked when Mary got back into the car. Mary actually laughed at that; she didn't think she'd ever heard that question from the reporter's side before.

The parking spot shuddered and detached itself from the rest of the pavement, creating a downward ramp into the underground tunnel as Dawn gripped the steering wheel, her eyes round.

"Record away," Mary said.

The basement was just as she'd left it. She hurried through the workout space with Dawn on her heels, the reporter's jaw hanging open in wonder. When Mary suggested she take a few photos for the OperativeWatch website, she thought Dawn might actually start drooling.

Mary didn't linger in the workout space. She hurried through the sitting area and past the hidden guest rooms, straight to the corner of the basement that had once served as her personal tech haven. Gadgets were strewn about everywhere; she'd thrown as much as she could into bags when she'd left here last fall, but she hadn't brought nearly enough.

The sight of all her toys made her want to cry with relief. Even after losing the System—she still had the program, but there was no rebooting the incarnation that had helped her at

Aries—she still had a few friends left in the world, after all. Inanimate though they might be.

Dawn followed her into the room, looking around. "This is all you needed? To get into the house?"

Mary started throwing drawers open, looking for discarded cameras and lenses. "I need to call a press conference," she said. "A fake one."

Dawn frowned. "A fake one."

"Don't worry, I'll do a real one, too. But I need to do a fake one first to lure the Trap and her friends to me on my terms, and I can't put reporters in real danger."

"How will you—"

Mary held up a camera. "Holograms. If you'll help me get some data from your reporters friends."

Dawn's frown deepened, suspicion plain on her face. Mary supposed she hadn't given the poor woman much reason to trust her. And yet, just like Jeff had been there for her in North Dakota, Dawn was here for her now.

"Is that all?" Dawn asked.

Mary set her hands on the table and met Dawn's eyes. This was the difficult part, the part she hated. If she could think of a way to avoid it—to create a hologram that could walk the streets of L.A.—she'd do it. "I also need you to show up in person."

Dawn nodded slowly, biting her lip. "Because I always know where you are, and if I don't show up at the press conference then they'll assume it's a trap."

She connected things fast. "Exactly. I know it's asking a lot, and we'll do our best to keep you out of danger. And you can say no. We'll find another—"

"I'll do it," Dawn said.

Mary grinned. "I knew reporters weren't all bad."

"You could just say thanks."

Mary grinned. "Thanks." She yanked open another drawer

and started tossing strips of metal onto the counter. Getting the retirees to the press conference was the easy half of the plan. Even with El on her side, she wasn't sure it would matter if they couldn't somehow deal with Diana and her poison. The striped wounds across Mary's torso throbbed in agreement.

She had half an idea—the seed of an idea—but she wasn't sure she had the parts. It would be a complicated invention, one she'd have no way to test until the real deal. And it wouldn't contain a single needle.

"Those parts are for the holograms?" Dawn asked.

Mary shook her head. "This is something else." No need to frighten her any more than she needed to; Mary intended to get Dawn out of there well before any fighting began. "Can you start calling your reporter friends? I'll tell you how to get full scans for the holograms, sitting and standing."

Dawn picked up the camera and turned it around in her hand. "Just call me Igor," she said. "I'll get to work."

Eloise sat on the overstuffed chair in the corner of the cabin's living room, the gray cat wedged between her leg and the armrest. The creature purred softly as she scratched its ears, wondering if this was what normal life looked like. Dad frying onions in the kitchen, wearing a checkered apron. Miles Davis pouring a tune into the background.

And the Knife, contentedly heavy in the back of her mind. Almost sleepy, if she had to guess, as if its recent successes had worn it out. That part, certainly, was nothing like normal.

Eloise sighed and picked up her phone. Heart in her stomach, she dialed the number her father had given her for Agnes.

"Don't hang up," Eloise said, when Agnes answered. "I need to talk to you."

Agnes's answering huff of breath might have been a scoff, or a sigh. "I'm not sure what there is to say, El."

"Mary has a plan to bait the LIO retirees and round them up," Eloise said, the words tumbling out of her mouth far too quickly. Agnes and Mary had been friends, once.

A pause. "You spoke to Mary?"

Eloise scratched the cat behind its ears, and it snuggled closer against her leg. "I did. It's a good plan."

"But you need backup."

"It wouldn't hurt."

Across the room, Dad added chicken to his onions, keeping his gaze studiously on the frying pan though certainly he could hear every word Eloise said.

For a long moment, Agnes didn't say anything at all. Eloise wished she could see where Agnes was, whether she was bent over a lab table or sitting at home with a book. She knew Agnes had a wife and daughter, but she'd never met them. It was hard to picture them.

Had Agnes taken her family away to whatever safe house Wave had stashed her in? Were they being protected? These, Eloise thought, were the things she should have been focusing on from the very beginning. The things she should have checked.

"You don't trust us," Agnes said finally, her voice sad. "We showed up in Vegas to help. We got there before you did, with the same intention—to *help*—and you couldn't have caught those guys without us. And still you don't trust us."

We, we, we. She hated that Agnes meant Wave. "I couldn't just let you take them."

"Right. Because *you* run the sanctioned enhanced human holding facility, right?"

It sounded bad, when Agnes put it that way. It sounded very bad.

"If you trust us," Agnes said, "you could help exonerate us."

Eloise folded her hands in her lap as her father hummed softly along with Miles's melody. She wanted Agnes's help, but she wouldn't lie to get it. "I'm not sure I should do that."

"I know," Agnes said, sounding tired, "and that's why I can't help you."

The line went dead. Disappointed, Eloise tossed the phone

on the table beside her. The cat startled at the noise and zipped away, rushing across the room and up the stairs.

"No luck?" Dad said as he stirred the food, and Eloise got up to join him in the kitchen. She leaned back on the counter, allowing herself to savor the cooking smells for a few breaths.

"I can't blame her," she said. "But I'm barely holding onto the whole 'sanctioned organization' thing as it is. If I suggested that Travis Bertram ask his bosses to clear Wave, too? They'd riot."

Dad tossed her a smile, his dimple popping deep into his cheek. She'd only been here a few days, and already this was beginning to feel normal. But then she'd catch an expression like that one, notice his dimple, his new wrinkles, or his graying hair, and she'd be struck all over again by the magnitude of her grief. How much she had missed him. How much time they'd lost.

"Vegas aside, I'm not huge on ops anymore," he said. "But I'll be on call. If you need me."

She wanted to ask why he no longer used his powers—or so it would seem, anyway—but it felt like crossing a line. Too personal. Too sensitive.

So instead, Eloise just nodded. "Thanks, Dad." She stepped across the kitchen to kiss his cheek, wondering how Mary would respond when she saw her old mentor again.

Eloise had a feeling Mary might be angry about what Dad had done, innocent or not.

"I guess I'd better give HQ a call," Eloise said, returning to the abandoned phone and half wishing for the cat to return. "Let's see how many league operatives we can fly to L.A. on short notice."

Nathan arrived back at LIO HQ to the tune of his sister's voice, not only in his head and his memory, but booming out of half the screens in the place. He hurried through the corridors while team members paused to watch her talk, clustered around corner screens and watching her on their phones.

"The League of Independent Operatives isn't capable of handling enhanced threats in this country, or anywhere in the world," Chloe was saying. "They should be stopped... brought up on charges... enhanced humans are dangerous."

Dangerous. The word echoed along the hallways, even as the news anchor brought in a nervous looking national security representative to rebut Chloe's claims.

A couple of weeks ago, no one would have taken Chloe seriously; the EAEA had hardly been able to get in the door to speak with politicians. And now she was getting major interviews? That couldn't be a good sign.

The calm Nathan had summoned during the six-hour plane ride vanished, his head swimming with grief and fatigue, anger and fear. He didn't know which to give precedence to, so he let them all come until his hands shook with barely contained rage.

Nathan passed the worried team members, brushing off their questions—he didn't know how to answer them, anyway—as he hurried to the prison level.

The doctor glanced up from his desk when Nathan entered. Dr. Gordon, Nathan had learned, still studied the practice of healing in as much detail as he could—hence the books, the piles of papers. Despite the fact that his powers were regularly dampened since coming to LIO HQ, he still worked to help people.

Dr. Gordon took one look at Nathan's face and stood, concern creasing his brow. "Officer," he said. "Are you all right?"

"The story you told me about St. Louis," Nathan said. "Is it true?"

Dr. Gordon adjusted his glasses. "I'd hardly say otherwise even if it wasn't. But yes, it's true."

Nathan turned to face Jo, who probably already knew his intention. She sat on the bed, her hair floating free around her face, a trio of Tarot cards spread across the blankets. He couldn't see their faces, wouldn't understand them, anyway.

"Is there anyone here who'd dangerous?" he asked her. "Aside from Jenna Carpenter, and the Las Vegas prisoners?"

"The Vegas prisoners," Jo repeated. "Didn't you hear? They don't need the serum any longer. I wouldn't release them, but I wouldn't call them dangerous, either."

Nathan paused to glance down the row to where the pair of Vegas troublemakers were being contained. "How is that possible?"

"Without examining them," Dr. Gordon said, "I can only hypothesize that it means their powers were somehow temporary. Your lab has sent scientists down several times to evaluate the situation."

Nathan swallowed a wad of nausea. Had the EAEA

somehow manufactured temporarily enhanced humans? How was that even possible?"

One thing at a time. He turned back to Jo. "The Wave operatives," he said. "Are any of them dangerous?"

She met his gaze with her clear blue one, and she shook her head. "They are not."

Nathan went to the panel in the wall and typed in his credentials. He could feel Jo watching him, the doctor's expression still concerned.

Nathan selected their cells, and every cell—except for Jenna's—that housed a Wave operative. Dolly had framed them, jailed them. Assumed guilt, because the Pearl Knife said so.

If the U.S. Government wanted LIO to handle their fates, that was exactly what Nathan would do. With a deep breath, he opened the doors and let them go free.

STANDING in a hotel lobby made of glass walls, Mary almost felt as if she'd come full circle. The house in Malibu had been a false front, little more than a set where she'd spent years acting, whether anyone was watching or not.

Jeff had been right. She'd used glass as a prop for years. And she was using it again—only this time the press was in on the joke.

Cleared of civilians, the hotel lobby extended skyward in a tall silo. Balconies graced the levels above her like lacework, palm fronds reaching over their railings as if trying to touch the glass dome that capped the whole tower.

And before her, a sea of chairs was filled with reporters. Recognizable ones, all, not faceless fakes but actual known news professionals from as many outlets she and Dawn had been able to find. Designing the holograms had been a challenge, even with the cooperation of the models. It hadn't been easy to make them look solid, or place projectors where they wouldn't be noticed immediately.

They'd still be noticed, likely in minutes if not less. But Mary didn't need them to last forever. She just needed them to give her the element of surprise.

Outside, the palm trees that dotted the street waved in a sudden gust of wind as clouds marched on the sun, the sky darkening. Anomalous weather for Southern California.

Mary wiped her hands on her pants, wishing she could have worn Coral's getup to this little party. But that would have ruined the illusion she wanted to create, so instead she had on loose black pants and a loose red blouse with white polka dots. So far from her Mary O'Sullivan persona, with all its slinky dresses and overpriced yoga attire. So far from Coral, too.

It made her feel like a target. But it also made her feel... free? Besides, she needed the puffed-out sleeves to hide the gadgets she'd managed to cobble together in the Malibu house.

Mary stepped up beside the platform and checked her watch as the audience made fake restless motions. Dawn had done a good job collecting holograms from her reporter friends, especially once she'd dangled the promise of a real press conference. Though Mary had heard one of the reporters ask what he'd get out of it if Coral died in the fight.

A few of them were still sharks, clearly. But Dawn had been right; most of them simply wanted to help.

Mary rubbed her hands together and stepped up to the platform, heading for the podium with her smile turned on bright. What would she say, if she actually had to start talking to a sea of pretend press?

She could consider it a practice run.

When the first raindrops spattered against the glass, Mary actually gasped. Silly. It did rain here, just... not very often. Lightning lanced across the sky, and Mary looked out to see Dawn hurrying along the street, ducking her head against the pattering drops. Right on time.

Dawn plunged through the revolving glass doors as the rain intensified, rivulets streaking down the walls, the thin palm trunks along the street bending close to double in the wind.

Carlisle. He was using the weather to distract her. Clever. Mary brushed her hands on her pants as Dawn slid into an empty seat in the back row and gave her a nod. Mary hated risking her—especially after hearing the way she'd cursed out the 'what if Coral dies' guy—but she'd get the reporter out of here as soon as she could. That was her first priority today, even if it meant the retirees escaping again. Though she certainly hoped they wouldn't.

The rain pounded harder, and Mary tapped the microphone with an index finger.

The windows exploded in a hurricane of wind, glass pouring into the lobby from every side. Mary ducked behind the podium as Dawn threw herself under a chair, the holograms still twitching, unfazed by the glass that rained harmlessly through their bodies.

Mary leapt off the stage to reach Dawn, to get her to the route she'd secured through the lobby cafe. Diving through the useless sea of holograms, she shoved chairs aside. Eloise should be here any minute, if the Knife could do what she claimed.

Now would be good, Mary thought. It felt like a prayer.

A flicker of movement caught her attention from above. Still running, she looked up to see Monster swinging from one of the mid-level balconies. Grinning, he let go, dropping through the lobby like a blue-scaled gorilla. Or something. She didn't have an analogy for what Monster was.

He landed between Mary and Dawn, who wisely kept herself tucked under the nearest chair. The chair would be like dollhouse furniture for Monster, but it was better than nothing.

Wind screamed through the lobby as Monster turned toward Dawn.

Mary threw herself forward, but he'd aimed his landing well. He was going to beat her. Monster bent to fish under the chair, hooking his claw through the collar of Dawn's shirt and dragging her out into the open. The chair clung to her back, and he tossed it away with his other hand, yellow eyes fixed on the wide-eyed reporter.

"Sneaky," Monster said.

A shimmering thread sliced through the air between Mary and Monster, and he paused, quirking his head. Expecting Dolly, perhaps? A heartbeat, two, and then Eloise stepped through the portal—a *portal*—as if out of empty air. The Pearl Knife glowed at her side, luminous, and Eloise had never looked more powerful.

The silver thread winked away behind her, and then the Pearl Knife was cutting through the back of Monster's hand. He roared, dropping the reporter as blood poured through the gash.

Dawn scurried away, chest heaving with fear, and Mary pointed to the back of the lobby. "The cafe," she called, and Dawn ran.

Trusting the reporter to find her way, Mary stepped up on the nearest chair so she could look Monster in the eye. He was caught between her and Eloise, a fly in a web. The back of his hand was bleeding freely. "Sent you to do her dirty work, did she?" Mary said.

Monster grinned, and his teeth looked sharper than she remembered. Did he file them? How would that even work? "This work is all mine," he said. "You think a little cut can stop me?"

Monster launched himself at her, but the Pearl Knife sailed before him, opening a portal that landed him on the other side of the room. That was a very cool trick. Mary jumped off the chair, landing next to Eloise as Monster pulled himself to his feet with a snarl.

Together, the two of them could best Monster.

As if in answer to her arrogance, the other retirees

appeared, climbing over the ruined windowsills, their boots crunching on glass as they came forward to face Mary and Eloise. Diana, Monster, Rocker, the twins. Carlisle must be controlling the weather from elsewhere, but Goldi was with them, her hair glittering.

Mary had a special surprise rigged especially for her. Even so, it might not be enough.

Eloise kept her eyes trained on Diana, who was peeling off her red gloves. Mary really wished she had Coral's outfit. Or something more than a bunch of untested tech. And the Knife; based on what El had told her, that thing had power behind it they'd never dreamed of.

If anyone could wield the blade, it was El.

"OK, no problem," Mary said. "Just you and me against six angry and experienced enhanced independent operatives. Expected a few more on our side, but that's cool."

Eloise just smiled. She seemed relaxed, almost eager—not at all surprised at having stepped through a *portal in the air,* or like someone who was likely about to lose a fight. Very badly.

Maybe El was thinking she could get them out with one of those portal things. But Mary didn't want to run. Mary wanted to win. That was the whole point of this.

"Care to negotiate, Eloise?" Diana said. "I'll gladly trade your life for Mary's, out of respect for your mother."

The Knife, which had been figure eighting through the room as if checking for hidden threats, arched back with a vengeance, shining so brightly that Mary could hardly look at it.

"Did you tell it to do that?" Mary asked.

Eloise shook her head. "It gets protective."

Diana tucked her gloves into a pouch at her waist. "I'll take that as a no. What a shame. Goldi?"

The illusionist clapped her hands, and the room went dark.

One moment they were staring at the next generation of supervillain nursing home residents, and the next everything was pitch black. Even the Pearl Knife blinked out of sight.

Illusion. It had to be. Clever, too; Mary hadn't expected that. In the disorienting first moment, the retirees were already moving. Mary could hear their footsteps crunching over the glass.

She reached for the trigger in her pocket, and someone fell into her, pushing her sideways. One of the twins, not that she could tell which one. She met them blow for blow, not really caring where her hits landed. But whoever it was, they could clearly see her. An interesting dimension to Goldi's powers, creating two separate realities. What else could she do?

The twin punched Mary hard across the jaw, knocking her off her feet. She rolled back up to stand, aware that the fight would end way too quickly if she couldn't activate her little toy, but her opponent was relentless. The twin grazed her cheek with a punch, and Mary risked aiming for a knee to the gut. She must have gotten close, because she was rewarded with soft flesh and a grunt, giving her a chance to reach the switch in her pocket.

An intricate pattern of ruby laser lines cut across the room in every direction, slicing through Goldi's illusion. The lobby reappeared, tipped over chairs and all.

Mary had spent almost a full day installing the laser bulbs at the correct angles.

The twin—it was Brenda—sprinted back toward Mary as Donny appeared on the other side. Fully rested as she was after a couple of days in Malibu, if still sore around the middle, Mary took pleasure in every hit. She still didn't know how they were going to win this—she had a sense of Eloise and the Knife in her peripheral vision, fighting Rocker, Diana, and Monster all at once—but landing a punch to Brenda's lip felt good.

She didn't know what kind of hero felt good about hurting someone else. Maybe the kind of hero who'd been held down and tortured by these people.

Maybe the kind of hero whose parents they'd murdered.

Or maybe the kind of hero who knew she was about to die by their hand, and didn't mind sneaking in a few hits before she did.

As the thought crossed her mind, Eloise extricated herself from her fight, the Knife sailing before her like a bodyguard. She leapt back, hands outstretched, and if not for the fire in her eyes, Mary would have thought she was surrendering.

Eloise would never surrender LIO to these people. Because that was what they wanted, wasn't it? The golden age back, their status returned. The recruits. HQ. All of it. And unfortunately, Mary had given them the opening they'd needed to do just that.

Donny used the distraction of Eloise's movement to try and undercut Mary's guard. He aimed a punch, and Mary defended herself, batting him away. To Mary's surprise, Donny stepped back, trading a confused look with his sister.

For a moment, Mary didn't understand. Had Brenda disobeyed whatever move he'd telegraphed to her? She'd never seen that happen before.

Mary risked glancing away from the twins, and her eyes landed on Rocker. All flesh, no shapeshifting limbs. He was staring at his fist, as if its mundane shape disappointed him greatly.

And then Mary looked at Eloise.

The Knife was glowing green, of all things, and Eloise's brows were drawn together in concentration, her dark eyes reflecting the emerald light of the blade.

And suddenly, Mary understood. She didn't know how it was possible, but Eloise had stolen the retirees' powers.

ELOISE COULD FEEL their powers pulsing through her, not in a way that she could use herself—though perhaps, if there were fewer of them, she might be able to do that—but in a way that begged for direction. In a way that made her think that, if she chose to, she could make puppets of them all. Her mother had done that, for ill. Maybe Eloise could do it for good.

With a thought, the Knife flickered—almost as if leaving this plane for a moment—and Rocker's body shifted to stone. The same material as the floor. Goldi was weeping, not that she'd participated in the fight. Eloise sensed the great illusions she could weave through the magician, the strength of Monster's enhanced body. She could use his strength to lift the others, all of them, to throw them across the room. She could use his strength to carry them away, and no one would be able to stop her.

The mind reading was more illusive, so she merely held onto it. Built a wall between the twins while they stared at each other as though uncertain the other was really still there.

To Eloise, it felt like holding a stable of racehorses in her mind and trying to keep them from running. She felt as if the wrong twitch of a pinky could turn everyone in the room to stone. She could still feel Rocker's power, his presence, pulsing through her like a heartbeat. Could he transfer it to others? Could she mix and match them all?

The Knife beamed comfort into her mind, a steady reassurance. Between the two of them, they'd handle the rush of power.

Diana set a hand on her hip, surveying her companions as if trying to piece together what had happened. "Clever," she said slowly, and Eloise realized the one thing she didn't feel: Diana's powers. The poison. That was inconvenient, and yet she almost felt relieved. What would the poison feel like in her mind?

It was easy to guess why it didn't work that way; the same way Monster would retain his physical properties—his hard scales, and his size—Diana's finger poison couldn't be controlled by the Knife. It was part of her body, a physical trait.

Did that mean that the power-suppressing serum wouldn't work on her, either? It worked on the sticky-fingered Wave operative. It ought to work on Diana.

Either way, Eloise had the distinct feeling that the field was now even. Eloise, Mary, and the Pearl Knife against Diana and a half-strong Monster?

She'd take those odds. And if she was lucky, they'd have backup soon.

"Why do you think Ranger isn't here?" Diana said. "He's with your mother. And Dolly has residual powers. They'll come for us, and when they do, we'll take back the league."

It was what they'd been angling for all along, really. Undercutting her authority, stealing her mother away. But nothing about today's league belonged to these pretenders. Eloise was the one who'd wanted to transform LIO, but with operatives like Ire, like Nathan? And her loyal staff team? Diana could kill Eloise right here, but it wouldn't matter. The old guard would never get HQ back. They'd never have LIO.

Eloise could control Ranger's powers. As for Dolly, unless her residual powers created some kind of inadvertent feedback —the Knife sent a tremor of nerves through her mind, which Eloise's heart echoed—Eloise doubted her mother would kill her, if it came down to it.

Eloise didn't move. Mary stood beside her, every muscle coiled, and Eloise found herself wishing she could see Mary's expression. Was she horrified? Never mind. She held the rushing powers calmly, allowing them to rush through her consciousness and trusting the Knife to help her handle them. "If they come, we'll be ready for them."

Mary had managed to keep her mouth shut while Eloise and Diana traded barbs, which hadn't been easy, particularly when Rocker shifted into stone *and stayed that way*. At Eloise's command, apparently.

The Pearl Knife really could steal powers, allowing Eloise to control them. The implications... it was too much. Will's innocence, for one. Still, the idea of it made Mary shiver. Monster was doubled over in the middle of the overturned chairs, and Goldi was still weeping openly. The twins looked as if they might join her.

If someone had to have this power, Mary figured it might as well be Eloise. She'd never abuse it. Even now, Eloise could be using the retirees' powers to have them attack each other—and they'd have deserved it, too—but she didn't. Mary wondered if the thought had even occurred to her.

"You might as well surrender," Eloise said to Diana. "I promise I'll give you the nicest cell."

Diana smiled in a stretched, pressed kind of way that made Mary wonder if the poison could be somehow infecting her brain. "You know," she said, "I don't think I will."

Without prelude, Monster attacked. One moment he was

bent in half on the floor, the next he was leaping for Mary with teeth bared, claws set to maul. The Knife intercepted him, slicing a strip of red across his arm, and he roared, turning on Eloise. Exchanging a glance, the twins joined him.

Mary sidestepped them all and aimed for Diana.

The Trap had her fingers bared, black poison leaking from her fingertips, and Mary swallowed a wad of bile as her still-fresh injuries pulsed a warning across her chest, and the palm of her hand. Diana had nearly killed Mary the other night, and now the Trap was staring at Eloise with murder in her eyes.

Mary threw herself between Eloise's three-on-one fight—or two on three, if Mary counted the Knife as a separate entity, and maybe she should—and pushed herself forward, kicking Diana's knee out from under her and knocking the other woman to the floor. Leaping after her, Mary almost managed to pin her to the floor, but the Trap slapped a palm to Mary's neck, and Mary fell back, screaming as her skin burned in response.

She thought Diana would run for El, take down the immediate threat. Instead, the Trap attacked Mary, landing on top of her. "Eager to finish our fight from the other night?" Mary asked.

Diana laughed. "I suppose you would call that a fight. But it was more of you getting your ass kicked than a proper battle, wasn't it?" She reached for Mary's hand, as if to emphasize her point. But Diana's insistence on opening sentimental wounds left her exposed, and Mary used the opening to punch her in the face, throwing her off balance.

Diana righted herself quickly and pressed her fingernails into Mary's shoulders. "I can't believe my luck," she said, as Mary struggled to throw her off. "I get to torture you twice."

A person-sized streak blurred into the room and flashed straight into Diana, knocking her off Mary and into a pile of chairs. Mary leapt to her feet, expecting Steve—she didn't know why, but he'd been there with El in Long Beach.

But it wasn't Steve who materialized now; it was Flick. Mary's eyes widened, and she felt her mouth drop open. She'd imprisoned this guy, unfairly it seemed, and he'd just saved her life.

No wonder Diana had wanted to find him. He wasn't on her side.

Flick nodded to Mary before rushing over to help Eloise with her part of the fight, though El seemed almost a blur herself as she and the Knife whipped around. The Pearl Knife was always amazing, but this... Mary had never seen El fight quite like this before.

The room filled abruptly with LIO operatives, and Mary caught sight of Ire's red hair, Steve flashing to Eloise's side.

And Nathan, leading a crew of people Mary didn't recognize. She'd thought there were only half a dozen recruits, or so the news had said, but there had to be thirty or more people streaming in behind him. Who were they?

There was a part of her that couldn't believe he'd come. On Eloise's orders, no doubt. Nathan wouldn't have come here just to help Mary. He met her eyes across the space, a flicker of attention that passed too quickly. There were other matters to deal with here. He had a bruise on his cheek, and she wondered vaguely if it was from their fight in Long Beach.

Diana groaned, and Mary ripped her attention from Nathan to face her. The fight might essentially be over, but the Trap was still a danger, and would be until Mary took care of her.

She moved toward Diana. Still on her back among the chairs, the Trap shot a wad of poison at her that she avoided easily. Diana sported a long cut on one of her cheeks, and she was breathing hard, though whether in pain or anger, Mary couldn't say.

Diana pulled herself to her feet, staggering slightly. "You never fit in," she said. "You ruined the league. You. Will, taking time away from the rest of us to train you. Dolly, pretending to treat you like a daughter. You never had enhanced abilities. You never mattered."

"I used to think so," Mary said. "But then I realized the truth."

Diana wiped the back of her hand across her mouth. "And what is that?"

Mary tore into the loosely sewn threads at her cuffs, opening her blouse sleeves to reveal a pair of metal cuffs. One on each arm, they deactivated with the touch of a button, strips of metal that detached from her arms before locking together to form a pair of closed-off clamps. To Mary, they mostly looked like mittens. Or socks, like the ones parents placed on an infant's hands to keep them from scratching.

Diana laughed, but at last it sounded forced. "Not this again," she said. Expecting more failed torture devices, probably.

That was the idea. But these cuffs were different than that last, clumsy attempt. Activated, they were drawn like magnets to Diana's poison, and they surged toward her. Realizing the danger too late, Diana tried to scramble back, but the mittens zeroed in on her hands, and she shrieked in rage as they locked themselves firmly over the her toxic fingertips.

Diana shook her hands as if she could throw off the cuffs, screaming in anger, but it didn't matter. She could shoot poison all she wanted. It wouldn't make it through the cuffs, and they wouldn't detach without a passcode.

Diana took off for the broken windows, heedless of the glass, but Mary caught up with her easily as the cuffs pulled the

Trap's hands around behind her back while she fought wildly against them. But their magnets were too strong for her, and when they locked themselves together—that was the genius of them, really, the handcuff function—she finally lost her balance. Mary couldn't help cringing as the Trap's knees hit the glass.

"The only truth about you is that you never mattered," Diana spat, as if harsh words could change her fate, or wound Mary any more than already had been.

And then they were surrounded by the group of unfamiliar operatives—Mary really hoped they were LIO—who lifted Diana to her feet and marched her toward the doors.

Mary let them take her. "I'm a genius and a celebrity," she said. "And you're nothing at all."

ALL ELOISE COULD THINK, as she arranged for Ire and the others to escort the prisoners back to HQ—their powers suppressed, their anger not so much—was that she'd rarely seen LIO make so many enormous messes in such a short amount of time.

The hole in the ceiling—ceilings?—in Las Vegas had been dramatic, there was no denying it. But the destruction in this hotel lobby was at least equal to that. Every first-floor window had been blown out, and glass lay scattered across the floor. It was almost pretty, sparkling in the afternoon light, if you ignored the rest of the destruction. Several of the balcony railings above hung at odd angles, and one had crashed into a planter of ferns near the check-in desk. There was glass and blood and destroyed furniture. Everywhere.

Eloise wondered if her mother had ever caused this much damage. She wondered how long it would take Travis Bertram to call.

And she wondered about Nathan. His sudden arrival, and his not-so-mysterious entourage. She found him on the sidewalk, loading his team into vans. He had his hands in his pockets, and he kept shooting glances back to the hotel lobby.

"Thanks for coming out here," Eloise said.

He just blinked at her, shaking his head, as if he wouldn't have considered anything else.

"So," Eloise said. "You let the prisoners go." It wasn't a question; she'd recognized Dr. Gordon as he healed injuries on crew and restrained retirees alike. She knew the others as well, their faces, their names. She knew their official stories. She knew there was more to it.

Nathan nodded, lips pressed together as if he half expected a reprimand. But he'd dealt with something that Eloise had considered doing a hundred times herself. Through more official channels, maybe, but she thought she understood what Dad had meant when he'd encouraged her to embrace LIO as a true team. To let go of her obsession with protocol, the illusion of control. They *were* supposed to be independent operatives, weren't they? Dispensing justice where no one else would.

Eloise smiled and gave his shoulder a pat. "You'd better help me with the paperwork."

She turned to go, but Nathan caught her by the arm, holding her back. "Is she OK?"

Eloise studied him, the way his eyes were pinched with concern, his fingers trembling on her arm. "She's fine," Eloise said gently. "Come talk to her yourself, if you want to."

If Mary was even still here.

Nathan let go of her arm to drag his hand across his jaw, shaking his head slowly. "I'd better not."

Eloise just nodded. No point in pushing the matter. "Call me when you get to HQ." She glanced around for Steve, hoping to catch a word with him, but he was nowhere in sight.

Back inside, Eloise found Mary behind the counter in the lobby cafe, coffee percolating in a machine the size of a vat. The smell was incongruous compared to the shattered remains of the lobby, but to Eloise it might as well be the scent of heaven.

She sat down at one of the tables—one of the legs had been shorn in half, somehow, and the table tilted at a dangerous angle—and after a moment, Mary joined her.

Together, they sat and stared out at the destroyed hotel. The cafe felt like it was a breath from collapsing onto their heads, and though Eloise's burdens had lightened considerably, they weren't completely relieved. They still hadn't caught Dolly, or Ranger. If Dolly had made a portal out of HQ, the way Eloise suspected she had? That might turn out to be a serious problem.

Mary just sat there, legs stretched out in front of her. Bruises still marred her face from the Long Beach fight, the purple marks swelling red with new hits from today. Eloise didn't know how she'd managed to escape Dr. Gordon, but if he saw her like this he'd surely make her submit to healing. Mary had dark circles under her eyes, and her fingernails were chewed to the quick. Eloise couldn't remember ever seeing Mary bite her nails, in all the time they'd known each other. The past few months had been rough on her. Or at least, the past few weeks had been.

"Travis Bertram is going to have a fit over this," Eloise said finally, looking back over the destruction of the lobby. That was probably an understatement; Travis Bertram was going to lose his mind.

"Nah," Mary said, stretching her hands back over her head. "I bought the place a couple of days ago. Believe it or not, I have no intention of pressing charges."

Eloise set down her coffee mug on the rickety table, where it clung, barely, by the grace of gravity. And then she started to laugh. She couldn't help it. It was one of those laughs that just bubbled out of her, unbidden and unstoppable. It might have been a release of stress, or adrenaline, or just that the idea of

Mary buying this place so she could legally destroy it was the funniest thing Eloise had ever heard.

Mary watched her for a beat, and she might think Eloise was crazy—and maybe she was, truly—but there was no stopping the laughter.

And then Mary started to laugh, too, until her face flushed red and tears streamed down her cheeks. They laughed until Eloise felt vaguely sick—it was worth it—and had to force a few deep breaths, her shoulders still heaving.

Finally, wiping her eyes, Eloise grabbed Mary's hand. "Hey," she said, "I'm glad you called."

Mary squeezed her fingers. "I missed you."

"We do better together." Eloise released Mary's hand and took another sip of coffee. It was true, and Mary had to know it. And now they came to the point. The crucial moment. Would Mary go off on her own again? Or would she come home? Eloise sipped her coffee again, stalling. "So."

The word hung between them, the rest of the sentence impossible to utter. Eloise pictured Mary getting up and walking away, disappearing back into this new, shadowed life of hers. Some other crusade, some lonely vigilante life. Or maybe a cabin in the woods where no one would bother her.

Eloise tried not to picture life at LIO in the long term without her sister—no matter how she'd tried to talk herself out of it, she'd always pictured Mary returning—but the thought was there, too sobering, and Eloise wished for the laughter again.

Mary looked at her hands, into the cup of coffee, and Eloise willed her to speak. After a moment, she did. "About Goldi," she said, then stopped. She brushed a shaking hand across her eyes. "It was an accident. I didn't mean to hurt her."

Eloise had thought they'd talk about Goldi back at HQ,

that there would be time for every explanation. But she was glad to know the truth. "I believe you."

Mary gripped the side of the chair. "I want to come back, El. If you'll have me."

Relief unfurled in Eloise's chest, and she grinned. It wasn't a bad day, destruction aside.

"So Will's alive?" Mary said.

Eloise let out a shuddering breath, her body still coming down after the adrenaline of the fight, the laughter. "He is."

"But he didn't show up today."

"He's trying to stay out of ops," Eloise said. She hadn't quite figured out why, though she'd very much like to know why he no longer used his powers. What Dolly had done to him... it wasn't his fault. But there'd be time for that. There'd be time to sort out everything. "But he's nearby. Wants to see you."

Mary sipped her coffee and smiled. Eloise had worried about her reaction to the news, but maybe she wouldn't hold on to anger, after all.

A shuddering vibration rumbled across the floor in a wave, and Eloise exchanged a glance with Mary. What now?

In the middle of the hotel lobby, a shimmering golden line split the air above the audience of destroyed chairs. Aside from its color, the line looked exactly like the threads the Knife wove when opening a portal.

Eloise stood, looking instinctively for the blade, but it was resting in its sheath at her waist. She withdrew it with a silent question, but the Knife sent waves of confusion back.

The golden portal widened, and Mary joined Eloise at the cafe door. "Dolly?" she asked.

Eloise frowned. "Could be." But Dolly's portal had been as silver as the Knife's.

On the other side of the portal, Eloise could see what looked like a kitchen. Or maybe a lab, with strange looking pipes, silver countertops. The same place Steve had glimpsed when Eloise had pushed the Knife back in Long Beach? The image was distorted, and as she squinted at it, a woman materialized on the other side and stepped straight through. She was tall, with long black hair, and Eloise might have thought she'd stepped out of the 1960s with that hairstyle, her flared-out pants, if not for the appearance of her companion. A too-pretty soldier type with his hair worked into spikes, he wore shiny armor across his chest, and covering his arms and legs. It wasn't Renaissance Faire, jousting-type armor, but rather... robotic looking. Like the mittens Mary had made to trap Diana, assembled across his body in dusty silver sections.

Two more figures followed the first pair, staying closer to the portal as if to jump back through at the first sign of trouble.

"I really don't see why I had to come," one of the cowering figures said, an older woman with a long silver braid trailing down her back. Her words didn't quite match the movements of her mouth, as if she were being dubbed over. Some kind of technology, to let them speak the same language? What language?

More than the portal, it was their clothing that made Eloise blink. Which, she supposed, just illustrated the intense strangeness of the past few weeks. Sure, they'd stepped through a portal, but more importantly they had on weird armor, metallic boots, and belts stuffed with tools or weapons—or both—she'd never seen before. The man had colorful geometric tattoos all over the backs of his hands.

"Who are you?" Eloise demanded. She let go of the Knife, and it hovered in the space between the two groups like a bodyguard.

The black-haired woman raised a hand as if to touch it. "I'm so sorry about this," she said, eyes locked on the Pearl Knife. "But we're here for the Blade of Starlight."

What, the Knife? The Blade of... what?

"Oh, is that all," Mary murmured.

The woman nodded, eyes pinned on the Knife. "You opened a portal. We followed its resonance."

"Sort of," one of the people behind her said. Who were they? Scientists? Wave operatives? Not, if Eloise had to guess, in those boots. Unless Wave had changed their aesthetics drastically since she'd last encountered them.

"Sorry," Eloise said. "The Knife's not for sale."

The black-haired woman blinked, eyes wide. "Oh, I don't have any money. I'm going to steal it."

Mary laughed. "Go ahead and try. It only recognizes its owner." With, apparently, a couple of exceptions. "It'll sear your hand off if you try to touch it."

The woman opened her mouth to speak again—to offer a deal? To threaten them?—but before she could, the pretty soldier leapt forward, holding a pearl-white box out in front of him. Eloise felt locked in place as Mary lunged to stop him, but he moved faster than Eloise would have thought possible, except from Steve or Flick.

It would have been nice to have one of them here now. Because before Mary could reach the thief, he clapped the white box around the Knife.

It shouldn't have been possible.

Eloise felt for the Knife, sent it a frantic image of cutting through the material, whatever it was. The blade didn't respond. She couldn't even feel its presence in her mind. She reached out, as far as she could. No images, no feelings, no rhythms or melodies. Nothing.

It was like reaching into a void. It was like reaching through thick nothing, the silence ringing too loud in her head.

Instead of cheering their friend on, or leaping to escape

through the portal, the black-haired woman's jaw dropped. "Oliver, what the hell—"

The Oliver person didn't stay to listen to the rest of the sentence. He didn't jump through the portal either. He launched himself across the room and leapt out the open window, heedless of the glass on the sill, and Eloise had the vague impression that the black-haired woman had been betrayed. With a cry, the woman ran after him, and Eloise had a sense that Mary was following, too. And the others. In what order, she couldn't have said.

Eloise's brain felt cleft in two. It wasn't pain that made her sink to her knees, cringing as she remembered too late that the floor was littered with glass. It was more like a fog, a thick one. She was vaguely aware of the portal blinking away. Ears ringing, knees smarting, she reached for the Knife. Her partner, her companion. Her friend. What had they called it? The Blade of Starlight?

Eloise reached out, and opened her feelings, and let go. When that didn't work, she begged. But it didn't do any good.

The Pearl Knife was gone.

Thanks for reading!

Visit http://katesheeranswed.com/free-books/ to join my readers group, where you can get access to my exclusive VIP reader library for downloadable extras and serialized short stories.

If you enjoyed *Anti-Hero*, please consider leaving an honest review on your favorite online retail site. Reviews help authors more than I can say!

ACKNOWLEDGMENTS

As I write these acknowledgments, it seems the whole world is sheltering in place due to coronavirus. I hope all my readers are safe and well, and that by the time you read this the world will be on its way to healing. That may be an optimistic hope, but I'm not afraid to share it.

At this moment in history, I'm extra appreciative to the people in my life who support my writing and all my creative endeavors.

I'd especially like to shout out my wonderful editor, Lynn O'Connacht, whose insightful comments make all the difference. Lynn's the kind of editor who can fix a comma while musing thoughtfully on both character arc and word placement. I'm grateful for our in-depth conversations. My writing improves every time we work together.

Writing friends, what would I do without you? Thanks to Sara Rauch, Jessie Kwak, Chace Verity, Maria Z. Medina, Leigh Landry, Stephanie Eding, Tyffany Hackett, and C.E. Clayton for keeping me sane—from outlining to draft one to finished product. And on to the next ;)

They may never see this, but there are folks out there providing incredible support and information for indie authors.

I'm grateful to Joanna Penn (the Creative Penn podcast), Mark Dawson & James Blatch (the Self Publishing Show and Self Publishing Formula courses), Lindsay Buroker, Jo Lallo, and Andrea Pearson (the Six Figure Authors podcast) for all they do to make this a vibrant and positive community.

My family's always cheering me on, so I thank them every time: Mom, Dad, Susan, and Shana, thanks for being the best. And I owe extra special thanks to all my cousins and extended family. The Sheeran clan is one special group—and so are the Sweds!

To Moshe and Milo, I love you guys forever <3

Kate Sheeran Swed loves hot chocolate, plastic dinosaurs, and airplane tickets. She has trekked along the Inca Trail to Macchu Picchu, hiked on the Mýrdalsjökull glacier in Iceland, and climbed the ruins of Masada to watch the sunrise over the Dead Sea. Kate currently lives in New York's capital region with her husband and son, and two cats who were named after movie dogs (Benji and Beethoven). She holds an MFA in Fiction from Pacific University.

You can find more of Kate's work, and pick up a free short story collection, at katesheeranswed.com.

 facebook.com/katesheeranswed

 twitter.com/katesheeranswed

 instagram.com/katesheeranswed